THE
LOVER
OF
HISTORY

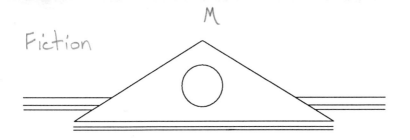

THE
LOVER
OF
HISTORY

◆

Jonathan Dee

Ticknor & Fields

NEW YORK

1990

The author thanks the following people for all their help and understanding: John Herman, Frances Kiernan, Amanda Urban, and *The Paris Review*.

For information about permission to reproduce selections from this book, write to Permissions, Ticknor & Fields, 215 Park Avenue South, New York, New York 10003.

Library of Congress Cataloging-in-Publication Data

Dee, Jonathan.
The lover of history / Jonathan Dee.
p.   cm.
ISBN 0-89919-946-1
I.   Title.
PS3554.E355L68   1990
813'.54—dc20   90-11061
                                    CIP

Printed in the United States of America

BP   10   9   8   7   6   5   4   3   2   1

The author gratefully acknowledges permission to quote Stanza XXV from "In Time of War" by W. H. Auden. Copyright 1945 by W. H. Auden. Reprinted from *W. H. Auden: Collected Poems*, edited by Edward Mendelson, by permission of Random House, Inc.; and passages from *How the Other Half Lives: Studies among the Tenements of New York* by Jacob A. Riis, the Belknap Press of Harvard University Press, 1970.

for Denise

Nothing is given; we must find our law.
Great buildings jostle in the sun for domination;
Behind them stretch like sorry vegetation
The low recessive houses of the poor.

We have no destiny assigned us:
Nothing is certain but the body; we plan
To better ourselves; the hospitals alone remind us
Of the equality of man.

Children are really loved here, even by police:
They speak of years before the big were lonely,
And will be lost.

    And only
The brass bands throbbing in the parks foretell
Some future reign of happiness and peace.

We learn to pity and rebel.

      —W. H. Auden,
       In Time of War

THE
LOVER
OF
HISTORY

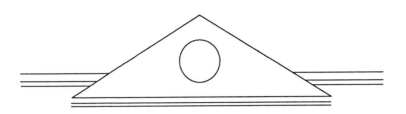

WHEN nothing else demanded her attention, Kendall slept. She worked at night and never said no to friends; so sleep, though she got enough of it, was often a matter not of routine but of opportunity and pleasant surprise. The morning of October eighteenth—a date commonly remembered now—was such a time. Kendall's shift at the station was over, Warner had just left for work, and she didn't know where Julian was. Outside her apartment building, newspaper rolled slowly in the wind, and the sun traveled unobstructed up the sky, lighting the city's short corridors one by one. But the city at morning was too loud for open windows. Dust circled in the sunlight that warmed the backs of her legs. Her hair fell evenly, as if she were floating on water, across the small cushions and the soft arm of the couch. The lights were off. The television spoke quietly in the corner.

The phone rang ten times and stopped; Kendall drove her forehead deeper into the cushions. On the television screen, a small jet drifted to a stop on an airport runway. A hundred or so men and women, most of them in military uniform, a few others with cameras, stood a respectful distance away, behind a weak velvet rope barricade. Microphones on poles waved lazily like cattails beside a lake. A red staircase on wheels was rolled up to the door of the plane. Kendall liked to have the television on when she was alone at home. The noises it made were reassuring. When someone else was in the apartment with her, she seldom watched.

The sound of drilling rose from the street below, muted by the closed windows. The phone rang again. Kendall shouted into the pillows. Then she got to her feet and, pulling at her eyes with her thumb and forefinger, walked to the kitchen and picked up the receiver. It was her mother.

Give me a second.

Were you asleep, Diane? I could call back.

Don't worry about it. Kendall opened the refrigerator door and, swinging the mouthpiece up near her forehead, drank from Warner's carton of orange juice. If you called back later I'd be asleep then too.

How are things? her mother said. I haven't heard from you in a while.

Things are fine. I just got home from work, so I'm a little beat. She replaced the carton and closed the refrigerator. What's up with you? Anything the matter?

Well, there's news. This is a news call.

Really. Kendall boosted herself with her free hand onto the kitchen counter. She lay down on the cool tile, bending her knees to keep her feet out of the sink. Should I be sitting down?

Laugh if you like, her mother said.

A tall man with white, wind-tossed hair—an American man—stooped to get through the door of the airplane. He waved, buttoned one button on his jacket, and descended. At the foot of the steps he shook hands with two men, embraced another, and walked with the three of them to a small reviewing stand.

I'm sorry, Kendall said. It's nothing serious, is it?

Well, it is serious. It's not bad news, though, if that's what you meant.

Kendall played with the cupboard door above her head. In the near silence she could hear the faint, unmodulated noise of the drill. So?

Is Julian with you?

Not just now.

Where is he?

I don't know. As it happens.

I'm just asking, that's all.

The white-haired man hunched slightly to get his mouth closer to the nest of microphones mounted on the podium. He began to deliver his message. Palm trees marked the distant end of the concrete runway, which shimmered in the heat like a sea. A dark stain appeared on the man's white shirt, and then three more. The screen image shuddered, and then rolled, as if the concrete had begun to heave. After a moment, in a formal confirmation of significance, this scene was repeated, again and again.

Are you watching TV? Mrs. Kendall said. I have it on here. Something's definitely going on.

Kendall slid down from the counter and walked out of the kitchen until she was stopped by the phone's cord. I can't see it from here. Listen, you always do this. I'm sorry if I'm not in a great mood, but I haven't slept. What's the big news?

It's about your brother, Mrs. Kendall said.

At a private high school uptown, in a neighborhood so solid he could not afford to live even within walking distance, Warner taught history. That morning, he stood at the front of a crowd on the Union Square subway platform, his feet on a wide, cracked strip of faded orange paint. He was a young man, and he dressed like a young man, in khakis, bucks, a jacket and tie. Across the damp tracks stood another crowd, as indifferent as a reflection. Many people read newspapers folded like road maps, stopping between stories to scratch a sleepy face with a knuckle or a wrist. Warner heard the faint thunder of an approaching train; after a few seconds he was able to determine that it was not going in his direction. He looked toward the tunnel across the tracks. Reflected pools of light spotted the rail; the lights began to move, then lengthen, finally joining one another. The roar increased. A woman frowned and put her hands over her ears. The tunnel, which described a slight curve, changed color suddenly, and a moment later, with a long, deafening exhalation, disgorged the train. It rested for a moment beneath the dark ceiling and the water-stained mosaics. The windows filled with broad backs in jackets. The engine hissed, and the train started off again. Blue sparks, large and silent, flashed along the rail. The windows seemed to empty as they sped by, until the line of cars vanished to reveal one unlucky man, standing alone on the vacant platform, out of breath and grimacing. Warner turned his attention back to his own newspaper, which was falling out of date, though the ink still blackened his fingertips.

Warner's own train was too crowded to allow him to raise his arms, so he put the paper in his bookbag and read the back cover of the book the woman on his left was holding. He read the ribbon of advertisements for roach powder and secretarial schools that ran above their heads. He read the initials, DAR, on the briefcase of the man standing in front of him, and then he saw the sign for Eighty-sixth Street and propelled himself through the doors.

Back in the sunlight, back above ground, he walked quickly, head down. A bald man stood with the ease of ownership in the doorway of a clothing store; he addressed half a dozen strangers, one of them a policeman. A taxicab idled against the sidewalk. Its passenger leaned forward, arms crossed on the front seat, utterly still. The driver did not ask for money, or for a destination. Scenes like these were everywhere and yet easy to miss. A crowd three-deep in places watched a mute store window full of televisions of all sizes. A light changed to green; the people on the corner, all but a few, were eavesdropping on a conversation and did not move. Warner kept walking.

A group of men and women stood, like children at a puppet theater, in front of a wooden kiosk, festooned with magazines

and sunglasses and jewelry, at the edge of the sidewalk. They
were listening to a small portable radio, turned up to the point
of distortion, set out on the small counter used to make change.
The men held their ties against their shirts with one hand as
they leaned forward in an effort to hear the low, crackling male
tone; their eyes were unfocused. Words were lost to car horns
or to static. The owner leaned against the kiosk's back wall, his
arms folded, a dark look on his face; clearly, if he could have
thought of a way to charge money for this impromptu service,
he would have instituted it. Stacked in front of the counter,
ignored, sat the morning's newspapers; their headlines spoke in
too small a voice.

Warner passed behind the group at the kiosk, walking fast.
He had to beat the students to school. The streets were stained,
damaged; they threw a glare into his eyes.

St. Albert's was on a quiet, residential side street, half a block
west of Madison Avenue, in sight of the low wall that runs
alongside Fifth Avenue and the park beyond. Its modest
entrance—the name of the school was not written anywhere
on the facade—was recessed from the street. At nine o'clock
Warner taught the tenth-graders, and he made it just in time
to walk with them into the classroom. Several of the boys were
as tall as he, and most carried bookbags. He headed for the big
metal desk.

For fifty minutes they talked about Jacksonian democracy.
Only a handful of the students participated; most knew so little
about the subject that they were afraid even to ask questions.
A paper was due that day, and so many had not had time to
do the assigned reading as well. Warner, who prided himself
on being thought of as a hard teacher, expected this, and understood; he did not pursue the ones who looked away from
him most desperately. One girl, named Alexa, stared into her
textbook as if nearsighted and slowly underlined certain passages, undoubtedly at random, a stratagem Warner remembered
from his own school days. He felt himself start to smile, and
hurriedly asked another question. At the bell, they filed past
his desk, left their papers in a kind of pile, and pushed one

another out the door. The papers had all been torn from spiral-bound notebooks; their left edges were frayed. Warner straightened the pile patiently. His next hour was free.

At ten o'clock the room was used for a French class. Chenet, the French teacher, walked in and set his briefcase gently on the edge of the desk. He opened it, and busied himself with its contents.

Did you hear? he said.

There is a reliable pleasure in being the bearer of important bad news. It has less to do with morbidity than with the easy acquisition of real responsibility. The American secretary of state had been shot to death a short time ago, remarkably short if one thought of the distance the fact itself had to travel — one third of the way around the world. The secretary had been in the first few minutes of a goodwill visit to a small island nation that had become influential through an accident of geography. No one had been caught, and Chenet, at least, had only the most general idea of whom to blame. For Warner's benefit, he recited all he knew, and waited. Leaves from the park, just down the street but invisible, blew as if magically across the stillness framed by the open window. Warner took his bottom lip between his teeth.

You don't know, he said, if there's a TV in the building?

Chenet was an older man, rather formal, and his face seemed able to move only along its three or four deep creases. He took a folder from his briefcase. I think Don Fales has a little one down in his office, off the gym. You might try there. I'm not sure it picks up anything but basketball games. One crease turned out to be the track of a smile. A girl walked into the room and dropped her books loudly on a desk in the back row. She was tall, with an elegant face and a boy's narrow body, and she wore a buckskin jacket. She regarded the sight of two teachers conversing with a look of exquisite, sullen distrust. Warner gathered his papers and left; on his way out he smiled at the girl, but she was looking elsewhere, at nothing.

The gym was below ground level, at the west end of the building. As Warner started down the hall, between the twin rows of metal lockers, the bell rang; the students before him parted and disappeared through the heavy classroom doors. In a matter of seconds, he was alone. He was not far enough removed from childhood for the feeling of walking through an empty school corridor, peering through the crosshatched safety glass at classes in session, to have lost its nervous thrill. He was not sure how much of the excitement he felt now could be traced to that. He took his time before reaching the stairs.

Fales had converted what used to be a trainer's room next to the basketball court into his office; students now had to take any minor injuries suffered during his class upstairs to the nurse. The walls were whitewashed concrete; posters advertising brands of sneakers and a few frameless photographs were hung with masking tape. There was a handsome old oak desk, cleared of absolutely everything, a low, ripped, leather chair, and a knee-high refrigerator, with a black-and-white television on top of it. One side of the rectangular room, the long side adjacent to the court, was dominated by a sturdy plastic picture window, which bore the smudges of many errant basketballs. Warner, in the hall, had heard Fales's whistle blasting on the court, so he walked into the office without knocking. A young math teacher named Lewis, whom Warner didn't know very well, straightened up in Fales's chair. In his right hand he held a cigarette, which had already filled the airless room with smoke. The television was on. Warner hopped up onto the desk.

What's going on? he said.

Not much, Lewis said reflexively; I guess you heard about Sheffield.

Just that he's dead, Warner said. He stole a look behind him, through the window. Does Fales know we're in here?

He knows I'm here.

Warner moved closer to the wall. Something about gym teachers, he said. I don't know what it is.

Lewis smiled. You know, he said, I'm sorry, I'm not sure I know what your first name is. Is it Robert?

Yeah, or Rob. Either one.

I'm Mark Lewis.

Nice to meet you. Actually, I think we've met before. You teach math, right?

Lewis nodded as he blew out a mouthful of smoke. You know the press was all there to cover the visit. They got the whole thing on film.

You're kidding me, Warner said. The two of them looked at the screen, where a man holding a microphone spoke against a background of palm trees and tall white buildings. Have they shown it?

That's all they do is show it, Lewis said. Over and over. They don't have any idea what's going on, there's been no kind of statement from anybody, but they feel like they can't just go back to game shows or whatever, I suppose. It's kind of revolting.

Lewis took a Coke can out of the wastebasket and dropped his cigarette into it, where it hissed.

Warner craned forward to look at the screen. An airplane landed on an empty tarmac.

Here you go, Lewis said. He turned away from the set toward the aquarium-sized window, where a basketball game was in progress. The boys carried it out with fervor. Fales, in a black-and-white striped shirt and gray shorts, ran easily up and down the court with them, always a step or two behind. His whistle, tied on the end of a black shoelace, was wrapped tightly around his fingers. Slowly, though, Lewis gave in, and turned back to the image, rescued from time, of the shooting. The brute repetition had begun to introduce an element of tragedy, as if the secretary of state had been condemned to relive the moment of his death for eternity.

Jesus, Warner said.

Seen in slow motion, the secretary of state — the newsmen used all three of his names now, an honorific conferred on the famous dead and their assassins — seemed to glance down for a moment at the blood seeking new vessels in the fibers of his shirt, before closing his eyes and sinking behind the podium.

I don't know, Lewis said. I mean, this is starting to turn into pornography. It's certainly as boring.

Warner didn't answer.

Lewis waved the smoke away from his face. He seemed to feel that this kind of weary callousness was a necessary attitude, and Warner, to some degree, could sympathize. Too much of what came between him and an event such as this was designed to manipulate him, to gain access to the unthinking part of him in ways that were both crude and mysterious.

The secretary of state stepped off the plane again. Well, Lewis said, I'm not learning anything here. He stood up, brushed at his pants, and opened the door. He and Warner looked at each other. See you, they both said.

Warner took over the chair and turned up the volume. He was glad to be alone. He watched patiently. The signifiers of importance—hastily scheduled speeches, unexpected tears, slow motion—were not interesting to him. That such an event would have consequences, in his own life, was what he believed in. He was a teacher of history. His roommate, Kendall, worked at one of the all-news radio stations; she might know something more. He thought of calling her, but she would probably be asleep.

After a while, the network ran a string of commercials, if only to give everyone a rest. The clock on the office wall showed that there were seventeen minutes until Warner's next class. He turned around to watch the basketball game, which he imagined was a close one, though he had no idea of the score. He was twenty-six years old. At midcourt, biting on his whistle, Fales glanced in at him, or seemed to. The boys ran back and forth in the window like some museum diorama meant to depict youthful desire. The little room, though, was close to soundproof. All that reached Warner were the high shriek of the whistle, the low boom of the basketball, and occasionally, if it was very loud, a more midrange, human sound.

When Warner got back to the apartment that night, Kendall was sitting in the living room with a closed magazine in her lap. He dropped the two newspapers he'd bought and his bookbag on the long trestle table they had bought to eat at but used mostly as a dumping ground. Its surface was covered with catalogues and old mail. What's up? he said. He went to the refrigerator, picked up the carton of orange juice, raised his eyebrows, and put it back; he selected an apple instead. He leaned against the jamb at the entrance to the kitchen and regarded Kendall. She fought the impression, as she often did, that this was a man who had somehow obtained a key to her apartment.

What's up? he said.

She forged a smile.

Do anything exciting today? he said. It often took a few questions of this nature to get her to acknowledge that he had returned home; he wasn't so much concerned with an answer as with breaking her silence, which he thought inconsiderate.

Nothing, she said. Slept.

Warner walked in and sat on the couch across from her. They sometimes did things simultaneously — reading, or just sitting in the living room — but never together, so that there seemed always to be a quiet battle going on for occupation of the room. They were polite about it, more likely to retreat than to press the point. This passed for compatibility. He took a bite of the green apple, then wiped his mouth with the back of the same hand.

I guess you heard the news, he said.

Kendall looked up, confused for a moment.

The shooting and everything, he said.

I heard some of it.

You think anything's going to happen?

Hasn't it already? she said.

Well, yeah, but I meant do you think anything's going to happen as a result of it? How do you think we'll react?

We?

Warner frowned. I don't know, I thought maybe you'd heard something. You didn't call the station or anything?

She looked at him. Call the station?

Yeah.

No, I'd just as soon — I'll hear enough about it when I get in.

The light in the room was fading. He held the apple core between his thumb and forefinger and looked helplessly around, finally leaning over to balance it on the floor. The refrigerator clicked on and hummed loudly for a second before waning.

Actually, Warner said, the president's supposed to be on TV, right around now, I heard.

Kendall stood up, took one step to switch on the set, and kept walking toward the hall, which led to the bedrooms. I'm sorry, he said, I don't mean to kick you out, I can —

No, it's okay. I'm going out in a few minutes anyway. She had just decided this.

Julian?

No, just some people from work, just dinner.

Where is he lately?

Oh, he's around. I'm sure you'll run into him. She smiled and turned to go again.

You don't want to watch this? he said.

She sighed. That's okay, I'll just — I'll see the whole text of it when I get to work, I'm sure. Warner took her discomfort for embarrassment at not taking an interest in things she knew to be important. I mean, she said, would you want to come home from work and go to night school? That's sort of it.

Kendall and Warner had become friends two years ago, after running into each other three or four times at the student housing office at New York University. Both were looking for a place to live; both sheepishly admitted that they were in fact not students and had been driven to such dishonesty by their frustration with the search for an affordable studio apartment. The next time they met there, Kendall suggested they have lunch afterward; at a pizza parlor on University Place, she mentioned to him that she had seen, in the past few weeks, plenty of one-bedroom apartments too expensive for one person, but big enough for two. Warner stopped chewing and nodded in agreement. She asked him what he thought about the two of them sharing a place. He said that sounded great to him. He thought she seemed sweet and generous, though her looks influenced his appraisal of all these things.

The apartment had been advertised as a large one-bedroom; they had answered the ad posing as a couple, not to seem like more traditional tenants but to disguise their intention to put up a wall in the bedroom. Warner had been excited by the game, though he never let on. He kept hoping for some sign of authenticity in her attentions, but she was not even a very good actress. As the landlord went on about the unspoiled nature of the neighborhood and his regret at not being able to accept a personal check as their security deposit, Warner had imagined the two of them there as the wall went up; he saw himself standing dangerously close behind her as she stood on tiptoe with the measuring tape, his hands free to calculate, his mouth full of nails. This sexual daydream would, he knew, have been a disaster had it come to pass. But even now, at times, he felt he would be willing to poison the friendship—which, after all, was not one of his close ones—in return for the feeling of being taken seriously.

Of course, any romantic advance would have had to come from Kendall, and it was not about to. Warner was paralyzed by the very self-image he wanted to overthrow. The wall had gone up, with an ill-fitting, makeshift door in one corner, and since the wood was by necessity so thin, they had moved their beds as far from it as possible.

Hers was the bedroom with the closet; his had the window. Kendall had set up lamps in the tiny room, to compensate, and now as she changed for work she turned them all on in the hope of rousing herself. Getting dressed up was purely a symbolic act, for her own benefit, to help keep her working life, which she hated, separate from the balance of her hours. No one on the night shift at the station was required to look even presentable, since they had no one to impress at that hour but each other. A few workers routinely showed up in outfits that they would later wear to the gym, or in the clothes in which they had awakened.

Kendall walked back into the hall, still trying to decide where to eat dinner now that she had committed herself to leaving. Warner was intent on the image of the seated president. She opened the door. I'm off, she said. Warner waved. The elevator kept her waiting. She decided to go to a diner that was just a block or two out of her way; it was inexpensive, and if she ate there and then walked to work, she would be on time but not early. The elevator door opened on what looked like a small, overfurnished room. There was a standing lamp, an easy chair, a wooden end table with two plants on it, a box marked Plates and a box marked Records. Standing behind the lamp was a man she did not remember ever seeing before.

He smiled at her. She could step only a few inches inside the door. When the door started to close, it hit her on the heel, and opened again automatically. The man looked slightly embarrassed and held out a hand, to no particular effect. The door hit Kendall again; laughing nervously, she sat in the chair. The door finally closed and they started down that way.

Moving in? she said.

The man shook his head. Out. This is the last of it. I have my brother downstairs helping me.

How long have you lived here?

Four years. You live here, right? I think I've seen you.

Kendall sat facing the door, with the man standing behind her. On the eleventh floor, she said. Where we just were.

Nice to meet you.

The elevator stopped, and Kendall got out of her seat, brushing her skirt. Another man, unmistakably his brother, was waiting in the lobby when the door opened. He nodded at Kendall, lifted the box of records, and laid it in front of the door, to hold the elevator. Each brother took an end of the bulky easy chair; Kendall flattened herself against the wall of the narrow lobby to let them pass and then watched them walk with small steps out the front door of the building, also propped open with a box. After a moment, she went back to the elevator, where the door beat impatiently against the heavy box, and picked up the two plants, which, with their stiff strands of wire braided into a hook, still looked as though they hung from some nail. At the mirror by the front door, she smiled at her reflection; holding each plant by the hook, palms up, she thought she looked like Justice. The two brothers were struggling to push the easy chair into a small van already crowded with furniture. She walked over and balanced the two plants on the fender. The one she had spoken to in the elevator looked at her, surprised; then he laughed.

Thanks, he said. Mighty neighborly.

She shrugged, and turned back in the direction of Sixth Avenue.

The diner was called the Lamplight; eating alone seemed the norm there. Customarily it was full of older men, but the oldest people there were always the waitresses. Kendall ordered a bowl of mushroom barley soup and some bread, and the waitress, a white-haired lady in new high-top aerobic sneakers, walked soundlessly away.

From the windows of her parents' house — or, better, from the cool, warped steps in front of it — the sun would still be visible at this time of day. The house was just a few hundred yards from Lake Michigan, to the east of it, and as a child, unable to fathom how the sun might fall behind the planet, she had theorized that it fell, slowly and grandly, into the lake, where it went out each night like a match. Her brother Sam had actually encouraged her in this belief, though he was older and knew better. She wondered now, as she had not wondered in years, why he used to lie to her like that, whether it was out of some impulse of cruelty or because he simply preferred her version of the world. Often, he would sit with her on the steps as it grew dark, speaking to her in the same friendly yet uncontradictable tone she would later recognize in some of her teachers, until their mother called to him to bring her inside. In New York, the sun disappeared from the canyons of the city by the middle of the afternoon; somehow, though, it went on lighting offices and stores and apartments for hours afterward. At certain times, like some spirit, it was visible only in one or another of the city's many mirrors, forty stories or more of darkened glass.

Traffic up Sixth Avenue was light, and the buses strained along, followed by kite tails of paper and grit. As Kendall walked north, the time, flashing from the top of a building on Times Square, was always in her vision. But the pace and congestion of that part of town were still far from her. She strolled up the avenue, past the mysterious warehouses, the bars with sheet-metal windows, whose plastic signs were each lit from within by one yellow light bulb, past the Spanish restaurants, the rows and rows of repeating posters refusing to peel from the temporary wooden walls of a construction site. She came, as if walking toward the present, upon the larger, more recent buildings, the soaring hotels, proudly incongruous, hoping to lead by example. Gradually the sidewalk filled with men and women still leaving work at this hour; they shouldered past her to get to the end of the day.

In the building that housed the radio station, night workers were required to sign in at the reception desk in the lobby. The guard was away from the desk — they, or their supervisors, often seemed to take their job less than seriously — but Kendall signed in anyway. The studios were on the twenty-first floor. A dozen or so people poured out of the elevator when it arrived at the lobby, but Kendall rode up alone.

The elevator door opened on the increased activity that always accompanied an important news development; as a general rule, though, the extra motion did not correspond to anything other than a heightened sense of responsibility. The process by which words came into the studios and left again, condensed in one voice, was unchanging and did not respect the words themselves. The elevators faced a reception area dominated by a great, semicircular white desk, which was unattended at night. For the night shift, the station's own security guard patrolled this area. The guard, who wore a kind of imitation police uniform with his name, Shannon, written on a black bar above his heart, didn't like to sit at the desk, apparently thinking it undignified; he sat on a tall stool to the left of the elevators. Above the desk hung a large brown audio monitor bracketed to the wall near the ceiling. The monitor was turned off. Leading away from the reception area was a maze of corridors laid with stiff, short-haired carpet and flanked by thick doors with printed white cards affixed beside them.

Kendall had an office to herself, though it was not exactly her own. Since the station operated around the clock, the same desks and the same recording equipment were used by two and sometimes three people. Dan Pedraza, who had her room during normal working hours, was neat, but his presence was ghostly. Both their names were on the card by the door. A framed picture of Pedraza's family balanced atop an old reel-to-reel tape can on the metal bookshelf, but he was not in it. An empty package of Marlboro cigarettes was in the wastebasket. Kendall laughed at herself as she realized she was looking in the trash for signs of him. She opened the window, though she smelled no smoke.

Pedraza had left a note, pinned to the phone by the receiver: Halfway through Jeff's review of All the Rage. Two more inserts, as marked. Not much, Dan P. She found, without even having to turn her head, a tape marked JVD Seg 10/20–24 and another labeled All the Rage Ints 10/8. Pedraza always left things in perfect order, not, she imagined, out of courtesy to her but because it would have bothered him, on the bus on the way home, not to have left everything exactly so. She hardly knew him.

The sound of horns, so far below as to seem plaintive, rolled through the open window. The walls were laid with squares of white, soundproof cork, which had enticed her on those days when her job seemed more than usually depersonalizing to bring one of her own tapes to work, turn it up until she could feel it in her chest, and dance. The floor was covered by the same stiff gray rug that smothered every inch of the twenty-first floor, pouring under every door, into every closet, with the uniformity of a flood.

She sat and looked at the telephone.

Oh, Julian, she said, you fucker, where are you.

She racked the two tapes and played back the principal. The voice of the station's film critic, a cheerful, ugly little man, began abruptly. — *above this morass in the role of Ethan, the young man who tries to cope with his nightmare visions of his war experiences, visions which persist long after he has come home. Perelli brings such vibrant life to what might have been a hackneyed role that he not only survives this disaster of a film but actually rises above it; his performance, in my view, is the real subject of the movie. I talked with him recently about how he is handling this critical acclaim at such a tender age. . . .* The critic sneezed loudly. *There!* he said, *I got the whole thing in. Saved somebody the trouble of splicing, even with my nose running. Whoever's doing this, you're welcome.*

Kendall smiled. Gesundheit, she said. She rewound the tape with her index finger until she reached the word *age.* Typed on a sheet of paper next to the tapes were the excerpts from the interview with the actor Perelli which she had to edit into the final copy. The first words she had to locate were *It's just a matter of practicing your craft. You can't worry about satisfying anyone but your director and the actors you work with, and yourself.* She played the tape of the interview from the beginning and listened.

The soundproofing of the room sometimes made her uneasy; the quiet reminded her of the quiet of someone listening at your door. If something were going on elsewhere in the station, she wouldn't be able to hear it. She wondered if anyone was wandering around in the hallway. She wondered who else was on that night.

Oh, the tape said, *he was a total professional, a joy to work with. I was a little awed at first, because of, you know, his reputation. I see a lot of what gets written about him. But it's just not true.*

Seven months of this sort of work, in an environment she had, before starting the job, inaccurately imagined, had led Kendall to think of what was called news as simply the sum of the labors of her fellow workers and herself. It was a commodity that the station produced. She did not believe that it touched her and had to take it on faith that it touched anyone at all. Her life away from work was what varied, what she could control, and therefore what merited her attention. To work here, she had left a job at a recording studio, where she worked long and irregular hours, depressed by the sight of the musicians who weren't successful, and by the sight of those who were. At least now she had a window.

She had lost track of the tape. *I would*, it said, *I would like to do Broadway, just to shut some people up. But I don't feel I have to prove anything to myself. And of course I don't consider film acting to be any less legitimate. If it's good, it's good, that's all.*

What an asshole, Kendall said out loud. The construction of the room encouraged her to talk to herself, to swear or sing with no chance of being overheard, as if she were inhabiting her own head. Tell me, she said to the tape player, what do you think you'd be doing for a living if you weren't good-looking?

She reached out and turned the tape player off. The traffic sounded like water running far beneath her window. There were just under seven hours left in her shift. She would have to phone for a cab to come and meet her, rather than go out into the street and hail one at that hour, in that neighborhood. She felt depressed and angry. A small on-air monitor hung on the wall behind her; she tilted back her chair and switched it on.

Colozan, the nation in which the secretary of state's body still rested, was maintaining a somewhat ominous silence. But the group, if not the man, responsible for the assassination, one of several restless factions within that nation's government, had been, a United States government spokesman said, tentatively identified. In his emotional address a few hours earlier, the president had faced the camera and said that a measure of a country's greatness was its unwillingness to be bullied. All ships and submarines that habitually patrolled that part of the world had been placed on full alert. It was the kind of act that could mean anything at all; it consisted, in fact, mostly in the words themselves.

In the last hours of that morning, as Kendall lay asleep in her bedroom, a key turned in the front door lock. Julian walked in and, hearing no greeting, put his bag down gently. He went into the bedroom, paused a moment, and closed the door behind him, to maintain the night. He stood beside her bed and stepped out of his clothes. The weight on the edge of the mattress woke her; she opened her eyes, lifted her face to him, and then let it drop back into the pillow. They struggled into each other's arms and told each other nothing.

Geoff Collier was named after his father, and ever since his mother had divorced the man when the child was two, she had felt a little foolish at having sentenced herself to this reminder of youthful love. She had loved the boy energetically, partly for that reason. As a baby he had given shape to her life, since there was, at that time, nothing else to counteract his influence. When he was at the age when anything taller than himself was simply something to climb, she had once quite by accident burned him with the bottom of a pan filled with hamburger. He bore a small white mark on his forearm, near the wrist, for the rest of his life. Though no one blamed her for it — least of all the boy, who was so young when it happened that years later he would have to be told how the scar had gotten there — his mother considered the mark, covered by clothing only a few months out of the year, an ineradicable sign of reproof for not loving him enough to protect him even from herself.

He was never a wonder in school. His obvious intelligence, as it manifested itself elsewhere, was at first a source of exasperation to his mother, later a kind of solace. When he was in the eighth grade, she left town for a week on a business trip. The business required only three days; she spent the remaining time enjoying the company of a man who also lived in New York and who wondered how they had been brought to such a pass, leaving town in order to avoid cheapening themselves in the eyes of their children. On the Friday she was away, Geoff invited nearly everyone from his class and from the class ahead of his to a party that night at his house. He went home after classes, made himself a ham sandwich for an early dinner, washed the dish, and then took his mother's instant camera and wandered through the apartment with it, snapping a picture in every room. Saturday afternoon, after a long bath and a tentative cup of coffee, he took out the photos and reconstructed the apartment to match them. His mother found out about the party a week or so later from the doorman of the building across the street. Her own doorman had been prevailed upon, it seemed, to keep quiet. She went home that night with punishments in mind, but as happened to him so often at home and elsewhere, and as he had expected, when he told his story he was forgiven.

He was wildly popular in school, even among the teachers, who could see in him with fondness what they, as children, either had or had not been. He got by on charm and on the love he was well aware he inspired. He was tall and even handsome. On the strength of a personal interview, he was admitted to Bennington, and to a few other small colleges as well. But Bennington was where he meant to go. His mother saw his departure as the start of the majestic season that would end her life. She saved her tears for the long drive home. In his first semester he made friends without much effort and also discovered learning. A curriculum just broad enough to accommodate him finally married his interests to his capacities. His roommate finished midterms a day earlier than he did, and with Geoff's permission threw a small party to celebrate. Geoff studied through the party, in his room, rather than go to the library; he liked being able to take a break every once in a while and go into the living room to talk to his friends. At about ten minutes to one the noisy discovery was made that there was no more beer. Several guests, all drunk, got up to drive to the convenience store for more; Geoff was alarmed and offered to go himself. He took the keys to his roommate's car and walked out into the clear cold, which in just a few weeks, he was told, would come to stay. He rolled down the windows. He enjoyed the cold air roaring through the car, and the feeling of not studying. He pulled out to pass an oil truck, and he and the driver of another car, moving much more slowly in the opposite direction, died together without reflection. The driver of the oil truck slowed down but did not stop; he heard the sound behind him and radioed a call to the local ambulance corps. He didn't need to see that.

The news of this, when it reached the students at St. Albert's, the high school that had graduated Geoff just five months before, pushed the recent events in Colozan, already a hemisphere away, even farther from their minds. Meals were eaten in silence, and the boys cried in gym. Warner had never had the Collier boy in a class, but he remembered him. He had spent the night preparing to lead his seniors in a discussion of the current crisis in international affairs, which, he planned to tell them, threatened, in his opinion, to involve them. Instead, the newspaper articles he had photocopied stayed in his bookbag, on his desk. Out of consideration, he did not ask questions, and read straight from the textbook the chapter he had assigned, in a flat, steady voice, as if these were words they all knew by heart, whose very sounds consoled.

In a restaurant on the Upper East Side, Julian reached toward the breadbasket in the middle of the table. Kendall took his downturned hand between her thumb and little finger and scratched it lightly with her nails. He waited patiently, his hand closed around a roll; when she released him, he brought the hand to his mouth and ate. It was Tuesday night, the start of her weekend.

How were your parents? she said.

They seemed fine. My mother's apparently decided to have

the whole first floor of the house redone, so we had to eat every single meal in a restaurant, which was kind of a drag. Though they obviously thought I'd like it, the way I would have liked it when I was about eight, I guess. And then when we were home, there were these two guys working in the kitchen, about twenty hours a day. Pulling up their pants, helping themselves to what's inside the refrigerator, so it wouldn't spoil, they said, when they had to unplug everything. My parents didn't say a word to them the whole time.

It would have been nice to know where you were, she said.

He closed his eyes. Why, he said. Did you think something had happened to me?

No. Don't be like that, okay?

I'm sorry. I should have told you, you're right. I did try before I left, but you're right. It's just I didn't have any jobs the whole week, so I decided to go.

She picked up her glass of wine, swirled it aimlessly, and finished it. She wanted to let him know everything was all right without forgiving him.

You don't have to explain it, she said. I think it's wonderful that you're so attentive to them. Julian took the train out to his parents' home quite often, and she didn't think it was wonderful at all. She couldn't discover what it was about them that drew such scrutiny from him; he didn't show such detailed curiosity, as far as she could see, about anything else. They weren't very old, or sick, and though she would never have asked him to admit it, he didn't seem to have great or even usual affection for them.

There's a weird kind of tension between them lately, Julian said. They don't exactly fight. The big sore point between them seems to be old age, and I don't see how they're going to resolve it. You know my father's birthday was last month, his sixty-fifth birthday. My mother tried to make a little party out of it, make it a cheerful occasion, invite a few friends over. Well, my father was extremely cheerful in his way — he started making all these jokes at the dinner table about dying, about going over to see the family plot, making up joke epitaphs. He thought he was being jovial, he thought he was going along with it, you know? By the end of the party, my mother wouldn't even speak to him. She kept getting up to go to the kitchen and bang things around. Everyone there was made fairly uncomfortable, I think. I'm not sure if it was because of his jokes or her reaction to them.

Yeah, you had told me about that, Kendall said.

It's pretty much the same thing that happened his last birthday. The waitress came to clear their table; Julian put his fork down on his plate just in time for her to sweep it away. She was coldly beautiful, with short black hair and a forbidding sense of fashion; his eyes followed her as, without having said a word, she walked away.

Though it was October nineteenth, the night, like the last few nights, was so warm that every slight breeze came as a relief. Kendall wore a white sweater vest; even in the restaurant light, her bare arms shone. They had picked a restaurant with sidewalk tables, separated from the pedestrian traffic by a low fence, to enjoy the night. But too many others had the same idea — the warm weather seemed to carry with it a warning that it could not be enjoyed for much longer — and so the best they could do was an indoor table at the front, flush against the window. The view was the same, and the air was cool enough inside. But Julian felt uneasy, separated by glass from another young couple, sitting outside just a foot or so away. He could not help feeling he was being looked at; the glass itself had something to do with it. Sometimes, the moment he picked up his knife or his wine glass, the man outside would do the same.

Kendall wanted dessert. She caught the eye of the sharp-haired waitress, who listened to her order and went away without nodding. Julian never dared to tell Kendall how the naturalness of her eating habits excited him, since he was not sure he could explain it even to himself. It seemed to hint at some animal nature; when she was hungry, she ate. She didn't care to deny herself. Women who ordered dessert had always held a sexual fascination for him.

She put her foot on his and pressed quickly. It wasn't a

particularly tender gesture, but she trusted him to know her intent.

My mother called yesterday.

Julian looked up and smiled. You make it sound so ominous. My mother called yesterday.

She says my brother wants to come to town in about six months. To visit me. She gave him my address.

Jesus.

The waitress brought something constructed out of chocolate, thick and immobile on the plate. It had a comic aspect.

She really did that? Julian said. She didn't even ask you? That's amazing.

The couple at the table outside got up to leave. Almost immediately, their places were taken by two girls, evidently college students. Julian sat back, as if to see more clearly. The girls slid their books under their chairs.

Maybe you could move, he said. Six months is enough time.

Kendall gave a sad laugh, one quick exhalation.

Let's not talk about it now, she said. I was going to try not to mention it at all until spring. Julian raised his eyebrows, but said nothing. She cut into the cake and offered him the first bite. He shook his head. She brought the fork back to her own lips and, with some effort, pulled the chocolate off it, still looking at him.

Right, he said. How's work?

Work sucks.

Really. Even with the shooting and everything?

What's it got to do with me?

The waitress was standing above them. Will there be anything else, she said, looking at Kendall. Kendall looked at Julian and then shook her head. Just the check. The waitress took out her pad and figured the total without moving. Kendall and Julian exchanged smiles as if in secrecy.

They leaned over to look at the check where it had dropped on the table, and took out their money. Kendall calculated the tip; when all the money was counted out, Julian looked at the pile of bills critically and threw in another dollar.

Outside, he breathed the clean air loudly, enthusiastically, and Kendall lifted her face as if to the sun. She took his arm as they walked toward the corner.

Great night, he said.

Are you coming home with me? she said.

He pretended to look thoughtful. I don't know, he said. I haven't been invited yet. I'm basically a very polite person.

Kendall halted him, put her hands on his neck, pulled his ear to her mouth, and invited him, with a seashell sound.

Since it was late, they took a cab; the driver, unprompted, got onto the nearly deserted FDR Drive. Kendall and Julian rolled down their windows and sat holding hands, looking in opposite directions. The drive ran along the edge of the city, at its waterline. The buildings seemed to undulate above them as they rode; at one point they passed underneath a collection of apartments anchored to the ground by four strong pillars, like a giant tooth. After that, the city seemed to slope down toward the river again. Only the hardier elements — playgrounds, warehouses — came down close to the water's edge. Tugboats and Coast Guard boats rolled through the surprisingly turbulent water, through the shaky reflections of the thousands of harsh lights burning on the far, concrete shore. To the south the lights of the Brooklyn Bridge hung against the dark sky. It looked as though the bridge itself were made of light, magically substantial, as in an architect's dream. The cab driver, it became clear, had picked this route for his own release; he drove as fast as he pleased down the wide, empty road. The meter ticked like a watch.

In the apartment, Warner sat in the easy chair facing the door, a stack of notebook paper balanced on its arm. He held a red pen between his fingers, like a cigarette. He smiled at them when they walked in. Julian went over to him and they shook hands, as they always did. Kendall turned the locks.

Grading tests? Julian said.

Papers. I think I've hit the wall, though. I try to save the ones I think will be good for last, to keep me going, but I'm not going to make it.

Julian stood in front of him, hands in pockets. Kendall busied herself across the room, looking through the mail. So how's the teaching? he said. You still liking it?

I am, yeah. Although it was a little rough today. A kid who graduated last year and was up at Bennington was in a car crash just last night, got killed, and so the whole place was kind of somber. Very somber.

Man. A kid you knew?

I never had him in a class or anything. I knew him mostly by reputation. You've never seen anything like the reaction of these kids, though. It's unbelievable. They just stop talking. It's like suddenly the air weighed more. And this guy was popular, but they couldn't all have known him, I mean some of them weren't even at the school last year. I don't know. I never had anybody my age die. There's going to be a service for him Friday.

That's awful. Julian tried to let the proper amount of time pass. Hey Rob, you remember my friend Holly, right? That you met?

Holly, my God, yeah, sure I remember. She's not somebody you'd forget. What's she up to?

Well, who can say. But she's throwing a party at her apartment two weeks from Monday, if you feel like going. Kendall thinks she can get somebody at work to switch nights with her, so we'll be there.

Kendall went into her bedroom and closed the door.

That sounds great. Thanks, I'd love it, Warner said.

Julian took his hands out of his pockets. Warner continued looking at him, not expectantly, but out of politeness; he wasn't particularly anxious to get back to his students' compositions. Through the window, across the street, Julian could see a man at his kitchen table, reading a newspaper and occasionally slapping at it.

So, Julian said. Goodnight.

Goodnight.

Kendall sat on the bed, waiting for him. He closed the door. I don't know why you're like that, he said. He's not so bad.

I hate him.

No you don't.

I hate him when you're here. Julian frowned to keep from smiling, and started to unbutton his shirt. No, she said. She stood and unbuttoned it for him, slowly, sensually, and with some difficulty. She placed a kiss on each new perfect spot of skin as it was revealed. He felt the muscles in his stomach tense.

She jerked the shirttail out of his pants. He drew his arms behind him, and she slipped the shirt off. When she pulled the top button of his pants smoothly through the buttonhole he felt the game overtake him; he reached urgently for the back of her sweater and pulled it over her head. Her kisses ran again like a bead of sweat down his chest and stomach.

They found the bed. Each freed a hand and tested the other's readiness. Julian broke out of her arms and knelt above her; he wedged one hand beneath her, into the small of her back, and tried to turn her over. Let's try something new.

With little effort, and no resentment, she resisted him, and stayed where she was. Smiling, she reached out and switched off the light on the table by the bed. She grabbed his arms and pulled, and he fell on top of her. They laughed. It's always new, she said.

Warner got up at seven-fifteen. In the shower, he leaned against the wall and rubbed his eyes. He dressed, leaving his tie loose, and followed his own wet footprints back to the bathroom to make himself a cup of instant coffee. The water from the tap there got much hotter than the one in the kitchen. There was no sound from the other bedroom and wouldn't be for several hours. With fifteen minutes to spare before the last possible moment he could begin his walk to the subway and still be on time, he crouched in front of the television set and turned it on, at the lowest possible volume. His desires to avoid disturbing Kendall and Julian and to save himself the embarrassment that always seemed to attend watching TV in the morning were about equal. He watched and listened until his legs were sore from his posture; and then he switched off the set and stood up. He felt a real sense of moral alarm, not only at the events he had seen and heard described but at the great edifice of image and language which had been constructed to try, he felt, to keep him from understanding what was happening at anything other than the most ambiguous, symbolic level. Warner felt as if someone was using his name without permission. He wanted to know, in all earnestness, why he had not been consulted.

Angrily, near tears in fact, he gathered up his tenth-grade papers and clapped them into the eleventh-grade textbook. He went over in his mind the Wednesday schedule—tenth grade, then ninth, then study hall, then the seniors, then study hall again—to make sure he had everything, closed his bookbag, and left for work.

At about eleven, Kendall woke up. She had to grope as quietly as she could, in the lightless, windowless room, for her watch on the bedside table. She enjoyed the luxury of not having to be anywhere. Julian, no matter what position he fell asleep in, was curled up with his back to her by morning. She got up on one elbow to look at him; his eyes were pressed into his upper arm near the crook of the elbow, the hand hanging defenselessly. She placed an experimental kiss between his shoulder blades. He didn't move. On some lazy mornings this was an exquisite challenge, to bring him up out of sleep as slowly as possible, yet with an erotic thought in his head, as if she had produced in him a dream. Now, though, she felt she had to go to the bathroom rather badly. She lifted the sheet an inch or two and slid out.

Later, waiting for Julian to get out of the shower, Kendall cleared two armfuls of debris from the table and threw them on the couch so that they could have breakfast. They had coffee and cranberry muffins, and Kendall had half a grapefruit as well. It was past noon, and hotter than the day before. They didn't talk much, but they smiled appreciatively at each other, and Kendall crossed her legs in such a way that she could swing her foot and kick him lightly in the calf.

After the meal, Julian stood at the sink and did the dishes; she waited behind him with her chin on his shoulder. She brought the fan out from her bedroom and set it up in the living room. They both stood in front of it with their arms out. Julian took a step behind her and put his arms around her stomach.

I think I'll head home, he said. He felt something shift.

How come?

I haven't been there in six days. Just to see if everything's okay.

What could possibly be not okay?

See if there's any messages on the machine, any jobs. Sometimes offers come in the mail, not often, but still.

He had taken up a position where he couldn't see her face, which he knew was exasperated and sad. She didn't feel dependent on him — she only wanted to be with him, for the pleasure to be found in that; but she would not be reduced to asking him to stay. She wanted to avoid even the appearance of dependency. He made much of his need to spend time alone. Time alone was time away from her; that was not faulty reasoning, she felt, and she could not be anything but hurt by it.

Whatever you want, she said.

He held her for a while longer before going into the bedroom for his wallet and his keys.

At the door, she felt her frustration spilling over and tried to temper it with an ironic tone, a half smile. Don't you worry about me, she said. I've got lots to keep me busy here. If you want to be a call, I expect I'll be here all fucking day. But he wouldn't accept those terms; they put him in the wrong, and made him angry. He pretended not to understand. I will, he said. He kissed her. I love you, he said. She nodded and closed the door.

Available taxis were almost always in good supply on the stretch of Sixth Avenue where Kendall lived, so Julian stood and waited for one with all its windows rolled up, a promise of air conditioning. He had other vices, but the only one he would readily acknowledge was his love of taxi rides, probably because, deep down, he didn't really consider it a vice. It provided a time for quiet contemplation and a chance to see the city. He rarely walked more than ten blocks. He was put off by the subway, and never bothered to figure out the routes of the slow, fitful buses. He told himself that he made up for the extra transportation costs by not having the sort of job for which one had to buy clothes.

His cab was cold enough to pack a snowball in. The driver was Chinese, or Korean, a good omen for Julian, who hated cabbies who tried to engage him in conversation. Talking to passengers seemed to be an inclination of the American-born. For some reason, Julian found these garrulous drivers impossible to contradict; he would hear himself mumbling agreement with the most inane or distasteful opinions, and would wind up angry at himself. It might, he sometimes thought, have had to do with the helplessness inherent in being driven somewhere. One rainy night he had actually agreed to attend a Buddhist prayer meeting at a cabbie's apartment, and for the last few blocks of the ride, keeping an anxious eye on the street signs, had repeated a simple chant from a small book the man held up for Julian's benefit as he drove.

The Asian driver turned his head to hear directions. Sixty-eighth and Third, Julian said. The cab pulled out into traffic. Julian sat looking out the window, his elbow resting on the door, two fingers through the strap. They rode up to Twenty-third Street and turned east, past the confusion of cars and pedestrians caused by Broadway, past Madison Square, whose emptiness seemed odd and temporary. The weather brought out certain people and kept others inside. There seemed to be less movement; people put their packages down on the corner and pulled their shirts away from their bodies when waiting for a light. Yellow taxis darted in and out of each other's company like fish. On Third Avenue, in the Forties, red brake lights started to go on. Julian slid into the center of the back seat to see through the windshield. The cab slowed down but never quite stopped. The first thing Julian saw, above the level of the cars, were horses' heads, and above them, policemen. The horses were still. The policemen looked calm, but their expressions were a function of uniform; the white helmets and dark aviator sunglasses kept their faces well regulated. The backs of their blue shirts were spotted with sweat.

The traffic, as far as Julian could see, was not terribly heavy, but everyone wanted a good look down the side street as they passed. There, within the familiar blue, scarred police barricades, a small sea of people boiled, waving signs and fists at a handsome four-story brownstone. The building bore no flag or seal of any kind, only a small gold street number above the mail slot in the door. All the blinds were drawn; the windows on the bottom two floors were barred. The demonstrators, those that Julian could see, were mostly of student age, ten years or so younger than he was; those who were visibly older were almost exclusively women. As the cab crept along, the scene in front of the brownstone rolled out of sight. Horns began to honk, behind them, in front of them.

Outside his building Julian paid his fare. The driver counted out change and returned it through the window.

To hell with them, huh? he said.

Julian smiled and nodded. He walked into the shade beneath the front steps and sorted through his keys. Julian rented the basement apartment in a rather valuable townhouse owned by a young couple by the name of Camp, who occupied the upper floors. The Camps had insisted on installing an alarm system for him, which he knew was prudent, but which made him feel at times as if he were living in a bank vault. He switched it off. He pushed the door open and bent over to pick up his mail— two residual checks, two bills, and a letter from his father, the contents of which had already been described to him on his visit home. Inside the apartment it was musty and hot; he pulled open the windows. Because of its sunken position, the apartment got direct sunlight only a couple of hours a day, and those hours had passed. On the table in back of the couch, the small red light blinked on his phone answering machine. There were four calls from Kendall, wondering where he was, a few hang-ups, probably also from Kendall, and a message from an engineer named John Caravella, whom Julian knew. Caravella had a job for him, on a soda commercial. It was a chorus part, so there would be no auditioning. The session was on November ninth, almost three weeks away. Julian called him back immediately and accepted, with thanks. He made a good living singing, good enough, with a little help from his parents, to afford him a space in this part of town, but he could never lose the apprehension that each of these calls might be the last.

He was alone, with the whole day to fill. He lay on the couch and thought about sleeping, but he had slept enough. He swept the apartment, but much of the dust refused to settle. He tore the receipts off the top half of his royalty checks and stuck the checks in his wallet. In the silence, he thought about the soda commercial. He wondered who else would be there. Restless, he convinced himself that he needed to rehearse, even though he would not see the score until a few days before the session. He closed the windows. He went to the phone and dialed the Camps' number upstairs; as he had hoped, there was no one at home.

So he stood behind the couch and he sang. He sang Lush Life. He sang Runaround Sue. He sang Crazy. He sang Catch That Pepsi Spirit. He sang When Will I Be Loved?

The elevator doors opened on an empty room. The receptionist's desk was unoccupied, and the guard was nowhere in sight. Beyond the desk, the halls were vacant. It looked just like an ordinary suite of offices on a weekend, except for the monitor on the wall, which was switched on and spoke of a city council motion. Kendall walked down the quiet hallway to her office and closed the door.

Pedraza had left her no instructions. Tape hung as still as an icicle from a full reel on the deck. She threaded it and listened. Human voices spoke loudly, in an effort to be heard over street sounds. It was the raw material for a man-in-the-street segment, gathering strangers' responses to a single question. In transferring the material from cassette to reel-to-reel, Pedraza, to save tape, had cut out the question, which of course had been repeated on the original over and over again. He had left two or three seconds of silence between each answer. Kendall listened to the voices roll through the room. *Absolutely, I think this kind of stuff can't be tolerated, we have to take a stand. When I was little, my father used to tell me to pick on someone my own size. No comment. I think this is the same kind of macho bullshit, excuse me, that we've come to expect from this administration. I say all right, I say it's about time, we've got to avenge one of our own. Let's go down there and kick some ass. Well, I'm too old to get drafted anyway, what do I care?* There were at least twenty such answers in all, far too many for a segment of this kind, which was generally kept to thirty seconds. Kendall searched the desk again for a piece of paper with instructions on it, the reporter's or the producer's notations of which responses they wanted to use. *Oh, I can't say anything about that, no. Excuse me.* She reached out and turned the tape machine off. She pulled out every ball of paper from the wastebasket and smoothed them on the desk with the outside of her hand, checking both sides. She found nothing.

Kendall sat back. Well, she said out loud, I can't be responsible for this.

She stood and took a walk around the room. Reels of tape stood in metal racks around the walls, higher than her head. She trailed her fingers along the edges of the reels, as if they were a fence. At the window, she stopped and looked down at the bright street below.

Though she disliked her job, and made much of the fact, she was forced, when taking stock of her life, if not to like the office itself then to give it its due. She had nowhere else to go. The apartment, secured only for a year at a time, forced her into an awkward and unwanted intimacy with a man she had barely known when they decided to live together, a man she barely knew now. She did not feel alone in her own home, even when she in fact was. She was never more than a welcome guest in Julian's place. She could never open a drawer there out of curiosity; when she came to stay the night, she brought a bag. She did not feel as though she could ever go home to her parents. There was too much pressure there; they would be too glad to see her. This dusty, silent room was best, all hers, unburdened by any presence but the evidence of Pedraza.

There were plenty of other tasks with which she could fill the night, but she wasn't ready to go back to them. Though she was absolutely safe from blame, she rehearsed her excuse for not having the man-in-the-street edit ready. Beside her own reflection in the darkened window she saw red lights blinking on her phone; few of the phones in the station actually rang, since there were tape recorders going all the time, and the sound could easily and mysteriously reappear somewhere. She went back to the desk and watched. The lines seemed to be ringing endlessly; for some reason, few of them were being picked up.

Her own line was clear. She lifted the receiver, held it in the air for a few seconds, and then called Julian. His answering machine was on, but that was no proof he wasn't home. Sometimes he screened his calls. As his recorded instructions hissed in her ear, she tried to imagine him standing in his kitchen, hands in his pockets, watching the phone, and his expression when he heard her voice.

Hi, it's me, if you're there pick up. . . . Guess not. I was just bored at work, for a change. I hope you had a good day, I wound up sleeping most of it. Listen, I don't know where you are or what time you'll get in or anything, but if you want to come down. No, I mean I'm asking, will you please come down? I'd just really like it. If I don't see you, I'll understand. Bye.

She hung up, and wondered how much more she could bear of calls like this. They were both careful not to take certain privileges for granted; instead of respect and gradual intimacy, this policy seemed to lead to confusion. They had been seeing each other for eight months, and she still had to take a deep breath after calling him. Julian seemed able to endure it.

Kendall looked again at the blinking red lights on the phone. The sight of them was unsettling, just as the sight of the empty reception area and Mr. Shannon's vacant chair had been. The silence all around her had begun to seem unnatural. She wondered if there was any traffic at all on the other side of the heavy door.

And then she began, slowly, to connect her feelings of personal dread with the general air of dread that surrounded her. She knew that they were not the same, but they were similar enough to make her wonder if the circumstances of her life had not been suffused by some larger emotion. Though she felt her own fear and sadness no less keenly — in fact, more keenly now than ever — it was strange and powerful to feel, for once, so attuned to her surroundings. It occurred to her that the source of things might be found outside herself. A curiosity awakened, or was born, in her.

She opened the door and stepped outside. There was no one in the hall. She looked up and down, but she knew where everyone must have been. Her footsteps made the faintest noise, absorbed by the carpet and the walls. Some doors were closed, but most were open along the route to the red On Air light.

About half of the night shift had gathered in the engineer's room; the guard, Shannon, perhaps in deference to the job he was neglecting, stood nearest the door. All eyes turned toward Kendall when she came in, then turned back again. The studio, one of two that the twenty-first floor housed, consisted of three rooms, rectangles flush against one another. The rooms were connected by doors stuck into the corners of the common walls, and by two enormous, soundproof plastic windows. From the room where they stood, it was possible to see all the way through to the back wall of the third room, a small studio unto itself which was used for live interviews and the like. The walls were laid with squares of white cork; notices, typed lists, and cut-out cartoons were pinned directly into every surface. In the engineer's room, the wall opposite the window was dominated by a large metal skeleton that held several tape decks, an equalizer, and other equipment. Against the window was a mixing board, which controlled the microphones, sound levels, the various tape players, and an intercom. The night engineer, Samuelson, sat at the board under a heavy set of headphones.

On the wall behind Kendall, to the right of the door, hung a monitor, its silver switch tipped up. Samuelson had turned it on for the benefit of everyone who had stopped work to come in to watch as well as listen. There was a small digital clock on the board for Samuelson to refer to; a large clock on the wall behind him read eight fifty-nine. A commercial was airing; from the monitor, voices recommended a Broadway show, first a man, then a woman, then a child.

In the middle room, the announcer sat by himself, taking the opportunity to fidget, smoking a cigarette as quickly as he could. He had stopped using his real name when he had first applied for a job as a broadcast journalist; his name was Tim Meriwether now. He sat behind a small Formica desk, in a noiseless wooden chair, perhaps four feet from Samuelson, with the glass between them. The small red bulb on top of the board was dark and cooling. He saw Kendall and waved to her.

Meriwether was one of four men, with voices as near to identical as possible, who took six-hour shifts as the station's anchor. He had begun this career in college, reporting on trustee meetings and conference basketball tournaments for the campus radio; he had majored in broadcast journalism and hoped to land a job in television. But he was forced to acknowledge before he even got started the obstacle his looks presented to his hopes. Meriwether was unconquerably fat, thick-lipped, with an ill-fitting head of hair. His fingers and hands were beefy, and he was easily made to sweat. Items of international importance could not be transmitted through such a vessel. He did have a rich, unstumbling voice, and so he remained on radio. He grew to enjoy this mask, and, perhaps to enhance his sense of deception, let his appearance go to utter waste, dressing in his most comfortable clothes, putting on more weight. He seemed to enjoy his job, and was unfailingly pleasant to everyone at the station, though, understandably, he didn't like to talk much right before or after going on the air.

Visitors were grudgingly permitted in the center room with Meriwether, but few came in unless they were sure they could escape before the red On Air Light went on; they were afraid that some instinct would betray them when total silence was required. Meriwether read from notes that lay spread on the table before him. They rustled if he picked them up, a sound easily caught by his microphone, so he kept his hands on his thighs. The notes were replaced periodically, during a commercial break, by a young man or woman from the newsroom. A schedule of advertisements and recorded segments, in the light type of a computer, was taped down on all four sides to the corner of the table.

As the last scheduled commercial began, Samuelson lifted his hand and pointed his index finger straight up in the air. Meriwether smoked furiously for a few more seconds, then stubbed out the cigarette in a heavy glass ashtray that held some loose papers in place. Smoke continued to rise from the ashtray, straight as a chimney in the airless room. He raised his hands above his head, grabbed his left wrist, and stretched. The members of the staff who lingered in the engineer's room leaned back against the soft walls, their arms folded. They stopped talking. The station's theme music began to play, six quick notes, backed by the sound of typewriters. Meriwether brought his hands down into his lap. A few men and women were visible now in the less crowded room at the far end of the studio. Samuelson's finger came down and pointed through the window. The red bulb went on.

Good evening, it's one minute past nine o'clock. Continuing with our top story, the White House has now confirmed reports of conflicts involving United States Marines on the beaches of Colozan. Reports are being received from foreign journalists that the fighting continues at this hour, shortly before dawn on that island. The combat, which began at around four o'clock this morning, Eastern time, came only hours after the hurried evac-

uation of all remaining U.S. citizens from the island, including all American journalists, none of whom have been permitted to stay aboard any of the U.S. Marine and Navy vessels positioned offshore. They are, at this hour, all on a U.S. transport for home. White House spokesman Bernard Helliwell said that quote concern for the personal safety of all of the citizens, including the reporters unquote, was the only consideration in their removal.

Helliwell also read a statement from the president this afternoon, which cited what he called incontrovertible evidence linking Colozan's government to various crimes and violent acts against Americans around the world, culminating in last Monday's assassination of Secretary of State Alan Hayes Sheffield. Helliwell declined to specify these other acts or the evidence linking them to Colozan, saying only that to do so would pose a security risk at this time.

Today's combat follows the White House's announcement, early this morning, that Marine and Navy vessels had been ordered to land at Colozan City. According to the official announcement, this order came from the president in response to a direct request from a faction within that nation's government. Again, White House officials declined to identify the faction or individual through whom the request was made, claiming that it would place the lives of those involved in immediate danger. No independent confirmation of that request had been obtained. The time is nine oh four. Back after this.

Samuelson hit two switches simultaneously, the red light went off, and without a moment of silence, the sound of a commercial was heard over the monitor. A couple of people left the studio. Kendall looked around the room at those who remained, but their expressions were stingy. This is how it happens, she thought, then thought again, and decided it had never happened this way before. As the commercial came to an end, the engineer prepared to play a second. He hit the button, and, able to rest for a moment, leaned back in his swivel chair. His eyes met Meriwether's eyes. Expressionless, they examined each other.

Soon Meriwether's voice resumed. *Congressional reaction has been largely critical, with several House members, including the Speaker, calling a news conference of their own in which they maintained that the president had taken over power reserved for them, in waging war on a foreign nation. The president, who has declined to meet with reporters since the first announcement of the Marine landing, responded to those charges in a written statement, saying quote to say we are two nations at war would be to legitimize the tactics of the Colozan government, in their own eyes and in the eyes of much of the world. We cannot be at war with those who refuse to fight their battles in the open. This is a retaliatory act, an act of preventative self-defense unquote.*

Response from world leaders has been mixed. Several Western European governments, including France, Italy, and West Germany, have approved resolutions condemning the military action, while England and Israel have pledged troop support if necessary. The White House has not responded publicly to these offers. The Soviet Union quickly issued a statement this afternoon, through its embassy in Washington, denouncing the attack as cowardly and unjustified. But many Soviet affairs experts in this country agree that the language of the statement is comparatively mild, and whether or not this new strain in relations will result in any significant action is the subject of much speculation. Later in this hour we will have Dr. Edward Givotovsky, a professor of Soviet studies at Columbia University, in the studio to discuss the possible effects of today's developments on relations between the superpowers. It's fourteen minutes past the hour.

Meriwether's shift ended at midnight. Kendall knew she could find him in the employees' lounge, a loose collection of comfortable chairs near a black and silver urn that heated water. There were small towers of Styrofoam cups piled upside down on the table, an open box of doughnuts, and wicker baskets filled with instant coffee and four kinds of tea, Meriwether's weakness.

He smiled at her, and watched as she made herself some

coffee. He had filled the room with cigarette smoke. His large legs were crossed awkwardly.

Playing a little hooky? he said. She laughed as she sat down across from him but said nothing in response. They sat in silence for a while. The two of them were very friendly, but not close, and Kendall was not completely sure why she had come.

So how about all this, she said.

Pretty scary. A little exciting, too, I hate to say it. I mean in terms of coming to work.

Do you suppose it'll go on for long?

Who's to say.

Think it could ever get to the point where there'd be any kind of a draft? When was the last time that happened?

Why are you asking me?

She looked at him. You're right, she said. That's stupid, isn't it? It just seems like you'd know. She folded the plastic coffee stirrer between her fingers. That must happen to you all the time.

Not really. He smiled, trying to save her from embarrassment. No one ever recognizes me unless I talk, and even then, it doesn't happen that often. I suppose if you were on TV or something, that kind of thing would happen a lot more. It's nice, I guess, not to have to deal with that. The people who listen to me on the radio, sometimes I think it might be a serious shock to them if they ever met me.

Do you ever try to imagine them? Kendall said. I mean, do you think about the people who're listening when you're speaking? Or do you just think of it like talking into a tape recorder?

I try not to imagine them, at least when I'm working, not because it doesn't matter to me but because it's distracting. It can slow down my delivery. Even tonight, having everybody in the studio, I really had to concentrate. He shook his head. That was weird, wasn't it?

Dr. Givotovsky, the Columbia professor, wandered into the room, and bent between them for a doughnut. Meriwether nodded to him and waited for him to get out of the way. The professor sat down, looked at both of them, and smiled, with his mouth full.

But, Meriwether said, sometimes when I'm not working, especially when I'm on my way here or going back home, I wonder, who listens to the radio? Especially at a time like this, when you can look at the television. Everyone would rather see a picture of something than have it described to them, right? If the only pictures you can see are the ones your government provides, that's okay, it's better than nothing. And those pictures will be showing up in a day or two, I can promise you. So who listens to an all-news radio station at night? People in cars. Or highbrow sorts who don't want a television corrupting their apartment. People in cabs. Near my building there's an all-night vegetable stand that always has us on, so I think of them. People waiting for sports scores. I don't know.

Dr. Givotovsky pulled his chair closer to them. He had a rough line of sugar on each lip.

But you have to be careful to drive these people out of your head, Meriwether said. If you're sitting there talking about how the dollar is down abroad, and you start thinking about some woman standing in her kitchen staring out the window and listening to how the dollar is down abroad, well, that's a good way to lose your place.

He turned somewhat impatiently to the professor, as if hoping to make him say something, to erase the impression that he was shamelessly eavesdropping.

The professor swallowed. That was fun before, he said, pointing with the doughnut in the direction of the studio. Thank you.

Not at all. You were very good. This is Diane Kendall, an engineer here.

Kendall smiled politely.

Don't let me interrupt, the professor said. I just can't seem to walk past food without stopping.

No, no, it's good you came, Meriwether said. We were just talking about the invasion. Kendall was asking if I thought there might be any reinstitution of the draft. He reached behind him and filled his cup with hot water. The rim of it had been chewed lightly. Kendall's question already seemed ridiculous to her, and she was embarrassed to have it brought up again.

Oh, heavens no, it's extremely unlikely. That's not a very big country, you know, and our forces are very strong, stronger, frankly, that I care to think about. I don't know where they all come from. Besides, he said, you wouldn't have much to worry about on that score, would you? Being a woman.

Well, that's not how I meant it, she said.

I suppose, the professor said, that it would be of some interest to the mothers of the land. But any son you would have would have to be in diapers.

Kendall shook her head.

Married?

No, Meriwether said, sounding mildly annoyed, Kendall's unmarried.

I was speaking more theoretically, Kendall said.

Givotovsky seemed amused by the other man's protectiveness; he looked at him and said, What about brothers?

They both turned to look at her.

What about them, she said.

He means do you have any.

She was often asked this in conversation, and usually answered no. But she wanted to consider Meriwether a friend, not someone to whom the answer made no difference. Her brother hadn't left her mind all week, and so it was harder than usual to dismiss the fact of him. Besides, she wanted to set a good example for herself by not attaching too much importance to him. None to speak of, she said, and laughed.

None to speak of? Meriwether said.

I have one brother, eight years older. I don't think he's in much danger of induction, though. He's spent the last seventeen years in jail. It's been a long time since I felt like I knew him. More than seventeen years, anyway.

What's he in for? Givotovsky said.

Please, Meriwether said, maybe she —

It's okay. Well, among other things, he was convicted of assault, though at first they were charging him with attempted murder. So between the fact that I haven't seen him in so long and the fact that he could do, or try to do, something like that, it's hard for me to really think of him as a brother. In the conventional sense.

After a while Meriwether said, Well, on to other topics. But no one said anything. He tossed his cup, its brim destroyed, into the wastebasket and took a new one. More coffee, Kendall? he said. The professor laughed softly. She shook her head no.

How about for you, professor? Meriwether said. Givotovsky smiled, his teeth slightly parted, and laughed again. Meriwether gave him a questioning look, which he tried to keep friendly.

I'm sorry, the professor said. It's just that voice. That great, stentorian, announcer's voice — to hear it in normal conversation, to hear it say, How about some more coffee?

It's funny, isn't it? Meriwether said.

Most of Warner's students came to class Friday in suits, a disconcerting sight. They lived in a theatrical world, a world of important surfaces; their clothes meant a great deal to them, and reflected not just how they wanted to be understood by others but how they understood themselves. It was clear that, to them, these sharply creased fabrics and dark ties were the emblems of suffering. They wore expressions of weary and difficult bravery. Warner tended to think they were overdoing it; but as the day wore on and their sadness showed no inconsistency, he decided eventually that his own approach to loss was something he must once have learned.

There was something chastening about the students. After an initial attempt, in his morning classes, to break through their utter acquiescence and get their attention, his own speech and movements slowed, and he began to examine himself. He too wore a black suit, the one he had worn to help carry his grandfather's casket, but it only made him feel restricted, and he wore it now only because he had decided it would be too much trouble to bring it to work and find somewhere to change before the memorial service. He had been trying, since hearing the news in the faculty room three days ago, to better remember the Collier boy. By Friday afternoon, his emotions were such that he did not need to. Grief is not contagious, but it seldom fails to produce in others a feeling of sorrow, as well as a conviction that that sorrow is familiar and deserved. Like an actor preparing for a difficult scene, he had imagined that this loss had somehow befallen him, so that despite the sense of a gulf between his students and himself, he was able, through this natural if somewhat dishonest process, to join in the mood of quiet preparation.

The afternoon's classes had been canceled to allow everyone to attend the service. In the last period of the day, Warner talked politely about the chapter he had assigned the day before. When the bell rang he stopped talking in mid-sentence. Okay, that's it, he said. See you Monday. Usually he had to shout these words. Some of the students had closed their eyes for a moment at the sound of the bell. They stood up slowly, one or two at a time. The boys shook their wrists, trying to get the strange clothes to settle. The girls were beautiful; they filled Warner with sadness. They stared at nothing—or at him, as if he were nothing—until they allowed themselves to be brought to their feet by the touch of a friend, usually a boy. The degree of casual physical contact between the boys and the girls at the school in general was looked upon by Warner with longing and regret. It took nearly five minutes for all of the last class to leave. Again, their grand reluctance came close to seeming ridiculous to him; still, here in the face of it, there was no way to believe that it was not genuine. No one spoke as they walked out, arms around one another, or holding hands. Their attitudes were classical. One girl let her head fall like a late sleeper onto the level shoulder of some boy.

Warner's own reluctance to go to the church translated itself into lazy movements—closing books, straightening and re-straightening papers. When he felt, as he did now, that a particular class had gone badly, that nothing was learned, he most often traced it, rightly or wrongly, to some failure on his part as a teacher. Today, in the atmosphere of grandiose sadness which helped him to see himself from a greater distance, and less clearly, he blamed it on the failure of something much larger. He believed as strongly as he believed anything that history did not simply matter, it was the material of which one was made. But the lives of these children — lives of unacknowledged privilege — made that belief difficult to transmit. The notion behind it would seem strange to them. They were bright children, sometimes astonishingly so, and, as he had seen today, sensitive to at least certain brands of injustice, certain kinds of tragedy. He wondered at the depth of their present suffering. Why, then, could this natural understanding of suffering not be radically broadened? Yet already, even at this young age, it seemed much had been done to discourage them from seeing their world as relative to other worlds. Their teachers had been entrusted with the job of making the past not just interesting but inescapable. Today he felt that the job was impossible; he had not been given the tools, the tools did not exist.

For days now he had been trying to bring the news of another hemisphere into his classroom — current events, an easy trick compared to the reanimation of lives and events already long past. But he could not do it. Rather, the only ways in which he could do it were sensational and pointless. The boys in his classes were nearing draft age, for instance; what if attention to the fighting were suddenly to become a matter of personal safety? Or, he could say, what if it were your country, and a foreign army had landed on the beach down the block from your home and started shooting? He refused to do this. He did not want to teach smart young people to see conflict only in terms of how it affected, or might affect, themselves. The true lover of history is on both sides of every battle. In this sense, he held their looks and their manner against them; he did not want to be part of all that taught them to see the world as a series of mirrors of their own desires.

It pleased Warner to have to wear his sunglasses in the glare of the afternoon. He set out unaccompanied for the church, which was on Lexington Avenue. He walked in the valleys formed by affluent homes, on blocks where the houses shaded the trees. The sun was behind him, and floated before him in the tinted windshields of parked cars, moving, as he walked past, slowly from right to left. A telephone rang in an open window.

A line of people waited patiently to one side of a machine that dispensed cash. Just inside the plate glass front of a diner, a dark man stood scowling at the street from behind the counter; two letters from the name of his restaurant were printed in shadow on his white shirt.

The church, built of stone more than a century ago, looked as if it belonged on a village green somewhere; instead, it shared one wall with a stationery store and another with a restaurant. Warner approached it, patting down his hair, sweat dampening his suit. A crowd on the steps and out onto the sidewalk waited to enter. On the sidewalk stood a furrowed black message board on a thin metal stand, with white, spiked letters: 3 PM A CEL-EBRATION OF THE LIFE OF GEOFFREY COLLIER. The crowd on the sidewalk formed a black gate for pedestrians, many of whom waited until they were out of earshot to start speaking again.

The girls stood together in groups of six or eight. They wore black dresses that might, under different circumstances, have been considered alluring — the only black dresses they owned. They had begun to cry. They moved in slow circles, their bodies brushing against one another, gazing off across the street. Plainly they did not want to go in.

Many of the boys wore proper black suits, bought for them by their fathers, not for any specific occasion but rather to impress upon them the fact of a complete wardrobe. Some of them, though, were dressed in a touching parody of mourning clothes — tuxedo jackets, skinny black ties, black denim pants. The clothes were a gesture, like an armband. To a man, they wore sunglasses.

Carl Tatum, the chairman of the biology department, walked past Warner and nodded. A sweaty sheaf of yellow legal paper was doubled in his hand. He was recognized by an usher and waved through a side door.

In another ten minutes Warner was close enough to the entrance to be in the shade. He stood with his feet on two different steps. Organ music escaped from the church. He saw that part of the reason for the delay was that all the guests were being asked to sign a register as they entered. When his turn came, he took a pen from his jacket pocket and signed his name, using his first two initials in order to fit it into the space. The line on which he had written continued into a righthand column headed Remarks. He wrote Teacher, and left his pen there for others to use, to hurry things along.

As he entered the church on its lefthand aisle, a white-haired woman handed him a program. The only light came through an elaborate skylight high above the crowd, and, for a few minutes more, through the open doors. The stone kept the building remarkably cool, considering the temperature outside and the heat generated by bodies, which numbered perhaps four hundred. Nearly all of the remaining seats were in the wooden balcony, which ran ten feet or so above the pews, along the rear and side walls. Beneath the sound of the organ, the crowd murmured softly, but there was quite a bit of last-minute motion in the seats, cautious waves, quiet, rocking embraces. On the column to the left of the pulpit hung a wooden board with runners, into which were pushed wooden blocks with painted white numbers; in gold letters at the top of the board were the words Hymns For Today. The white numbers corresponded to those on the program in Warner's hand.

He spotted one empty space against the lefthand wall and made for it. Excusing himself, he shuffled past the others in the pew — a married couple, their two small children, and another, older man, who also appeared to be sitting by himself. One of the children remained standing on his seat and turned around to get a good look at the crowd, until his mother made use of the most threatening pronunciation of his first name in her repertoire.

Geoff Collier's body, too disfigured to be put on view, had been buried the day before yesterday. At the front of the church was a thick barrier of flowers. The organist, invisible, held one last long note and stopped.

Slowly, the Reverend Paul McLaren rose from his chair, walked onto the pulpit, and straightened the microphone. He made brief remarks of welcome. The organ came to life again; on its first note, half the people stood, while the other half looked anxiously to either side and stood a moment later. The first two lines of A Mighty Fortress Is Our God were accompanied by the gentle rustle of the softened pages of the hymnals.

There would be a reading by the reverend and then a series of tributes to the dead boy, five in all. One of the speakers was the teacher, Carl Tatum, and one was Stephen Honeywell, the headmaster of St. Albert's. One was a student at the school, a senior named Clay Robbins. The first was Geoffrey Collier, Sr. The last was the mother, though many looking through the program did not realize it, since she had many years ago gone back to her maiden name.

The reverend read a selection from Corinthians. We look not to the things that are seen, but to the things that are unseen. He had presided over a number of services like this, memorials for absent dead, though only once before had it been this crowded. He knew that these ceremonies tended to build a secular momentum of their own, and he did not mind. The days of a constituency that did not depend on a particular occasion were not entirely gone, but they did seem to him to be going, and the sight and sound of a church this full left him mildly nostalgic for a time he had never known. What he might have considered the trappings of his position — his clothing, his demeanor, the tone of his voice, even the look of the church itself — had become instead, in cases like this one, its essence; something about these things helped people to be receptive to the emotions they thought it was up to them to produce. But it was not for him to be dissatisfied with what help he could provide. The sound of his reading, enriched by the stone, soothed all the strangers in attendance; the sense of it, he felt, was there for his soul, and for the soul of the departed boy.

The family has asked, the reverend said, that some of those who knew and loved Geoffrey say a few words, in remembrance. The boy's father rose from the first pew and walked toward the pulpit. The reverend took one step to the side and waited for him. Mr. Collier was unsure whether to offer his hand, but the reverend found it anyway, and squeezed it with both of his.

I want to thank everyone for coming today, Mr. Collier said into the microphone. It's a great comfort to Geoff's mother and I to see that others saw the same things in him we did. Sometimes parents have a little too rosy an image of their kids. It's natural enough. I always thought I must have been one of those parents, because I really didn't think there was anything Geoff couldn't do. I guess it would be silly to think about what he might have gone on to do. It would kill me. But I would have to be very selfish indeed not to be able to content myself with the memories of all he did give to the world in nineteen years. That should be enough.

He went on in this vein for another two or three minutes. He was ashamed of his nervousness. Applause, of course, was out of the question; Mr. Collier walked with loud steps back to his seat, his face burning. When he had been asked if he would like to speak at the service, he had said yes readily enough, but now that it was over he considered the practice of putting a newly childless parent on a stage and asking him to perform a barbaric one. He could not remember a word he had said, but he could remember that while he spoke, the face, the athletic figure of his son had not once appeared before him. His new wife had suggested to him that talking about the boy would provide some relief, but he did not want relief of this kind. In fact, he did not want relief at all. He excused himself and slipped past his ex-wife, taking his seat on the other side of her. She did not look at him. It had been strange, two days ago, to walk into her apartment, a place he had never seen, and find her surrounded by friends whom he did not know, but who must have known some intimate things about him. He had expected that she might break down on seeing him; but, though it was true that the boy's face lived on in his, she had gotten up slowly from her kitchen chair, smoothing her dress, and had hugged him and thanked him for coming. He was a stranger.

There's no point, Carl Tatum said, in saying Geoff was a model student. He wasn't. But he always told me, and I understand told others, that biology was a particular interest of his, and so I got a year-long look, when Geoff was a senior, at just what his mind could accomplish when it found something to engage it. Tatum's breathing was off; he was not used to reading a prepared speech. He stopped for a moment, not taking his eyes off the yellow paper. The brief pause was filled with the sounds of unchecked weeping, hasty sniffles, soft gasping. Tatum looked up in confusion. He quickly brought his eyes down to the paper again. There is nothing quite so heartless, he read, as the ruin of all this promise and energy. We cannot rely on reason to explain it. He read these words, and the rest of his speech, so rapidly as to be barely intelligible. He read it the way a man might read a newspaper article to his wife, an article in which there is some particular point of common interest he is about to get to. In this case, Tatum was searching through his own words for anything that could correspond to this crying, and he did not find it. He felt suddenly foolish. We can only be grateful, he said, to have seen a flame such as this burn, however briefly, with such unusual light and warmth; and Tatum resolved, as he walked back to his pew, to read his speech through again when he was sitting down.

The headmaster's remarks, to his own chagrin, were much the same as the biology teacher's, even in the same sort of language; but he, too, had prepared a written speech, and it was too late to depart from it. The whole search for appropriateness seemed doomed; but the children, at least, did not seem to notice, or to care. Defenseless, they were equally affected, or unaffected, by everything that was said. They went on crying with abandon. In the center pew, four rows from the back, sat a black-haired, man-sized boy, his face wrecked by sobbing. His head hung down; a tear collected at the tip of his nose and dropped to the floor. That whole pew was filled with students, all of whom kept physical contact with the friends on either side, fingertips on a knee, a forehead on a shoulder. The black-haired boy picked up his head as another boy's arm came around his shoulder. They hugged one another, rocking slowly, each dampening the ridge of muscle that ran between the other boy's shoulder and neck.

Clay Robbins, one year younger than the Collier boy, a senior now, sat in the front pew with the other speakers; this cut him off from the suffering of his classmates, but then that was how he saw himself. Though a dark gray suit he had gotten for Christmas hung in his closet at home, he wore a more personal outfit, jeans that had been dyed black, dirty bucks, and a dark gray jacket with a barely detectable pattern in it. Geoff Collier and he had never been close friends, but they had liked each other, he remembered. The headmaster's surprise had been more than balanced by relief when Clay had come into his office to volunteer to be the student representative at the service. All the boy's obvious friends had already been asked; they were too upset to consider it. Clay had heard this, and felt he might be able to put what his classmates were going through into words. The fact that he was not too close to Geoff might, he thought, actually help matters. It might enable him to go beyond mere grief, beyond a litany of good memories, and get to the more abstract heart of their pain.

As the headmaster started down the steps, Clay rose, the spots high on his cheekbones already reddening, and made the unfamiliar walk to the pulpit. The high, vaulted ceiling seemed to have taken to itself the sounds of crying, as if birds had flown in before the doors were closed and could find no place to light.

On Tuesday morning, October nineteenth, Clay said, we all lost a bit of our innocence. It happened as we slept. A dark country road, no moonlight. A moment's indecision. And now we must, at an earlier age, perhaps, than our parents had to, face the fact of our own mortality. We must all find our own way to come to terms. As for myself, I have been, and am, consumed by a terrible rage. The anger takes the form of a question: Why have we been chosen? Why has death visited us, stripping us of all that we held to be true? How, given this awful knowledge, are we to go on living?

Many of the adults in the church frowned slightly in embarrassment, or shifted in their seats. Such words, they thought, tended to cheapen the tragedy that had brought them all together. The time was not right for public self-examination; this service was concerned with someone else, someone absent. The students, however, paid as little attention to what Clay said as they did on an average day at school. They went on consoling each other. Even more now than when all was right in their world, it seemed that nothing could touch them.

The narrow wooden balcony was about two-thirds full; the late arrivals, all of whom were students, were sent up there. To lessen the noise they made as they looked for a seat in the three steeply escalating rows of pews, the latecomers took off their shoes. In the righthand balcony, in the lowest row, all alone, sat a barefoot girl in a sleeveless black dress. Her blond hair touched her shoulders like fingertips. She looked dully at the pulpit. Another girl, dressed much the same, held her shoes in her hand as she walked sideways between the pews about fifteen feet away. She saw the first girl and stopped. Clay's voice filled the church. The seated girl, unbeckoned, turned and met the eyes of her friend. Without a sound, they ran the three steps to one another and embraced. They stayed that way, half sitting, not moving, in each other's arms, hovering like angels above the mourners sitting below.

Clay's own tears, which he had hoped for, had arrived. To the extent that I believe in anything now, he said, I believe in this: an abandoned highway; a roar of metal; a burst of light; and a flood of calm.

He walked down the two steps. The Collier boy's mother, a short, attractive woman, draped in black, stood up. She thanked him, and kissed him, and walked to the front of the church. For once, Geoff's friends turned and directed their attention to the pulpit. Some of them knew her well. She thanked the reverend and kissed him too, and turned her exhausted face to the congregation.

Look at you, she said. You are all so beautiful. You've got your heads up. I like that. She smiled. Her hair was black for half an inch at the roots. She was thin, and her face was at once youthful and lined.

You look even more beautiful to me today than you usually do. Geoff's father and I are so grateful to all of you for coming here to be with us. And to those of you who got up and talked. I know how difficult that must have been. But I heard some things about Geoff that I never knew. He was full of great stories, and he was right at the center of most of them. There are lots of them, I'm sure, that he never told me. I hope that now you'll tell me. I hope you won't stop coming over. Of course, you can't all come over at once. I mean, you've seen our place. She looked around her. It's okay to laugh, you know. Anyway, you can't all come over at once, which is why I decided to have this. I wasn't going to. But the important thing is to come together, isn't it? I hope that's one thing you can take with you when you leave today. The important thing is to be together. It makes things possible. It's made it possible for me to get through this. It's made it possible for me to say goodbye, which I thought I would never get the chance to do. Because he's a part of you, and so all of you together are him. I wanted to see him one last time. I mean that, I mean he is here, right now. I feel him as much as I did when his body was alive. This is the last time that will ever happen. I wanted to talk to him one last time, to tell him how much I love him, and how very grateful to him I am. Thank you all, for letting me do that.

The organist played a Grateful Dead song, and everyone was urged to take one of the flowers from the front of the church before leaving. Warner considered it, but the line was long, and he pictured himself holding a lily among the open newspapers on the subway ride home. It was three blocks, in the gentle late afternoon sunlight, to the station; he reached the entrance and went down.

Julian lay flat, his legs tensed, his face composed. Kendall, on her knees, her back straight, lowered herself slowly, until the backs of her thighs touched her calves. She said something. He put his hands on her hips, closed his eyes, and tilted his head back, his chin cutting the air. Her back was a perfect arch; she trembled slightly. They were a small boat under sail.

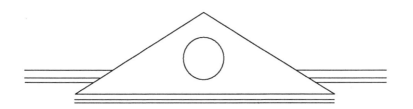

THAT fall, in the corners of the city, the forms of protest were considered. The university committees, the neighborhood coalitions, the antinuclear organizations, the church-centered groups, all had schooled themselves in how to draw attention to just such a revelation of what they felt were their state's true aims. What the protesters were less prepared for, though, was the overwhelming degree of public support for the brusque military activity in Colozan; indeed, one of the chief domestic battles was over the word to best describe that activity — war, peacekeeping, invasion, liberation, killing, protecting, aggression, defense. Whatever it was, it was largely a success, though perhaps not the complete and immediate success its planners had counted on; after ten days, what were called pockets of resistance were still being encountered. Videotapes and photographs, shot and supplied by the appropriate arm of the government, began to make their way back home, into the newspapers and onto the television newscasts. Though the media went as far as they safely could in intimating that these pictures were tainted somehow, they had little choice but to show them, and the images of American doctors in Colozan hospitals, of men firing rifles at offscreen enemies in their most cinematic manner, of the occasional wounded American serviceman, had their desired effect. But the great patriotic strength of the moment was drawn from the one unifying image for which no one could take credit—the violent death of the secretary of state. The short videotape of this, shown over and over again, entered the common imagination, and inspired a vague, collective lust for retribution, which could not be reasoned away. The simplicity of it was invincible, and the rush to embrace that simplicity was so quick and so widespread that it seemed almost as if the people had been waiting for such an outrage, dreaming of it. Even many of the dissenters could have admitted that they had wished, in a way, for these days. After prophesying doom for so long, only a genuine crisis could vindicate them. They had practiced, if only in their thoughts, long and diligently for this moment. And like their brothers and sisters, the architects of this new war, they had not practiced for the sake of readiness alone. The better they got, the more they desired, in their heart of hearts, to act.

In a hastily organized meeting on the steps of the Low Library, one Columbia student held a microphone while another read aloud a draft of a letter of condemnation which was to be sent to the president of the university's board of trustees. It called for an immediate, public disavowal of the invasion from the board itself, cancellation of classes for a daylong protest and symposium on resistance to the war effort, and the ouster of two particular trustees who also sat on the boards of corporations that manufactured weapons. Only about sixty students attended the meeting, to the great dejection of its organizers. When a vote on the draft of the letter was called for, several students left, and so many voices rose in such confusion that the young man who had read the letter put his hand over the microphone and shouted in the ear of the organization's secretary to send the letter just as it was. When he tried to move on to the next order of business, the din increased. Then the secretary pointed back behind the crowd. Four policemen were walking casually across the plaza toward them. They seemed in no hurry; two of them were eating. Nonetheless, a great, wordless shout went up from the students. The meeting came to order. Letters of support were read from the student presidents of similar groups at Berkeley, Northwestern, and Harvard. The policemen stood idly at the foot of the steps and watched with interest. As it grew darker, the plaza emptied of its normal traffic, and the group's proprietary feelings increased. A few left the steps to go home and study, but more came, made curious by the noise, to take their place. A hundred yards or so away, past the locked main gate, the street was quiet, almost menacingly so. A motion was made to form a strategy to occupy the main administration building at some unspecified future date. Since the details could not be discussed anyway in the presence of the police, the motion was passed. A young woman asked for the microphone and told the gathering that their crucial mission was to see to it that what she called business as usual was not allowed to continue on campus. Only by such force, she said, could the sluggish consciousness of their fellow students be raised. There was loud agreement. The members of the group believed in themselves utterly. Surrounded by chains, held in and made louder by the old stone buildings, their cries of joy and outrage rose well into the deepening night.

Far downtown, in a clean schoolroom filled with the glare of the setting sun, a gathering of neighborhood parents, mothers mostly, came after the school day was over to a meeting that had been announced on area lampposts and in store windows. There was no singing or chanting, not even a raised voice; they came because they were curious to see what others had it in mind to do. The tiny desks and chairs filled gradually; many chose to stand near the doors, so as to be able to leave without risk of offending anyone. At the front of the room a stout, white-haired woman with a youthful face and manner sat on the edge of the big desk which, during school hours, belonged to Mrs. Kimberly, the teacher who had shepherded this woman's own three boys through the second grade some years before. She

smiled and swung her feet slowly through the air as she tried
to enumerate the things the twenty-five of them there could
reasonably hope to do. A local copy shop had donated its services, and as maps of the neighborhood were passed around,
she asked who would be willing to distribute leaflets on the
corner nearest their home for an hour a day. Some raised their
hands. All of them looked at their neighborhood on a map as
if they had never seen such a thing before. Drawings of a kind
familiar to all of them, of racing cars and western shoot-outs
and smiling dogs and leaning houses, were taped to the walls
all around them. The shadows made their way across the floor.
A man standing against the wall nearest the light switch shyly
turned it on. The white-haired woman said with a smile that
soon it might come to pass that they would find themselves in
conflict with the law, and they must not be afraid of that. She
herself had been in jail numerous times. She said that it was
important that they see the law for what it was, an elaborate,
rickety construction that depended for its survival on the com-
plicity of people like them. No one else in the room felt moved
to speak. The woman talked in a pleasant voice about the root
causes of war, how the idea of it was inseparable from certain
ideas of governing, how the current situation was not an ab-
erration but merely a historical moment at which the true goals
of their rulers happened to find their highest expression. Only
one person walked out early, but when the meeting was over,
the rest of them left confused, and vaguely resentful, and dis-
inclined to act, as if unsure they could be counted upon even
to know what was expected of them.

Similar meetings took place all around the city. But among
those who took the most active parts in the protest, it was not
uncommon, after a day of sitting behind a card table on a street
corner collecting signatures, or holding a sign outside a government building, to return home and listen in panic to the
news broadcasts that indicated how solidly the country stood
behind its president in this time of national crisis. Many lost
heart; still, most of the organizations of dissent now found their

meetings swelled by people who knew little or nothing about them but who could not suppress a need to at least register in some way their opposition. For many, this did not go beyond attending one meeting, or supplying a group with their name, address, and telephone number. Some hung around and waited to be told what to do. The organizers worked feverishly. The more idealistic explained their sense of urgency in social or historical terms; but the more experienced among them knew the banality of what they were up against. They knew that these individual social awakenings, though genuine, were only temporary. Soon boredom would set in, and then there would be that to fight, too. They knew that while injustice is enduring, the sense of injustice is ephemeral. They had to collect these bodies and put them in the street, before the cold weather came, and the snow.

Although Holly Gordon was born in the city, she remembered from her infancy there only a few small, domestic pictures — the layout of her family's apartment, the soothing arrangement of pans hung on the wall in the kitchen, and the furious street she had to cross, one hand holding the hand of her teacher and the other holding that of a boy who might be anywhere now, to get from her nursery school classroom to the playground. When she was four, her parents moved the family to New Jersey, where their money could buy them a little more space, and a little more security. Holly did not have a happy time growing up there, and though she strove to make that evident to her parents, their inattention and fear of unhappiness kept it more or less her secret. As she grew older, she and her friends grew more ingenious, then brazen, in the lies they devised to help them escape from their parents for a night or a weekend in New York. She developed the idea, protected by loud music in her large bedroom, that she had been unfairly uprooted from the one place where she could have been truly happy. The key to her survival was an eventual return to New York and an immersion in just the kinds of experience her parents often said they were glad they didn't have to hear about anymore. Indeed, she passed through high school and one and a half years of college with the air of someone on her way to an appointment elsewhere. And now here she was, beautiful, popular, poor, resplendently unrespectable in activity and appearance, and feeling in general as though everything she had said and done in her life up to now was vindicated by her present happiness.

She worked in a nightclub, and since she did not get up for work until four in the afternoon, she often threw notorious parties on her nights off. The current one was scheduled for November eighth. Normally, at this time of year, she threw her Halloween party, which in many ways was the most famous of all; but lately they had become too famous, and the number of guests whom, costumes or no, she was quite sure she had never laid eyes on before, too alarming. So she had changed the date and told all her friends to keep it a secret. Now, early on the evening of the eighth, she sat drinking a rum and tonic in the living room of her apartment on Greenwich Street, which was already in the nocturnal phase of its own double life—rugs rolled up, furniture against the wall, music playing—and watched the setting sun erase the faces of the buildings across the river, turning the factories into smoking ruins.

After the sun was down, but before she had gotten up to turn on the lights, her friend Andre showed up. More than a year ago—she could not remember with which party the tradition had begun—Andre had designated himself the official first-to-arrive. He insisted this was done purely out of love for his friends and Holly's, since he knew how painful it was to be the first at a party and was willing to take that burden upon himself so others might be spared. He went straight to the pristine bar and made himself a drink. Glass in hand, he came over, kissed Holly on top of the head, and went to sit in one of the chairs that had been pushed up against the wall on the other side of the room. She did not move from where she sat; they talked for an hour or so, about the war, among other things. Andre made Holly promise she would come visit him in Canada if it ever came to that. Holly said she didn't think it would ever come to that, but if it did, there was nothing on earth, not even her love for him, that could induce her to set foot in Canada. Mexico, then, Andre said, and Holly told him that was more like it. Soon the intercom began to buzz, and gradually the vast loft filled. Every few minutes, as more and more people arrived, Holly would walk over to the stereo and turn the volume up a notch. Lines formed in front of the bar and the bathroom. Since there was only one bathroom, the kitchen was designated for drug use, and there was a line there, too. By midnight the intercom could no longer be heard in the apartment, and those waiting in the lobby would simply lean against the buzzer for a minute or more, patiently, waiting for a song to end or a conversation to lag upstairs, so they could be let in.

Just outside the building, the music falling softly around them on the sidewalk through the open windows, Julian and Kendall stopped and cautioned Warner not to stare at some of the other guests he would see; but he was already staring through the glass front door at a tall man, all in black, standing with his shoulder against the buzzer, whose hair was gathered by a thick band right at the top of his head, so that it fell in a graceful circle, like flowers in a bowl. The four of them wound up riding the elevator together. Warner stood behind the tall man and continued to stare, without contempt, but without reservation, either. He felt that anyone who got himself up like that could only have done so because he wanted to be looked at, and so to avoid looking at him was dishonest, maybe even, in such people's scheme of things, impolite. The tall man himself was staring at Kendall in an unabashed way; he had seemed enlivened from the moment he saw her press the button for the eighth floor. Julian did not seem to notice.

All of them were at an age where there were still two distinct sorts of parties. One consisted of time set aside for the practice of refinement, a display of social learning, sometimes at the cost of occasional awkwardness and misunderstanding—a tentative embrace of adulthood. It was the sort of social gathering that they were still growing into, and these affairs — cocktail parties, sit-down dinners — carried both the thrill and the distaste of something unnatural, something assumed. The other sort of party involved the total casting off of that learning; it was time set aside for a conscious, willful descent into instinct. Natural response — to drink, to loud noise, to the need for love of some kind — was allowed to rule. Essentially, what distinguished the two was music, or rather, the volume of the music; once speech was discouraged, anything seemed to go. At Holly's the door was left unlocked all night, since no one, not even someone standing near it, could have hoped to hear a knock. The whole intricate gathering, with all its ritual and cunning, was manifest in the other apartments in the building only as a steady, unsynchronized pounding of feet and of the music's bass line, as if a microphone had been placed to the heart of everyone there.

Warner lifted his hand to knock, but the tall man with the wheat-shock hair reached over his head, pushed the door open with his fingers, and shouldered his way through the crowd of friends and strangers, none of whom protested. The moment they stepped inside, Kendall put her hand through Julian's arm. Julian felt a familiar wave of disdain; but he knew it was wrong of him, and he was careful not to let his expression change as they pushed their way into the room.

The party was thick with people from what Kendall had always thought of, with admiration and some inaccuracy, as an underworld. One of the things she had always admired about Julian was his ease with these people, while not exactly one of them. There were gradations of dress, and she was comforted to see that she did not necessarily represent the most conservative point on the spectrum. In the conversations that she could see, rather than hear, the barriers of style obtained, though the crowds in the kitchen and outside the bathroom seemed more nondiscriminatory.

Holly waved from a few feet away, and the three of them waited patiently for her to reach them. I'm so glad you're here, she yelled, when she was closer. She was wearing what could have been her mother's prom dress, a restrictive, off-the-shoulder, found object, which certainly must have rustled, though it was not possible to hear it. She kissed a surprised Kendall, then was reintroduced to Warner and shook his hand with a formality that made him think he was being made fun of. Then she looked with a half smile at Julian, who stood between his friends. Hello, baby, she said. They did not touch each other.

She stayed long enough to extract from each of them, Warner included, a promise to talk later, just about worthless under the circumstances. Kendall took Julian's arm again and led him quickly into the heart of the crowd. Warner, thinking he might have missed a shouted instruction, tried to follow them but was cut off. He turned and moved sideways through the crowd toward the bar.

Near the wall on the other side of the room, Julian looked back and frowned. I really, he said to Kendall, I mean, I look carefully now, and I really don't see what he does to deserve that from you. I asked him here, he doesn't know anybody, and now I feel like an asshole.

They watched Warner standing with one elbow on the bar, bringing a beer to his mouth, his lips still moving to the words of the song that was playing, to show that he knew it.

I haven't done anything to him, Kendall said. Lay off. He's a grown-up, he can handle himself. I mean, you spend a lot less time with him than I do, and I'm happy to bring him along when we go out, too. But I don't think it's too much to ask that the three of us not hang out together every second, like we're the Marx Brothers or something. What do people think, I wonder? What does your friend Holly think?

Holly would probably be into it.

Still. Their faces were very close, his right shoulder touching her left to shield them from the noise. Still, I don't think it's unreasonable of me to want to be alone with you.

To her amazement, he laughed. Alone? He gestured to the room behind him. I don't know what you really mean. Is it just that you want to be seen alone with me?

Absolutely. Absolutely. I like to be seen with you. I like to be talked about with you. I like people to think of us as together. I don't know what's so hard to understand about that. She pulled her mouth away from his ear to look at him. Then she kissed him. I'd love a drink, she said.

The party thinned out a little around one o'clock, but then there was a new influx of bodies just after two, as people left the restaurants and clubs they had been to earlier in the evening. In all the buildings visible from Holly's large windows, the lights had gone out. The guests began the push toward dawn. Warner sat on a windowsill with a beer and watched a lone woman on Greenwich Street walk up and down the block twice, for no discernible reason, before stepping in the front door of Holly's building. He wondered if he was the only one present with a day job. He had taught before on little or no sleep, and did not enjoy it—the students seemed to follow him down into his own torpor—but it was the nearest thing in his life to a kind of physical daring, of adventure, and he was always proud to get through it. Behind him, the crowd churned in anonymous silhouette. He had met no one. He hated parties like this one, insofar as they seemed like validations of his own self-image. But he had few friends, no lover for longer than he cared to tote up, and these parties were opportunities, not to be missed or, in his case, wasted. Still, he wondered what he had seen in this one. He was getting drunk now, not out of spite but out of nervousness; he had recourse to no other activity—not dancing, not talking. It was either drink or stand like a mannequin. He pressed his forehead against the window. The few passersby hurried along on what at his hour, he imagined, could only be some shady, glamorous business.

I'm glad to see, Julian said to Holly, that everyone got the word about the change of date. You didn't have anybody show up here in a costume on Halloween, did you?

They were standing in a tight circle with Holly's friend Andre, another, rather lascivious friend of hers named Kim, who insisted that she and Julian had met before, and Kendall, who was fighting off her most paranoid suspicions about everyone there, including Julian, with whom she kept some kind of physical contact at all times.

I don't know, Holly said. Maybe. I was out all Halloween.

I'm sure a few did come, Andre said. Serves them right. They probably all came dressed up as Alan Sheffield anyway.

I hate costumes, Kim said. She looked at Julian with intensity, as if this were an important conviction that she sensed they shared.

Why so grumpy, handsome? Holly said to Andre. Aren't there any nice boys here for you to meet?

He made a sound of derision.

I'm afraid you'll have to forget about that cute Julian, she said. He's like an arrow.

Julian laughed, and looked at the floor. It was hard to imagine what might embarrass her. They had met a year ago, when she was wondering if she might not like to be a famous singer, in a small recording studio on Forty-first Street, where a casting director from an ad agency was auditioning singers for an American Airlines commercial. She didn't have a bad voice. She deserved to get the job, though that wasn't why she got it; she got it because the casting man fell in love with her. There was nothing so simple as flirting involved. She was a powerful woman in that way, a woman men would make mistakes for. Her charm was not in aloofness—that was much more common; she returned every attention she received with an interest that was so intense and so uniform that no man could possibly believe it was genuine. And that was what made her so attractive, so powerful; obviously a passionate woman, it became the mission of every man she met, or at least the unintimidated, to bring out the genuine in her. Faced with this, throughout a long rehearsal and mistake-plagued recording session, Julian had distinguished himself from the casting director, and, he imagined, from the mass of men, by abandoning his sexual feelings entirely, and being as indifferently friendly to her as possible. It had worked, and the two of them had become close friends.

He was good at such recharacterizations of himself, where women were concerned.

Andre went off to the kitchen, and someone asked Kim to dance. Kendall held on to Julian and looked around the room with mounting fury.

Holly pointed to the row of windows. Isn't that your friend over there?

That's him, Julian said. Rob. He's Kendall's roommate, actually.

He doesn't seem to be having big fun. Was it something I said?

No, not at all, he goes through — he does this at every party I've ever seen him at. He's a little underconfident, especially when it comes to women, I guess.

Shy?

Not so much shy. Just without certain social skills. When he's really got a lot going for him. He teaches. Very smart guy. Very up on the war.

What a turn-on.

No, come on. You know what I mean.

Well, that's too bad, because guys like that are usually self-fulfilling prophecies, you know?

You don't know anybody who might be good for him? he said. Kendall stared at him.

Maybe, Holly said. Maybe. We'll think on it. I don't know, some women really get into that. Guys with no self-esteem. I guess it puts them in a position of power. Personally, it arouses me not a bit.

The party spun on. Word spread that the liquor supply was dangerously low, so a few people, to ensure that they had enough for themselves, went to the bar and returned with the two-thirds empty bottles, holding onto them while they danced. It was impossible to get into the kitchen. Holly dragged great bags of garbage through the crowd, hitting the backs of legs with her foot to clear her way; when she reached the door, she had someone open it and then heaved the bags into the hall and shut the door quickly, as if worried that they might try to regain the apartment.

The dancers now were fewer in number but more dedicated. At twenty of three the first complaint from a neighbor came, in the body of a policewoman. Her appearance in the doorway elicited a roar of approval from the guests. She wore her cap tilted back, her badge hanging at a slight angle from the pressure of her breast through the stiff blue shirt; her hips were thickened by a circle of weaponry, her feet lost in shiny, painful black shoes. The sound that greeted her, as if she were wearing a particularly racy costume, seemed to make her angry. She was turning red; through the din she shouted that she wanted to see the tenant of the apartment. Holly promised to turn off the music and to hustle everyone out just as soon as she could manage it. But after all, she said, look at all these people. Some of them I don't even know. You may have to come back and help me. The policewoman told Holly that she did not want to have to come back.

Mothers, Holly said as she closed the door. If they think it's too loud, why don't they just come up here and tell me?

Not one person at the party seemed like someone Kendall would want to talk to; they bored her now with their theatricality. No gesture or article of clothing carried with it any spontaneity at all. The promotion of self-image seemed the only kind of contact they were interested in making. She wanted to get Julian out of there before she got any madder at him. It wasn't that he was ashamed of her. But he consistently seemed to forget she was there; he would forget to introduce her to friends, forget to include her in a conversation, go to the bar for a drink and stay to talk with someone for ten minutes. It was hurtful, but then, she couldn't imagine how she might bring this up without sounding like a child. So there was nothing to do but fume. She stood quietly, nursing a drink, and when he turned to look at her she smiled.

You're ready to go, aren't you, he said.

At another time, such evidence of intimacy could have made

her optimistic, but now she felt only a sense of failure. Concealing her feelings from him was a skill she had never acquired. She nodded. Whenever you're ready, she said.

While he said goodbye to some friends, she edged toward the door and stood there patiently, glancing at him quickly and with caution. He looked for Holly and couldn't see her. He spied Warner on the far side of the crowd of dancers, sitting on the arm of the couch beside and above a woman with a near crew cut and a sweatshirt with the sleeves cut off. She was leaning forward, watching the dancers, as if with great interest. She seemed to be avoiding a conversation with Warner. He, too, watched the dance floor intently, as though this was something they had agreed to do for a while.

The dancers were too self-absorbed to let Julian pass, so he went the long way around, turning his shoulders and spreading his arms to knife his way between them and the wall. He tapped Warner on the shoulder.

How's it going? he said.

Great. This is wild.

Listen. Kendall and I are packing it in. If you're ready to go, we can split a cab.

A few times before, Warner had come home late with them, from a party or a bar or a late movie. It was a scene that could bring him close to crying. The three of them would travel home in near silence, wedged into the back seat of a cab. He and Julian would split the fare. They would ride abreast in the elevator, then pace about the living room in a territorial way, throwing a wallet on the table, a jacket on a chair, yawning, smiling. Kendall would suddenly seem much happier. They would say goodnight as they walked together toward the bedrooms, separating at the last second. Kendall would close the door. Warner would take off his clothes, set the alarm, get into bed, and turn out the light. He would try to fall asleep instantly, which would of course ensure that he would stay awake for an hour or more. Then a belt, still in a pair of pants, would land with a muffled thump on the floor. There would be some indistinguishable human sound, maybe a word, maybe not, and then Kendall would laugh, and Julian would shush her. One shoe would fall to the rug, and then, just a moment before the other one fell, there would be the sound of the first depression of the bed.

I think I might hang out for a while, Warner said. I'm having a great time.

Julian tapped him on the thigh. So, see you, he said. You don't know where Holly is, do you?

Warner wasn't sure how it was possible for a man to be in the same room with Holly and not know where she was, but this sort of control was part of what he looked up to in Julian. He pointed with his beer bottle to the far fringe of the rough circle of dancers, just in front of a large speaker.

Julian walked over to the speaker and rested his elbow on top of it, leaning back behind it so as not to catch the full wind of sound. He watched Holly from behind and waited for the song to end. She always danced at the edge of such gatherings because her physical expression required a lot of room. Her dance was a sort of high-speed ballet, back bent, arms thrown out in graceful lines, hands hanging magically at ease, sudden spins, feet thrown up to impossible heights. It was a dance of sexual power. In motion, she was alluring, but also distant—it was like watching a movie of a woman dancing. He could see, over her shoulder, the face of her partner, no one he knew. Holly's dancing was self-fulfilling; it neither required nor acknowledged a partner. This man's presence had been forgotten, and so he was free to stare. He had stopped dancing almost entirely, too inhibited, as most men were, to try to match this display. He simply moved from foot to foot, like a time-lapse film of a man waiting for a bus. He watched Holly with an awkward half smile, and tried to stay out of her way. Julian was no great student of faces, but he fancied he could see that this man had been enslaved.

The music ended, and Julian was willing to wait for the poor partner to say whatever, in the course of the song, he had decided to say; but Holly saw Julian first and came over, leaving the other man to walk back, shaking his head, to the bar. She took a glass that wasn't hers from the top of the speaker and drank from it, breathing quickly. Sweat lit up her shoulders, and darkened the tips of her hair.

We're leaving, gorgeous, Julian said. It was fun, as ever.

She protested. Lightly, she took his forearm, and he was careful to keep looking into her eyes. We never get to talk, she said.

He laughed. A drumbeat thundered from the speaker beside them, and another song began. There are better places, he said.

She shrugged. And will Kendall be leaving, too?

Hilarious, Julian said. You really don't like her, do you.

I do like her. You always ask me that. I think she's lovely.

Lovely. Whatever. He looked past Holly to where Kendall stood near the door. Thanks again. Maybe we can have lunch this week, okay? We'll set our alarms.

He took two slow steps backward, hands in his pockets, and bowed slightly, before turning to walk out. Holly knew, and had always known, what this reluctance to touch her in even the friendliest way was about. She was flattered that he considered the danger real enough to be that careful, and she confessed to herself a small, sexual thrill every time he took those two steps away from her. She watched him make his way through the thinning crowd, touch Kendall on the shoulder, and close the door behind them.

The party lasted another forty-five minutes; the trick for Holly was to identify those guests who would need to be asked to leave, before it got too late and they began to fall asleep. She had no compunction about doing this, nor did anyone seem to hold it against her. Every one of her parties ended this way. The six or seven people who would simply sit motionless on a couch or the floor, having long ago ceased to have fun, would be neither offended nor glad to be kicked out; they took Holly's instruction in a passive, almost childlike way, as if their lives were a guided tour.

She had not guessed, though, that Warner, by the look of him, was one of these people; and, in fact, he was not. For his part, he was trying to ascertain why it was that he got drunk only when he hadn't planned to. The heat in the room and the need to do something with his hands had conspired against him, and he found himself in a calm hollow of self-absorption. The room, nearly empty now, was indefinably dirty; there was little garbage, but the floor was sticky, and the sun, beginning to rise on the side of the apartment where they could not see it, cast everything and everyone in a gray, heavy light. Warner sat in an old lounge chair covered in cracked leather. Not realizing it had been pushed against the wall, he rocked back a few times, hard, in an effort to make it recline. Without mirth, he laughed at himself. The room was a miniature skyline of plastic glasses and clear, not quite empty liquor bottles. A few stragglers sat across from him, some deep in conversation, some just staring. He had met none of them. The bathroom door had been closed for some time now. Warner was too drunk to do the arithmetic needed to figure out if more than one person was in there.

The sun rose a little higher, and the polluted western sky began to color remarkably. Soon the only moving thing in the room was Holly, as she put her home back in some kind of order. From time to time she would glance quickly, without stopping, at the others there, as if to remind them that their time would soon be at hand. Warner's eyes were fixed now on the motionless bathroom door. He felt certain that there were at least two people in there. In his state, that door came quickly to represent for him his exile from the kingdom of the sensual, from the delights that tortured him, which were his by right but were denied him somehow by forces too diffuse and too mysterious to see.

He saw Holly, fists on her hips, in the kitchen doorway, trying to separate reversible from irreversible damage. Holly had the self-assured stance of a ruler. She took for granted all that he could not have; he had heard stories about her, but even putting those stories aside, something about her face, her posture, her range of expressions, her air of easy power, the very lines of her astonishing body, told him that she lived a kind of life he wanted desperately. Watching her, he became angry.

Carefully, he stood up and walked to where he could see over Holly's shoulder into the kitchen. The sink was filled with wet cigarettes. Pools of alcohol lay calmly on the floor. The counters were scored with what looked like razor cuts.

Holly turned her head to see who was behind her, then turned back again. I took all my mirrors to a friend's house this afternoon, she said. I didn't hide them here—I tried that last time, it didn't work, they found them under my mattress. So I took them out of the apartment. And look at this.

Holly, he said. He tried to direct his breathing so she wouldn't feel it. He ran his hands through his hair, but there was not enough hair there to do it effectively, so he returned them to his pockets. Listen, can I ask you something?

She turned around. Something wrong?

No. Listen, I had a great time. Would you be able to have dinner some time this week? Or a drink, whatever.

Fine, she said. It'll have to be early, I go to work at nine. She smiled.

He looked at her smile as he had looked at the closed bathroom door. He could see he posed no threat whatever to her detachment; he was simply a free meal. Her estimation of him was apparent. He was instantly sorry he had asked her; already, he was dreading the time with her.

That's great, he said. He looked away, at the front door, at the strange arrangement of furniture, at the spent people murmuring, at the dawn.

I can't do it Wednesday, she said.

Back in Warner's apartment, the approach of day was like a signal to hurry up. Kendall and Julian had not spoken on the way home, or while undressing each other. It was a familiar quiet—not a fight but an expression of a mutual desire to avoid one. Now, abandoned to their bodies, they were as without resentments as strangers. Julian, for all his fatigue, was considerate and alert. She was given to a steady pulse of small, complaining noises of pleasure; but he knew that the highest moment for her came when her mouth would suddenly open wide to emit no sound, not even a breath. He hushed himself and watched her, to listen for, to feel—which he did, most keenly—the astonishing silence he could produce in her.

It was quarter to nine in the morning when Julian got out of a cab in front of the sound studio on Tenth Avenue, a brick box flanked by parking lots, a place he had worked at a dozen times before. He stood on the sidewalk, blinked exaggeratedly, and flapped his arms a few times, trying to wake up. Across the street, in the small shelter created by a concrete stoop, a man and a woman lay wrapped in several layers of clothing. Though the cold morning sunlight shone directly in their faces, they slept soundly and did not stir. A small fleet of shopping carts was tethered with string to the iron railing on the stoop. This stretch of Tenth Avenue was crowded with homeless people, but they never slept or even hung around next to the studio, at least not when it was cold; the wind that swept unobstructed across the parking lots was enough to compel anyone, no matter how tired, to stand up and move on.

Julian called his name into the scratchy intercom, and, with a loud click, was admitted. He knew from past dates where the hot water urn was and went for it. Sipping noisily from a Styrofoam cup of tea, waiting for the warmth to make it all the way through him, he walked through the carpeted halls and down the carpeted stairs to Studio B-11. On the way, he passed three of the studio's clocks, which were large and inescapable and checked once every day for synchronicity.

Through the crosshatched glass of the studio door he saw that just about everyone else was there. If he was the last to arrive, which seemed likely, there would be five other men and six women in the room. Bleary and cold, they sat on the risers or at empty music stands, talking and drinking, or walking across the root-like cables and wires on the floor, doing quiet vocal exercises. Everyone turned to look at Julian as the heavy door swung open and silently closed. Some said hello or smiled, others turned back to what they were doing. He had worked with nearly all of them before, though he knew only some names. It was possible to get to know them, if that was what one wanted; but one of the advantages of this type of irregular work was that it allowed him to choose his relationships with coworkers, and Julian generally chose to keep his distance.

Insofar as he liked to warm up, he did so by staying silent, avoiding conversation. He walked to a free spot against the rear wall, put his tea down on a disconnected speaker, and stood straight. Closing his eyes, he paid attention to certain muscles, until he was satisfied they were relaxed. He breathed deeply. He tried to imagine his throat — it helped not to know what it really looked like — as a clear passage, round as pipe, so smooth that a drop of water could pass through it without slowing down. His fingers lightly tapped a rhythm on the sheet music folded in his pocket. He had memorized the music, the way he always did. He sang a few notes, experimentally, wordlessly; the words of devotion to a brand of orange soda would only break his spell.

Folks?

A tinny voice came from a speaker fastened near the ceiling. Julian opened his eyes again. Through a large, rectangular pane set in the wall, he saw two men and a woman. The man seated on the left, with his feet up on the mixing board, in a cashmere sweater with no shirt underneath it and black denim pants, was Julian's friend Caravella, the engineer. A glinting silver chain hung from his left ear. Caravella drank coffee and looked as irritated as if this were the end of a long day, rather than the beginning. The second man was standing in the middle, leaning over the board, his finger on the intercom switch. Because he seemed a bit pressured and was doing all the talking, Julian guessed he was the ad agency man, an account rep for the soda whose praises they had been summoned to sing. The woman sat in a chair off to the right — from Julian's angle, almost offscreen, as it were — and watched with curiosity, as if, Julian thought, she had always wondered how these commercials were made. She had straight black hair pulled back in a tight ponytail, and wore a short black dress, stockings, and heels.

The agency man began giving instructions in a voice that was, for the benefit of the others in the booth with him, persuasive and kind; but no one paid attention. To the singers, the first sound of his voice was simply their cue to begin setting up. They stood up slowly, picking up headphones, still talking to one another. As the adman spoke, they arranged themselves in rough lines in front of the main microphones.

We need to get going, he said. We've only got the hall for another two hours, a little less. Okay, I know most of you, I've worked with you before, I know you'll fly through this. You've all seen the music. Is there anybody here who didn't see the music?

Again, he was speaking mostly to impress the woman with him, a company representative of some relative importance. When no one paid him even polite attention, he seemed a little anxious at the thought that the others were not playing along with him.

I'll take that as a no, he said. Okay, this isn't a particularly tough one. Though I think you'll like it. We're all very excited about it. All right, you seem to have things pretty well under control. I'll turn you over to John here.

His earring swinging, Caravella took his feet off the board and swung close to upright in his chair. He drank unhurriedly from his mug. Turning to the adman, he said, You want a couple run-throughs, sport? forgetting, or not caring, that the intercom was still switched on.

No! the singers shouted. In the booth, the men's heads jerked. The adman frowned. He leaned forward, one hand holding his tie, and the red intercom light went off.

The singers watched them as if they were a silent movie. Julian had rushed, when the general movement began, to a spot in the front on the far left side, to have a better view of the woman from the soft drink company. Hers was a well-tended beauty. He watched her as she listened to the two men; she seemed to be amused in some way that she was trying to keep to herself. She leaned forward and offered some remark. Detached from sound, the movement of her face seemed slow and graceful. She sat back and tugged at the hem of her dress. Julian looked in at her, not listening to the ordinary grumbling that was going on around him. He felt unmistakably sad, the sadness that was always his experience of beauty, the sadness by which he had known Kendall the first time he saw her—though he told himself that, in this case, what disturbed him was the thought that a third or more of every day this woman graced was devoted to the flogging of an orange soda.

God damn it, I hate it when we get these types, a man at the end of Julian's row said. He spoke to no one in particular; his eyes were on the booth. He wore a silver glitter tie. We'll be here until sundown. I'll be eating these fucking jelly doughnuts for dinner.

Yeah, but how will we know? a woman behind him said. Who knows what time it really is in here. My own feeling is that all the clocks are controlled by the receptionist. She can be ordered to slow them down or speed them up. Everyone we know could be dead by the time we get out of here.

No, a woman next to Julian said. No way. This guy's a clock-watcher if ever there was one. If he has to pay us any overtime, or book another hour, they'll kick his ass all over his tiny office. If we sang this thing like twelve Bob Dylans, if it was five minutes to eleven, he'd take it.

There was a ripple of laughter; two singers unfolded their sheet music and actually sang a few bars of the jingle in imitation of Bob Dylan. Other imitations, remarkably good ones, sprang up—Stevie Nicks, Tom Waits, Ethel Merman. In the absence of some immediate reason for them, the lines began to break up, subtly but definitely, as if the singers were magnets that someone had tried to lay end to end. There were two clocks they could see; one above their heads and one in the booth, visible through the window.

The singers ranged in age from their early twenties to nearly forty. For many of them, primarily the younger ones, commercial singing was a way to keep in trim and pay the rent on the way to some more artistically inclined, independent career — backup work, club dates, theatrical choruses, a hookup with a band. Sometimes this plan was not an illusion; mostly it was. The older ones were past the age when they could reasonably hope that they could get, or even deserved, any real break. Perhaps it was fair to say that some of them had had bad luck, or missed certain opportunities, or had actually been treated unfairly. But most of them felt as if there was a hole in their lives when in fact there had never been anything there to miss. All of them had technical skills in abundance; the only thing lacking, the only thing that could possibly have been lacking, was the soul or the individuality of an artist. This was a terrible thing for anyone to have to discover about himself. Some took it well and some did not. They were not distinctive voices, no matter how hard they worked, or wished, for it. And so they could not help but resent greatly having to sing with each other, being forced to aspire to sound as much like one another as possible. It seemed a cruel joke at their expense.

All that was left of their dream of uniqueness, of the artist's estrangement, was this false disobedience, petulant demands, the misbehavior of children in a classroom. When this brattiness manifested itself, it made Julian feel embarrassed, and old for being embarrassed. He tried not to join in.

Hey Andy, someone in the back said. Hey Andy, you know I saw your name in the Voice a couple of weeks ago. You had a gig?

One of the youngest men smiled proudly. Just for a night, he said. You were probably pretty tied up that night? Couldn't make it down?

Yeah, well, it was eight bucks. For eight bucks I can get a Billie Holiday record. Nothing personal.

Everyone laughed, and the laughter seemed to produce more movement away from the lines they had originally formed.

It was at a place called the Blue Hour, Andy said. Anybody ever worked there? It's no bargain. There was actually a space heater on stage, near the piano. This accompanist they had for me, some drunk, between numbers he'd lean over and turn the heater toward him, and then during numbers I'd walk over and turn it toward me. The crowd loved it. Maybe I'll use it again when I'm playing Carnegie Hall.

Crowd? the woman next to him said. Crowd?

You know what I mean, Andy said.

It's a euphemism, the man with the glitter tie said, looking back toward the booth. Come on! The engineer and the agency man looked to be having a mild disagreement, in which the woman took no part. She gazed out at the singers.

Come on! Mustn't keep the talent waiting.

Mustn't make the talent unhappy!

We have important commitments to attend to!

What, are we here for our health?

What, are we here out of charity?

Perhaps so! one woman said. Perhaps we are here out of charity. Perhaps we are expected to perform out of the goodness of our hearts!

Quickly reforming their lines, they began to sing We Are the World.

The woman in the booth, who could not hear them but noticed that something was going on, mentioned this to the men. They turned to look; the engineer leaned forward, and the red intercom light went on.

After a moment, everyone in the booth laughed. Their laughter, through the speaker, sounded thin and remote, and the singers seemed chastened, rather than satisfied, by it.

They settled in to tape the jingle. The musical track they were working from was timed out at exactly twenty-six seconds — it had been sped up imperceptibly in the final mix — so all the chorus had to do was stay in time and hit the right notes. They did it perfectly the second try, but, as always, the agency man didn't believe anything could be perfect on the second try; so they ran through several more takes, gradually growing more dispirited, adopting and then discarding his various, uninformed suggestions.

The agency man had explained to them that the last of the eight lines in the jingle, Something Good Is Goin' Down, would be sung by a solo male voice, someone they had hired separately. He would come in later that week to lay down his one line. Each time through the song, hands pressing lightly on their headphones, they would reach a sort of crescendo on their last line and then let the music finish without them. There was something about singing only seven lines of an eight-line, rhymed lyric that would leave them irritable and distracted for the rest of the day. It was an unnatural kind of self-restraint, and after six or seven times through, Julian felt himself growing restless.

The adman told them how impressed he was with their skill and professionalism; he would be calling most of them again, he said. There was no way he could have told which of them had sung better, or even differently, than any other. Though the singers had brought nothing with them, they went about leaving the studio much more slowly than the people in the booth. Julian watched them through the glass. The woman from the soda company checked her watch, and, in one heartbreaking motion, reached both hands behind her head, held the elastic band apart with three fingers, and pulled her ponytail tighter. There was some shaking of hands, and the booth quickly emptied, except for the engineer, who did not look back into the studio, but went immediately about his business, scowling as if at his lack of privacy.

The singers put their coats on reluctantly. Two of them were trying to knock down a tower of empty Styrofoam cups with the remains of a jelly doughnut. A younger man produced from the pocket of his leather jacket a small sheaf of paper, along with a pen he had brought. It was an antiwar petition. The first man he passed it to read it, grimaced, and handed it quickly to the woman next to him.

Keith, man, what's this, she said.

It's a petition to the government to stop the invasion, Keith said. It's being delivered to Washington with about three hundred others from the city.

They ask for my address here. What's that about?

It's just for a mailing list. You'll get on the list to get more information about demonstrations, rallies, stuff like that.

I'll get on a mailing list for the fucking FBI is what I'll get on a mailing list for. I'm putting down a bogus address. I hope that's okay.

She passed it to Andy, who looked at it and then at Keith. He laughed. Very engagé, he said, and signed it.

The first man said, I don't know. I mean it's admirable to want to do something about it, but I think maybe it's better, just in terms of peace of mind, to divorce yourself from all the evil that governments do. Because if you try to do something about it, you're bound to fail, and then you have this sense of failure that you don't really deserve.

Pen, the man in the glitter tie said. Someone handed it to him.

Seriously, the first man said. The way I feel about it is, I am literally, in all honesty, not responsible for any of this stuff happening, so why go out of my way to make myself feel as if I am?

That's sort of a convenient attitude, Keith said.

I don't think so. I mean I do think it's convenient, but it's also the truth. I think it's a provable statement. It's just the way things are.

A few people left in the course of this exchange, waving goodbye, or not. The petition made its way around the studio. Julian took it and signed it without thinking about it, or even reading it. He considered the idea it expressed to be a simple one. The first man felt that he wanted to defend himself some more, though no one was really taking issue with him.

I mean, I'm upset by the war, he said. I'm very upset about it. I'm upset about it the way I'm upset about floods and fires and hurricanes.

No one said anything.

The man watched as Keith folded up the petition and stuck it back in his pocket. So what happens to that now? he said.

To this? I'm supposed to get as many signatures as I can by next Sunday and then bring it back to the Committee in Solidarity with —

No, after all that. What gets done with them?

They're delivered to Washington, by hand.

To who in Washington? he said. I'm not trying to be antagonistic. I'm just curious.

Keith closed his eyes. I don't remember exactly to whom. To the secretary of state's office, I think.

Just to some guy at the front desk there? What do you think he'll do with them?

What he'll do with them is not the point.

It's not? Well, then I'm confused.

Tempers seemed about to break the surface in the room. A few more people left, hoping to avoid any real awkwardness; others, grateful for the diversion, sat down again.

But then I assume, the man said, that the petitions aren't the extent of your involvement with this whole movement, right? What else are you doing? You plural.

Well, Keith said, for one thing, there's a demonstration set for this Friday night in Washington Square Park. I meant to mention it. I hope everyone who signed this will come. Some friends and I will be singing, and anybody's welcome to join us.

Singing? Really. What good will that do, do you think?

Hey, fuck you, all right? Keith said. If you don't want to go, don't go. Who cares what you think about it? Look, all I'm trying to do is the same thing you think you're trying to do. I am making it clear that I have no part in this. There are these people who represent you, in a very literal way, and if you sit around and don't say anything, you're implicating yourself in what they do, as far as I'm concerned. But for me, I want the record to be clear. I protest.

He was turning a little red, unused to having his convictions exposed in this way.

Well, I'm still unconvinced, the first man said.

Somewhere in the building was the woman with the ponytail and the short dress. Perhaps she had stopped for coffee. In spite of himself, Julian imagined leaving the studio and searching through the corridors for her. He would see her from behind and would walk carefully on the carpeted floor, so she could not hear how quickly he was moving. He would say, Excuse me, very naturally, so as not to startle her, and then he would say that he recognized her. But even as this fantasy ran its course, he couldn't manage to bring it fully to life. He could never go out after her. Meeting her, talking with her, seemed to have little to do with what he was feeling, with the particular kind of longing and self-rebuke that she awakened in him. He found that he could most fully imagine such a woman, such promise, in the one place he had seen her — remote, silent, undisturbed, in a window, sometimes visible, sometimes not.

Julian, what about you, Keith said, scanning the list, which he had brought out of his pocket again.

What about me?

Keith looked up at him. Can you come to this thing on Friday?

I can't, Julian said. I have to go out of town this weekend. To see my parents.

Oh? Keith said. Nothing's wrong, I hope?

Julian was taken aback by the look of concern on Keith's face. He laughed, surprised. No, he said. Nothing's wrong.

Since the day of the assassination, when Warner had surprised Lewis in the gym teacher's office, they had met every morning, without ever arranging or acknowledging it, in the faculty lounge during their common ten o'clock free period. The lounge was one large room furnished with mismatched easy chairs and threadbare sofas. No one cared about the haphazard look of the room; any sort of disharmony among colors or styles mattered little in the general relief over the chance to sit on anything not made of plastic or wood. A long bank of mail slots ran along one wall. On a low table stood a cylindrical coffee urn, silver except for a black band of plastic around the bottom, with one red electric eye, which, as long as school was in session, was never seen to blink.

Warner's fingers met around a large plastic cup full of coffee. Lewis drank from his own mug, which he kept in the lounge. It was white, with blue letters that spelled Louis. They stole occasional looks at the clock over the door. Classes started on the hour and were fifty minutes long.

So I live with this woman I met in the NYU housing office. We rented this big one-bedroom down near Union Square, and we put up a wall in the middle of the bedroom, so now there's two. Actually, she put it up, I'm useless at that stuff.

She put it up? Lewis said. That figures.

Yeah. You can bet it wasn't my idea.

She cute?

Very. She has a boyfriend, though.

That must be a drag.

Well, it's a little tough sometimes. This is a plywood wall we're talking about. But it's nice. I mean, it's good to at least have a woman around so I don't forget what they look like, you know?

I do know.

What they move like, Warner said, what they smell like, what they sound like.

They sat beside the window, the heat from the old radiator offsetting the thin cold draft from outside. A fitful, unpleasant wind, audible to them in its strongest, high-pitched gusts, swirled all along the block. The leaves blew madly up and down the street and sidewalk, scraping loudly over the pavement as if trying to get to the earth that still lived underneath.

You live right near here, don't you?

Walking distance, Lewis said. On Ninety-sixth and Lex.

The edge of the world, Warner said.

You know it. There's only one subway exit I'll even use. But I was able to get a studio there, so what the hell. It's a nice place, a lot nicer than I could afford if I were about six blocks further south.

I don't know how you can afford it now, Warner said. A studio, God.

Barely, is how. I haven't been out for dinner in about six months.

A student came into the lounge, balancing a stack of mimeographed papers. She glanced at them briefly, then turned and began to stuff one notice in each mail slot. The task was one of her extra duties as a scholarship student. They watched her as she worked, bending over, standing on tiptoe, then gradually bending over again, but even after she left, they showed no interest in the notice itself.

You know, Warner said, I never really even had the urge to live alone until I came here.

It's the only way to get any living done, Lewis said.

They looked up at the clock, which read ten forty-five.

Who've you got at eleven again? Lewis said. Freshmen?

Juniors.

That's a little more like it. He paused. So this must be an interesting time to be teaching American history, huh?

How so?

With the fighting and all.

Oh. Well, we're still back in the nineteenth century. It'd be a little hard to work it in. If they're still killing each other in May, we can talk about it.

In fact, Warner had his theories about this, about what might or might not be considered his classes' legitimate subject. But he had also begun encouraging in himself the idea that his mission in the classroom was a secret, even a subversive one; and so he was vague about it, even around Lewis, who was, it seemed, becoming a friend.

Lewis laughed. Maybe you could speed it up a little. Give them the Reader's Digest version.

I suppose. The industrial revolution in one hundred minutes, or their parents' money back. He swallowed the rest of his cold coffee, then tossed the cup with a practiced motion into the wastebasket underneath the table. Well, I do hope it's all over before we get to it, in class I mean. Besides, I don't think they let you teach it unless it's history.

I have to say, though, times like this make me a little jealous of you, Lewis said. It just makes teaching math seem even less relevant. In every class I've ever had there are two or maybe three people who have a real enthusiasm for what they're studying, and the rest of them have this look on their faces like they're not really sure how they got there. To tell the truth, most of the time those are the ones who have all my sympathy. That's the great curse of teaching math, you know. Your best students are all assholes.

Warner laughed. Yeah, that was pretty much my suspicion. Why do you teach it, then, if you don't like it?

I do like it. But then I think the only reason I like it is because it's the one thing I can really do well. It always has been. I have this aptitude for numbers.

You could be a banker, go into banking.

Different numbers, Lewis said.

The bell rang, and they looked at each other. Forward, Lewis said. They rose from their chairs.

The room in which he taught the juniors, 319, was Warner's least favorite among the several classrooms he was assigned. It was the largest, and it did get a fair amount of light, at least in the hour when he was there. But in this room, the desks, which were attached to the chairs, were the large and hollow kind, with tops that flipped open so that books could be stored inside. Warner liked to have his students arrange their desks in a circle, so he could make himself an unobtrusive part, save for those times when he became excited and would get up and walk around. But the huge desks made that ridiculous; it would have looked as if every student were trying to protect himself from the others. So the class stayed ranged in rows before him. It called to mind some kind of adversary relationship. He tried sitting on the edge of his own desk, but he still felt a great pressure to entertain when they were in this formation, as if he had been asked to warm up an audience for some better, unnamed act to come.

There were two students already seated when Warner arrived; they had heard his footsteps and were staring at him expectantly. The two were not friends, and had selected desks far apart from each other. Warner nodded to them, smiled, and tried to busy himself at his desk. The seven or eight minutes before the second bell were always hard to handle. The time belonged rightfully to the students, and they always seemed slightly defensive when he tried to make small talk before class started. So now he pretended that there was work he needed to finish before the bell rang. Head down, he could hear the students' voices fall suddenly, as they came through the door in groups of three or four and saw that he was there. They went on talking, as they settled at their desks, in an ironic, circumspect way that actually seemed to increase their sense of pleasure with themselves. If he lifted his eyes at some particular burst of laughter, everyone would gradually notice, and a put-upon silence would follow. If he lifted his head and tried to eavesdrop while focusing his attention elsewhere, out the window for example, they would begin to stare at him, and to get the idea that he was upset about something. They would ask him, with a familiarity so shocking it was touching, if he was okay, if there was anything they could do. So it was out of respect that he had settled on this ritual of simply sorting through everything in his bookbag in the minutes before class officially started. He felt it was the role in which they were most comfortable with him. He would write grocery lists, letters, reminders to himself, sometimes a kind of shorthand diary, which he would later ball up and throw away.

The bell rang, one or two conversations hurried to their conclusions, and then silence. Warner put everything except the textbook and a stack of photocopied paper back into the bookbag, which he slid under his chair.

Carrie, he said, would you pass these out please?

Carrie Ames, who had arrived late and so had the misfortune of sitting in the front row, stood wearily and took the stack of paper from Warner's hand. It was stapled together every three pages; quickly, she brought the lopsided pile to her face and sniffed it before handing out the papers. She moved with her customary slowness around the classroom, smiling or rolling her eyes at some stops, offering an impassive face to others.

You all read last night, Warner said, about Commodore Perry's opening of Japan in 1852. Didn't you, Walker?

The boy named Walker looked hurt, and nodded.

Terrific. Now, the text makes mention of the presents that the fleet brought for their hosts, but they don't go into much detail about it. I wanted to start today by taking a little closer look at this whole episode than you're given in the book. I think this will be fun.

Carrie sat down with a thump. Warner's voice had reached the level of volume and eloquence that came to him only in classrooms.

Now, he said. These gifts were ostensibly coming directly from the United States government, and so Perry introduced himself, when he landed, by means of a letter from President Fillmore. You'll see that it's on the first page of the handout. Eddie, would you read some of that for us, starting from where it's bracketed there?

Eddie Childs lowered his head and spoke without inflection the words of Millard Fillmore. *We have directed Commodore Perry to beg your imperial majesty's acceptance of a few presents. They are of no great value in themselves: but some of them may serve as specimens of the articles manufactured in the United States, and they are intended as tokens of a sincere and respectful friendship.*

Okay, Warner said. Now these so-called presents were of course of enormous value, not to mention of interest. Take a look, everyone, at the list of gifts on the next page. Notice anything significant about them, anything they have in common? Anyone.

He watched as all the students cast their eyes down as if reading or thinking. After a minute, it became clear that they were pretending to be lost in thought, afraid they would be called upon if they lifted their faces. Warner tried again.

Why these presents and not others? he said. What was the thinking behind all this official courtesy? Were these really tokens of friendship, do you think, or expressions of something else?

A girl named Meredith liked to serve as the tension-breaker at these moments of impasse. She raised her hand, and Warner called on her. It's mostly guns and liquor, she said. Is it supposed to remind us of what happened with the Indians?

That's a good point, Warner said. Sure. And, as always, there was an economic motive; the hope was that if the Japanese liked these free samples, they'd get hooked, and the trade routes would open up. That goes without saying. But what I'm trying to get at is what a tremendous, calculated, all-out assault of American culture this was. I mean, they brought an entire train over, by ship, complete with passenger cars and track to be laid out in a circle! Imagine that. Imagine the upheaval this must have caused in the Japanese culture, a highly traditional culture, quite hostile to outsiders. The most popular of all the presents, according to the report Perry submitted to Fillmore on his return, were the Colt revolvers. The Americans conducted races between the fastest runners the Japanese could come up with and the telegraph they'd set up when they landed. The Americans also said—I love this—that the Japanese were especially impressed by what the report called the utility of buttons. What do you think the Japanese officials thought about all this? Would they have been receptive, or would they feel their own order threatened?

A boy named Carter held up one hand, while the other wrote furiously in his notebook. He seemed annoyed. Are we going to be responsible for all this? he said.

Warner knew what was meant; still, he had to run his hand over his face, lest the boy think he was being laughed at. It was a wonderful question. He tried to think of someone he could tell it to who would appreciate it.

They finished dinner in plenty of time, but then they sat in Julian's dark living room and talked, holding hands, for so long that finally it became necessary to hurry. Though there were few dishes to take care of, there was a formidable amount of cardboard, and Julian went back into the kitchen to get rid of the garbage. Kendall stood, ready to go, by the windows at the front of the apartment. The blinds were drawn to keep anyone on the sidewalk from seeing in; she was tempted to open them, just to have a look outside, but she knew that Julian, who could see her from where he was, liked them that way, and so she did nothing. She could not be at ease in his home, even now; things there seemed off limits by virtue of their very interest to her. Nothing Julian had ever actually said had encouraged her to behave in this restrained way. She turned from the windows. She had an urge, when she was in his apartment, to open closets, to look through his mail, an urge she had never experienced with anyone else she had ever gone out with. She did not know what she expected to find there. She wondered if this air about him was simply mystery, or something else. Julian came out of the kitchen holding a large white plastic garbage bag, its top knotted closed.

Ready? he said. He walked over to her, dropped the bag by the front door, grabbed his coat, and kissed her with his eyes closed while he pulled it on. She stepped toward him and wrapped her arms around his chest as tightly as she could. He made a low sound of mock surprise, and pretended to try to button his coat around them both. She laughed, and tilted her face back an inch or two.

You could call in sick.

Don't tempt me, she said.

She walked to the easy chair and picked up her bag. Will we need gloves? he said. She picked hers up and waved them. He opened the door, swore at the cold, and waited with his hand on the light switch as she walked out, bending to get under his arm. As she watched him lock the door and stuff the bag in the trash can, she heard a door close above them, and then heels clicking on the steps overhead.

Julian brushed by her and stuck his head out from under the stoop. The heels stopped. Well hey, Julian, a man's voice said.

Without looking back at Kendall, Julian walked to the bottom of the steps. Hi Bill, he said. Hi Liz.

Kendall felt a wave of consternation. She went and stood beside him; he looked at her, and touched her arm briefly. Have you ever met my friend Kendall? he said.

The couple on the steps looked to be about Julian's age. They were a handsome pair, not glamorous but obviously moneyed; he looked at home in his suit, which he had probably, Kendall thought, been in all day. They were evidently on their way out somewhere. The woman was pulling off her right glove. No, she said, but we've heard enough about her. The woman's voice could have been described as practiced. I thought we'd never get to meet you, she said.

They shook hands and put their gloves back on.

Bill, Liz, Kendall, Julian said. Kendall, Bill and Liz Camp. My landlords.

God, I hate that word, Bill said, and laughed.

Me too, Liz said. Couldn't we call it something else?

I'm just walking Kendall to work, Julian said.

Property holder? Bill said. No, that's not so hot either.

Where are you two off to? Liz said. Someplace fun, I hope.

I'm just walking Kendall to work, Julian said.

I thought you never walked anywhere, Liz said. How'd she talk you into it?

You work nights? Bill said. What do you do?

I'm in radio, Kendall said.

No kidding, Bill said. Are you a disk jockey?

Engineer.

That's too bad. You've got a great voice.

Well, Kendall said, I'm running a little late, so. She found Julian's hand and squeezed it.

Where are you folks going? Julian said.

Just dinner, Bill said. A friend at the firm is quitting.

Well, have fun. He stepped aside to let them off the stairs.

We'll try, Liz said. You too. Kendall, it was nice meeting you. I hope we can get you two to come out some time, or even just upstairs for a drink.

Kendall smiled.

The Camps waved and started down the street, east toward Second Avenue. Kendall took a step and started to pull on Julian's hand; looking up, she saw he was staring after the Camps as they walked to the end of the block and stepped right into a cab, almost as if it had been waiting there for them. After a second, he turned his head, said Sorry, and began walking with her.

Kendall had never heard much about Julian's landlords, which now surprised her, since he seemed strangely fond of them. They didn't seem at all like the kind of people he would be friendly with. She and Julian walked to the end of the block in silence. Nice couple, Kendall said.

Yeah, they are.

They own that whole place? They seem a little young to be landlords.

They're that, too. Julian looked intently at the traffic light, waiting for it to change. He could feel himself becoming uncommunicative. Because he knew the effect this had on her, rather than out of any real remorse, he decided to say something more. She's pregnant, actually. Could you tell?

I thought so, Kendall said. I wasn't sure enough to say anything.

She's fairly far along, Julian said, but she hasn't really gotten that huge.

And she had that big coat on. Well, good for her. Good for them.

As was their custom, they walked west on Sixty-second Street, past the swollen river of Lexington Avenue, past Madison, until the street came to a dead end at the park. They turned south down Fifth Avenue. The cold kept things clean; it was as if each breath served to polish the air before them. Even the streetlights seemed wintry and clear, without their usual faint aureole of haze. There was no wind. The few dead leaves still on those trees that grew hard against the stone wall by the sidewalk hung like icicles above them as they walked on the park side of the street, away from the grand lobbies and the solitary doormen.

The sky was black, but the avenue, particularly once they passed the southern border of the park, was brightly lit, and crowded, in spite of the temperature. The forces of commerce had declared it the Christmas season, a little earlier again this year; shoppers stared past their own reflections in the windows, and the revolving doors spun like engines. An enormous sculpture, constructed of lights, hung dangerously over the intersection at Fifty-seventh Street, suspended by barely visible wires. Someone important was evidently under the impression that it resembled a snowflake.

The Salvation Army was out, ringing bells over Grand Army Plaza. Near them was a group of men, shouting with diminishing passion at passersby; among them, sitting on a chair, was a stuffed dummy in a striped prison outfit with a metal bucket over its head.

Jesus, Kendall said, don't tell me I have to start thinking about this already.

About what? Christmas?

She nodded grimly.

No, he said. I'm here to tell you that you do not have to start thinking about Christmas already.

As they stood waiting for a light, people shouldered past them to take one step into the street. Julian looked up uneasily at the mammoth snowflake.

So what do you want? Kendall said.

Julian laughed. I don't know. I can't think of anything.

Really?

Really. Maybe I'll just stand pat.

The light changed, and they crossed the street, not able to look at one another for the effort of avoiding all the people coming at them. There's nothing you can think of, she said when they were back together, nothing in the whole world, that you want?

There's still a lot of time, he said, to think about it.

The crowd on Fifth Avenue seemed to flirt with the distinction between festivity and surliness. As the two of them headed downtown into the heart of it, Julian could feel himself growing annoyed, not at anyone's discourtesy but by virtue of the physical effect of the continuous soft knocks against his feet and shoulders. Kendall struggled to stay close to him. She squeezed his hand hard through the rough glove.

Are you going home to your parents' this year? Julian said.

For Christmas? No. At least I don't think so. I already told them I wouldn't be.

Too expensive?

I think they'd probably pay for it if I gave them any hint I wanted to come, but I don't want them to do that. You're going home, right?

Sure. Do you really just not want to see them that much? Your brother's not going to be there, is he?

No, that's not for a few more months, she said.

They walked past the cathedral. Men and women sat on the steps, some in groups, some alone, many of them surrounded by shopping bags. They looked exhausted as the surge continued on the sidewalk below them. One man, shivering, silently hawked a series of sketches of the cathedral itself, executed in warmer weather.

I'd like to meet your parents some time, Kendall said.

They walked for a while without talking. When they had gone past the avenue's real glamor, and into a bright, quiet valley of discount camera and jewelry storefronts, they turned right and headed farther west toward Kendall's office. She did not enjoy the silence. She heard it as the sound of breakdown, of decay; she looked around her for something to fill it.

So that Liz woman was pregnant, she said. How old is she?

I'm not sure. Thirty. Twenty-nine or thirty.

It's hard to imagine. She hesitated, sure that he would take what she was about to say the wrong way; but finally her dislike of the silence between them overcame her caution. I think about that sometimes.

She had meant it in the most general way; but she was worried that he would hear it as some direct reference to the two of them. Certainly she thought about that, though her speculations about motherhood went well beyond it. She knew she was risking his anger, or rather, his withdrawal. But when, after a moment, she looked up at him, she saw that he was not angry in the least. He had heard her, but he was not paying her any real attention. Evidently he was already thinking of something else. How he could do this while holding her hand was something that gave her cause for astonishment; and this was not the first time. They walked the rest of the way toward Times Square, the evidence of each breath vanishing in front of them. She felt she had suffered a great setback. On the dirty side streets, the light was scarce; a radio played near a hill of garbage. A few lone prostitutes watched them go by, unmoved.

By the time they reached her office building he had sensed from her that he should be feeling bad about something, but he didn't know what. They stopped in front of the double glass doors and stood facing each other.

So, he said, another long night at work.

She nodded.

You must be dreading it, huh?

Well, not really. Not so much lately.

Oh yeah? he said.

And that was all. She listened, and eventually she smiled at him, in disbelief, in sadness. Yeah, she said. Ask me about it sometime.

She turned and pushed through the glass doors, and Julian watched her walk down the long corridor, past the unmanned security desk, toward the elevator banks. The door swung shut with a bang that made the glass shake, and the view wavered briefly before him. Uncomfortable, he watched her all the way.

Then the elevator doors closed and she was no longer there. He had been staring so intently down the now-vacant hallway that the bright, mobile face of the street came as a shock to him when he turned around. For an instant, he did not remember how he had come to be there. He was alone, and it seemed he had been transported from his home for no discernible reason, only to find himself, as in some dream, having to make his way back again. After a moment, the noise brought him to his senses. He managed a smile at his own confusion. Then he stepped out into the street, hailed a cab, and was gone.

The hours passed, and the clamor on Times Square faded, though never entirely. The cold grew worse. Indoors, movies were projected, televisions flickered, while outside, giant billboards dumbly flashed their messages to one another. They ran robotically, unmanned, perfectly safe and unattended. Some time in the night, high above them all, silent, as if sourceless, dropping into vision, snow began to fall.

Two Americans died early this morning when a car bomb exploded at a makeshift U.S. Army barracks in Colozan City. Pentagon spokesmen say that a lone terrorist, his face covered by a scarf, drove an American model jeep through the newly erected barricades at the entrance to the Army compound at about one A.M. today, Eastern standard time. The jeep then traveled some fifty yards across an open field and into the heavily fortified doorway of the barracks, where it exploded on impact. Corporal Arnold J. Foster of Kansas City, Missouri, and Walter Brock of Troy, New York, a computer specialist who was serving as an Army consultant, were killed in the attack. Thirteen other Americans, all soldiers, were injured, two of them critically. White House officials said they believed that the attack, which they labeled the work of quote terrorist thugs unquote, was most likely in retaliation for last week's Army raid of a guerrilla camp just outside the capital city, in which sixteen members of the opposition forces were killed. The driver of the jeep also died in this morning's incident.

Elsewhere, a violent clash between two sets of protesters outside the White House resulted in two dozen injuries and more than a hundred arrests yesterday. Two hundred and fifty members of the Committee in Solidarity with the People of Colozan taking part in a demonstration on Pennsylvania Avenue were met by a smaller group, calling themselves members of the Coalition for the National Defense, who attempted to block their way. The two groups exchanged angry words, according to bystanders, and people at the front of the two lines reportedly began to shove one another. Before the heavily outnumbered police could step in, what one officer described as a gang war had broken out, including the throwing of bottles and rocks. White House spokesman Bernard Helliwell called the incident deplorable, and faulted the Washington police department for failing to provide adequate security. Only one of the injuries is reported to be serious.

Rain continued for a record eleventh day in Santiago, Chile, where massive flooding has already claimed seventeen lives and left as many as fifty thousand homeless. The government's declared state of emergency has brought little actual relief for those in need of food and temporary housing, according to Ivy Hernandez, a director of the International Red Cross in Chile. Chilean officials replied in a statement issued to reporters yesterday that quote where the sky is concerned, there is little that can be provided in the way of relief unquote. The forecast in Santiago calls for a break in the weather tomorrow.

It's twelve minutes past three o'clock. More news after this.

Meriwether scratched his nose, then his elbow, then the top of his head, and took a deep, loud breath. The studio engineer tonight was a stranger, one of a parade of strangers who had passed through the studio while Samuelson was away on vacation in St. Martin. The engineer busied himself with tapes during the break and did not look at Meriwether, who felt oddly resentful of the man, of being pointed at and cut off and having a red light flashed on and off in his face by someone he didn't know. A few doors away, Kendall listened to some music she had brought from home on the state-of-the-art tape machine in her office. She had torn off some wire service copy with the idea of rewriting it, unbidden, in the hope of impressing some superior at the station with her desire to make more of her job; it lay untouched on her desk. Made to feel guilty by her own boredom, she watched the doorknob to make sure no one was trying to come in, as she listened to the raucous love songs sung by a man whose voice reminded her of Julian's. Julian, quiet, dreaming, undisturbed by the headlights that occasionally washed through the living room just outside his bedroom door, or by loneliness, slept soundly, in rhythm with the rest of the city, or most of it.

The time is three-sixteen. Continuing with the news, Mayor Fossey continues to fire back at critics of his controversial Operation Antidote. Sources inside the district attorney's office say they expect very few, if any, of the ninety-eight arrests made in last Thursday's drug raid to lead to convictions. In the surprise raid, the entire block between West End Avenue and Riverside Drive on Ninety-second Street was barricaded without warning, and everyone on the street was stopped and searched by police. The mayor responded last night by saying, quote, if the prosecutors prosecute as vigorously as their counterparts in the police department did their jobs, then I expect the guilty will wind up in jail, unquote. The highly publicized operation employed some one hundred and fifty officers in riot gear, mounted police, and one department helicopter.

The Heilman Art Institute in Denver has threatened legal action against Colorado's attorney general over the destruction of a painting exhibited by one of its students last week. The painting, entitled A Crossover Vote, depicted former Mayor Ray Hayward, who died in office last September of a heart attack, in a bra and garter belt. Last Thursday, Attorney General Kevin Feeney walked into the institute's exhibition hall, accompanied by policemen and photographers, and slashed the painting repeatedly with a knife. Feeney told reporters that he would welcome a chance to defend his actions in court.

And finally, police in Lattimore, Pennsylvania, say they have decided not to press charges against seven-year-old Owen Pine. Officer Edward Lyle of the Lattimore police department became suspicious last Saturday when he noticed that the car in front of him, which was traveling well within the speed limit, seemed to have no driver. He sounded his siren, and the car pulled over. In the driver's seat was young Owen, who, upon seeing the policeman, began to cry. He explained that he had been bored at home and had taken the car keys from his mother's purse while she was on the phone in order to go for a little drive. When asked where his mother was, Owen replied that she was at home, and offered to give Officer Lyle a lift. The officer declined. Coming up, we'll have an update on the weekend weather, and Sam Grace with all of last night's college basketball action, including a big win for St. John's at the Garden. It's twenty-two degrees and snowing in Manhattan. Back after this.

Holly seemed like the sort of woman who was rarely on time for appointments; still, Warner arrived at the restaurant five minutes early. He stood in his overcoat in the small entryway, holding a brown paper bag wet with snow, pressing himself against the wall to let other parties in or out, spreading with his toe the puddle of water forming under his shoes. At quarter past, she walked in, smiling, and kissed him on the cheek, which put him somewhat off his guard. The restaurant was a small Italian establishment in the West Village; Lewis had told him it was both romantic and cheap, and though Warner had been there once before himself, without finding it terribly romantic, he decided he must have missed something.

The restaurant did not take reservations, and so there was an awkward, if short, wait in the doorway while an older couple, accustomed to dining early, finished their coffee and paid the check. Warner tried not to stare at them as he waited, though it was better than staring at Holly, to whom he already had nothing to say. His feet were still a bit wet, and every so often he sniffled. The interior of the dining room was warm and smelled luxuriously of garlic and coffee.

Is there someplace to check these? Holly said. She plucked at the sleeve of her coat.

No, Warner said, I guess there isn't. I don't see any.

Their table was cleared and set. Warner, feeling himself beginning to sweat, took off his coat and folded it over his arm. He was wearing a tie. The restaurant was three steps below street level. The windows were steamed up in a way that suggested nostalgia; all that was visible outside was the glow from various lights — whether from streetlights or fluorescent signs or reading lamps in the windows of the townhouses across the way, it was difficult to tell — mysterious and somehow calming. The room was quieter than Warner had expected. It was small enough to make one aware of one's fellow diners, and so inspired, if only for that reason, a kind of discretion and intimacy. This had been an important consideration in his planning, with Lewis, of the evening; but now it seemed almost a drawback, a cause for anxiety.

Cute place, Holly said. You've been here before?

A few times, Warner said. He turned, grateful for the pretext to look at her. She did seem interested in his answer, though the answer itself was hardly arresting. She was, he saw again, quite remarkably beautiful.

The headwaiter seemed to understand this too, and to know the value of any such presence to his restaurant, or even to the world at large. He treated her as if she were royalty, and, moreover, as if he were quite used to serving royalty. With a confidential nod to Warner, he led her by the arm to their table. To Warner, one of life's great sensations was to arrive somewhere, anywhere, in the company of a beautiful woman. He felt an actual flush as the heads lifted all around the dining room; he tried to stay close to her and to look as indifferent as possible. She slipped off her overcoat as she walked. She was in the habit, Warner knew, of dressing to provoke, especially after the sun was down. Tonight, though, she seemed to have toned it down somewhat. She wore a short black skirt and stockings, a loose white blouse, and heels that, on someone else, might have seemed precarious. For a moment he was relieved, even flattered that she would have made this much of an allowance for him; but then, as he tried to imagine her standing in her bedroom, thinking about him and deciding what to wear, it occurred to him that her appearance could be interpreted in several ways. As was his instinct, at least where women were concerned, the interpretation least flattering to himself struck him as the most likely, and he chose to feel diminished by it.

The headwaiter was an appealing, classy figure; though his demeanor indicated that he could treat anyone in the world with the precise level of deference to which he or she was accustomed, his outfit — no jacket, a white shirt with the sleeves rolled, a loosened tie, collar button undone — suggested a busy informality, as if he had invited them into his home. When he had pulled out Holly's chair, she handed him her coat without a word; without a word, he took it away to find some proper place for it. Warner had already draped his over the back of his chair. He was awestruck. As they sat and smiled at one another, he wanted to say something about that scene, even if indirectly, perhaps by paying a compliment to the headwaiter; but he refrained, afraid such an observation would reveal something about him, some lack in him. Holly, he could guess, probably would not understand any contention that something unusual had happened.

A waiter had come up behind him. Would you like me to take that for you, sir? he said. He was pointing to the paper bag, which Warner still held in his hand. Oh, yes, thanks, he said, and handed it over. In the bag was a bottle of red wine. With a flourish, the young man, whose hair reached his shoulders, placed the bottle on the table and discreetly stuffed the damp bag into the pocket of his apron. He opened the wine, slowly, concealing any difficulty. Warner looked uncertainly from the waiter's face to the bottle to Holly. When it was done, the waiter poured two glasses and went away.

They don't have a liquor license here, Warner said. You have to bring your own wine, or beer or whatever.

Holly smiled.

You do like red wine, don't you? Warner said. I suppose I should have asked.

No, I love it.

I hope this is all right. Do you know anything about wine at all?

Just how much of it I can drink, Holly said.

It's one of those things I've always wanted to be an expert on. I don't really know how you'd go about it, though. Just something in your upbringing. There was a silence. Well, he said, and raised his glass slightly, unconsciously, before he realized there was nothing he could think of for the two of them to drink to. She raised her eyebrows. He smiled. To absent friends, he said finally. They touched glasses. The wine was all right, he thought, or at least it seemed all right.

So how is Julian? she said. You must see a lot of him, I guess.

He seems well. Working pretty steadily, lately.

He's over at your place a lot?

A few times a week.

They paused to order. Holly had scarcely looked at the menu, but she didn't seem to care much what she ate; she ran her finger down the laminated column, humming, and stopped at the first interesting thing she saw. Warner observed, in her dealings with the waiter, that she lacked the businesslike haughtiness that many beautiful women seemed to have. She looked right at the young man — who clearly believed himself gorgeous, and not without reason — as she spoke to him, and also as he spoke to her; but she didn't seem to be flirting with him in any way, or making fun of him. Warner knew little about such confident people, but he felt sure this had nothing to do with her being attracted to the man. She was without guile in these matters. If she were aroused by him, or bored, or entertained, or annoyed, the reasons for concealing this would not occur to her.

You know, Holly said after the waiter had gone away, I think maybe I have been here before. This is a nice spot. It reminds me of a place in Italy, a little.

What city? he said, feeling slightly foolish for asking.

I forget. Have you been to Italy ever?

Once, barely. In Turin for a whole three days. I was staying with friends, though, so I didn't get to see much.

You went to Italy for three days?

No, he said, not really. I spent one semester at the University of London when I was in college, and I just went down with some Italian friends over Easter weekend.

London, she said. What made you go there? Were you studying something in particular?

No. I can't remember why I did it, really. That's if I ever knew to begin with. Maybe just to be adventurous, maybe because I wasn't all that happy at school where I was. But I really loved it there, it turned out. That was probably the best six months of my life. I know we're not talking about very much life. But I was very happy there. I loved London itself. Have you been?

She smiled.

It made me think that maybe the whole idea of cities isn't such a bad one, he said.

Do you ever think about going back?

All the time, he said. Maybe not every day, but a lot.

Why don't you? she said. You don't seem all that happy here, if you don't mind my saying so.

She seemed entitled to say such things. I don't know what stops me, he said. I don't know what keeps me here.

In the cozy room, with a glass and a half of wine in him, Warner felt warm and secure, even relaxed. Holly gave no outward signs of wanting to hurry the evening along, or of wishing she were somewhere else. As far as he was concerned, it was the task of the world to provide for the entertainment of women like this, and if it had fallen to him to do so for a few hours, he owed it to beauty to work hard at it and not to let anyone down. He had no sense that this was an exchange. It was his job to keep her interested in being with him.

You work at one of the clubs, he said.

She named the place.

I've never been, he said, not that that means anything. I'm a little naive about that whole club scene. Is it pretty wild?

Wild? she said.

Well, I don't know what I'm asking, really. Let me put it this way. Do you ever see any behavior, does anybody ever do anything, that you'd consider shocking?

To his relief, she took the question seriously. Rarely, she said. But it's relative, of course. I don't know you very well, but I suspect we might be shocked by different things.

Warner laughed and poured out the rest of the wine. An erotic remark, he thought, objectively speaking. He had a definite but not insurmountable fear of unafraid, experienced women. She was too much for him. But then, it did not defy logic to think that women like her might have some temporary attraction to men whom they were patently too much for, men who could make no believable attempt to conceal their submissive position.

She did seem somewhat engaged now, and, if only to fill the time, she began to tell some stories of the nightlife he had always thought of as a country too distant to visit. He was shocked, one or two times, but only into laughter; she joined in with him, shaking her head as if able to hear these stories anew through his ears. They had nearly finished the wine by the time the main course arrived. Incredibly, she asked the waiter, whom she now owned, if there was any way he could get them another bottle. He looked around him, spoke like a spy to the headwaiter, and came back from the kitchen a few minutes later with a fresh, dusty bottle, much better than their first.

Unbelievable, Warner said.

Again, she acted as if nothing unpredictable had happened. This time, she poured for them. Despite her good mood, he could not help feeling a little uncomfortable.

I guess women like you are used to getting what you want, he said.

She looked at him with interest. Nothing he could say or do

seemed to hold any element of surprise for her. Maybe in the short term, she said.

In spite of all his warnings to himself, he was beginning to feel entranced by her. Thoughts of sex — stylized, idealized — were allowed to creep into his mind. He could hear himself, as it were, trying to establish the desires of a woman like Holly, so that he might then play to them. It did not occur to him, really, that she might want him; only that he could get her to think so. Sex was nearly always associated, in his mind, with this kind of beneficent deceit, whether one-sided or mutual. Hope in this direction was precisely what he had promised himself all day he would not give in to.

So you're a teacher? Holly said.

Right. At least for now. I don't know if I want to spend the rest of my life doing it.

Well, that's not the acid test for something, you know, she said. Whether or not you'd want to do it for the rest of your life. What do you teach?

History, Warner said. Mostly American.

Really, she said. Why that?

From most people he would have considered the question inane, or possibly even rude. He might have said, politely, Who can answer these questions? But she obviously believed that there was an answer to such a question — that if there weren't, he wouldn't be doing it at all. He wanted to do his best for her, and something told him that she would not hold any foolish answer against him, so long as it was honest.

Well, it's what I know, he said. You teach what you know. Also, I suppose you can't talk about something for four or five hours every day if it doesn't interest you, and history interests me. I honestly consider it not just more interesting but more important than anything else you're made to learn. It's the one great lesson. It will stay still for you until you understand it, for one thing. And to understand what happened in a particular place, and time, is a real satisfaction to me. You feel like you've done something for these people, in a way. It gives you a kind of power over seemingly unmanageable things. I don't know if any of this makes sense. If it's the story of a triumph, then that's a satisfaction. If it's the story of an injustice, then to see what happened and why and how, if it could have been prevented or if it was inevitable, that's a real satisfaction, too. It's a perspective you never get to have on your own lifetime, or on your own life. I mean, I don't know about other people, but I wonder all the time what this period in history, what our lives, will look like in a hundred years, what kind of perfect sense it'll make. And I kind of resent it that I'll never know.

Remembering that he was not talking to himself, he stopped. Besides, he said, it's what I majored in.

Holly laughed. You've lived with Kendall for, what, two years?

He nodded.

The two of you never went out or anything?

Oh, no.

So what is she like? Do you like her?

Predictably, Holly did not bother to hide her interest in the subject, or to mute the contrast between her curiosity now and her polite curiosity a minute ago. He felt his heart sink.

Yes, I like her. We're not as good friends as we used to be, I don't really know why. But we get along.

She seems a little possessive to me. Is that right, do you think?

Holly had straightened up in her chair; she leaned forward to hear his answer. He felt that he was being indiscreet, but now, when his standing in her eyes was becoming clearer, more than ever, he did not see how she should not have what she wanted.

She does like to be alone with him, he said. In fact, I hear them a lot, but I see them pretty seldom. Sometimes I think she hides him from me.

Really, Holly said. Really. That's interesting. Do you think the two of them are good together, though?

He thought he was able to see now why she had been so unexpectedly open, so friendly with him. It was not a date; it was as if some random circumstance had thrown the two of them together for a while. It was as if they were from two different nations, or two different classes of people, stranded together, as on a train or in a broken elevator, for a couple of hours. She had no compunction about letting her guard down because she knew that in a short while it would be over, and she would never be expected to do it again. All along, she had had other things on her mind.

I like them both very much, he said. I admire Julian a great deal.

She smiled, and sat back, as if aware that she had pressed too hard. Her elaborate earrings glittered in the candlelight. She took her eyes off him, and looked thoughtfully around the room.

She was interested in Julian. He rejected the idea that the only reason she had gone out with him in the first place was to coax information out of him. She did not need to speed things along. Her interest alone was a powerful force and would make itself known; it would do the work for her. She herself had no work to do. It was simply a subject that had come up at dinner.

You don't pretend very much, do you? he said.

Sorry?

Nothing, he said. Never mind. She had probably heard him anyway.

He saw his role now—the role of men such as him—and, with a combination of sullenness and shame, he would not step out of it. His face red from the wine and the heat, he paid the whole check and the tip, over no objection from her. The second bottle of wine was not included in the tab. The headwaiter, looking precisely as rumpled as he had looked when they had come in more than two hours ago, came over with Holly's coat and helped her on with it. He held the door for the two of them, smiling, and Warner walked behind her up the steps and into the cold night.

They walked a few feet to the corner, one of those silent curvaceous West Village corners where there are always parked cars but never any traffic. They were not exactly waiting for a light, since they were going in opposite directions. Out of a kind of spite, Warner asked her if she'd like to go have a drink somewhere.

No, I think I ought to be getting back, she said. It's my night off, it's the only chance I have to get to sleep at a decent hour. Thank you anyway.

An end of Warner's scarf blew across his face; slowly, he raised his hand and tucked it back inside his coat. The crosswalk signs switched their colored messages with an audible click in the stillness. How on earth, Warner wondered, was it possible for a man and a woman to fall in love with each other at the same time? The type of longing which is always as if from afar, always hopeless, an ideal, a condition of subjection, of powerlessness, seemed the essence of love, the definition. He was in love with Holly now. He had been so from the moment he realized he would never have her, would never see the ways in which her talent for the sensual could translate itself, what it could bring to bear. He would never see her enthralled, as she had enthralled him. He felt humiliated by the very order of things.

You can get home okay? he said.

Sure, she said, I can just take a cab. Thanks anyway.

Clearly, she could be engaged by some men. She was engaged by Julian. He had always thought of Julian and himself as friends, but he wondered now just how authentic such a friendship could be. It went against what he was taught, and what he himself taught, but there seemed to exist in the world a sort of natural aristocracy, having much but by no means everything to do with looks, of which Julian and Holly were members, and he was not.

And thank you so much for dinner, Holly was saying. I really enjoyed it.

You're welcome, Warner said.

The lights changed again, brightening the wet pavement, flashing on the snow.

So I'm sure we'll see each other soon, Holly said, and waited, kindly, until he touched her shoulder and kissed her on the cheek. She kissed the dark air beside him. He smiled, adjusted his coat, and turned northward, to find his way out of the quiet maze of streets.

It was cold on the corner, and dark; and the quiet seemed threatening in the way only urban near-quiet can be. But Holly was only ten or twelve blocks from her apartment; she did not have the money to throw around on cabs, and she felt a heaviness from the meal and a slight headache from the wine. She started west, crossing the empty street, against the meaningless light.

Her footsteps echoed loudly off the walls of the brownstones, their windows dark and often barred. A thin, icy coating of snow frosted the shiny black garbage bags along the curb. The bags leaned against the miniature fences that surrounded the small plots of dirt needed to keep the thin, hardy trees alive. A cat walked in and out of a pool of lamplight far down the block, startling her. She was not used to being startled. Above her, an airplane moved silently in its element, its colored lights vivid against the empty sky.

As she walked westward, the brownstones gradually disappeared, and the streets took on an industrial cast. On some of the blocks, light blasted onto the sidewalk from an all-night deli; beyond was a patchwork of lighter and darker shadows. These streets were not lit for pedestrians. Pure darkness, so rare in the city, seemed disproportionately dangerous, though she had to pass through it, her hands balled into fists, only six or eight feet at a time. She began to regret not having taken a cab. She was too close to home now—about five blocks—to take one the rest of the way; still, when she heard the wet hiss of a car on the pavement behind her, she turned and was disappointed to see it was not a taxi. She turned to face forward again. The car slowed as it passed her. A male voice shouted something that she could not make out. He sounded angry. She pretended, absurdly, that she had not heard anything. The car crept past her, its brake lights on, and then sped off.

She was not used to this feeling. Nothing was at hand to protect her. She turned the corner, and though it had been frightening to walk on the street alone, she was far from comforted by the sight of two men who stood against a fence, talking. Hearing the loud report of her heels, they turned to look at her. Perhaps, it occurred to her, she was witnessing a crime. Though she was already several steps past the crosswalk, she stopped suddenly and walked over to the far side of the street, even though this meant she would have to cross back again at the end of the block. As she drew parallel to the two men, she glanced at them, against her will. They looked younger than she was. They had not resumed talking. She locked her eyes forward and tried not to speed up or slow down. The obscure, old buildings on the dark street were not residences. They seemed an element of the menace. At the end of the block, she crossed again, and waited at the light, though no cars were coming, to try to calm herself. Lamplight made the graying, crusted snow glitter like a desert.

Nice earrings.

She snapped her head around in spite of herself, and just as quickly looked back across the empty intersection. The earrings swung and slapped against her neck. The two men were still not moving, and yet they were now about twenty feet behind her. She started across the street, and then, suddenly, wondering why she was pretending, for whose benefit, she began walking as fast as she could. The streetlights on the block ahead of her were bright, but the few storefronts were closed, with iron gates pulled down in front of them. The snow had stopped long ago, and the air was still. In a moment of panic, in spite of all she saw and knew, she was convinced that this was not the way home, that she would have to turn around and go back, or else keep walking until daylight through these irregular streets, which looked as though their residents had fled them to escape some catastrophe about which she had not been told. The lights that burned overhead now seemed to expose her. Again, unable to stop herself, she looked back recklessly over her shoulder and saw that the two men were now walking behind her, quickly, to match her pace. One more corner to turn. She was flushed, even sweating, but did not dare slow down to open her coat, even though doing so would have allowed her to walk faster. She heard a noise over her head that sounded like a helicopter, and she thought suddenly of Warner, who would have walked her home, who would have stood between her and the two men, stupidly, instinctively. She would have let him do it.

Her building was the newest one on the street, and though it had no doorman, the lobby was secure and brightly lit. She turned the corner and saw the light spilling out onto the street. At that moment, one of the men laughed, and giving in to everything she broke into a run. Her heels made it nearly impossible but she would not stop to take them off. She heard her keys beating in her breast pocket like some alarm, and in stride she reached in and pulled them out. She heard footsteps, or the echo of her own. At the door, she fumbled for the right key, then fumbled to fit it into the lock. In a flash of clarity, she saw how little time it would be before she would be embarrassed by her behavior, and that she would never tell anyone about it. Tears in her eyes, unable to make the key slide into the lock, she reached out and ran her hand roughly over the panel of door buzzers for all the apartments in the building. The key slammed into the keyhole, she yanked the door open, and by the time it had swung gently back and clicked shut, the street was empty again, and silent, except for the tinny, inquisitive voices that began to float from the speaker by the door.

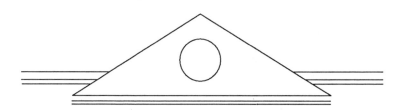

To Julian, the number of people who had to resort to travel on Christmas day always seemed surprisingly high; but there was nothing comforting in that, nothing to lessen the superficial air of sadness he encountered every year on the train to his parents' home. There was no real reason for this sense of loneliness, of abandonment, of longing—these were, after all, privileged people for the most part, and at every one of the fifteen or so stops in Connecticut, passengers were getting off to be met again by the families and crowded cars and warm, safe, expensive homes that invariably awaited them. They may not have loved these families, or the memories of these homes, but that was scarcely the point. Still, the atmosphere of despair and deprivation was as stubborn as it was irrational. It was, Julian had decided over the course of several Christmases, a function of the strange, collective quiet. Even on normal week-days, at rush hour, the trains were never exactly boisterous; but this was remarkable. Children sat beside their distracted-looking parents, behaving perfectly. The roar from an open door at the back of the car would come and go in a second; a minute later, the conductor would appear and ask in a hushed voice for one's ticket. Bags of presents swayed in the overhead racks or sat on the floor, bulging partway into the aisles. Julian was able to pinpoint this trip in advance as the single most depressing hour in any given calendar year.

It was a very sunny morning, cold, with no snow. Julian sat by a window, a shopping bag full of presents on the empty seat beside him, and watched the woods and the real estate go by. Twice, the hypnotic, rocking sound of the train was overwhelmed by a sudden slap of air as another train passed in the opposite direction. The small towns along the chain were set about five minutes apart; at each stop, the train would slow and pull up in front of a locked, darkened station house. People who had come to meet the train stayed in their cars to keep warm, invisible for the most part behind their tinted windshields. The parking lots were wreathed with exhaust, as the metal doors slid shut and the train glided northward again.

For the last few minutes of his ride, Julian took up his bag and stood before the doors. As the train decelerated, and the gray platform with its red-and-white signs pulled alongside, he picked out his father, standing beside his car in the lot, his breath steaming, shielding his eyes from the sun. A bell chimed as the train doors parted, and he stepped out into the cold. He waved, but his father did not see him. A tall man, he stood with his elbow on top of the car; he wore a bulky down jacket and corduroy pants. His dark brown hair was passing into gray. Car doors began to slam; quick kisses were exchanged, shivers mimed, and packages tossed or laid onto back seats. Julian waved again as he reached the stairs; this time, his father saw him and waved back broadly.

On the short drive home, Julian's face flushed as the car heater roared. He wiggled his toes. How was the trip? his father said.

Fine. Uneventful.

Right on time, his father said. It always is on holidays. I wonder why that is.

Julian's mother came out onto the porch when she heard the car. There he is, she said. Merry Christmas.

Get inside, Julian said as he kissed her. Don't be crazy.

She waited for his father to come in, then closed the door; together they watched Julian go over to the tree and unload his gifts.

No other bag? his mother said.

He turned around. No, I can't stay out this time, he said. I have a recording date tomorrow morning early, so I have to go back in tonight.

They gave you a job on December twenty-sixth? she said. Early?

Studio time is hard to come by. They get it when they can get it.

People have families.

What's the job? his father said, smiling. Anything we'd know?

No, it's not a real interesting one. It's a bunch of little promos for a radio station. A whole series of little four- or five-note things, singing the call letters, things like that.

I could wake you up early, his father said. You could go in on the first train in the morning.

Well, there'd be no point, really. I should go back in tonight. It's good to have as much sleep—

The phone rang, and Julian's mother excused herself to answer it in the kitchen.

So the jobs are still coming in, his father said. You're obviously building quite a reputation.

Well, Julian said, I don't know that reputation is the right word. It's more like I've gotten my name onto a lot of different computer lists.

Don't play it down. They know you, they know to ask for you, and that's no small accomplishment.

Julian's father measured his success as a singer strictly by the number of jobs he got, by the steadiness of his work and his pay. This was not, though, a principle that he applied generally, to others' lives or to his own; it was simply that he was willing to take any view of his son's life that would make him feel that it was happy and successful, because that was the feeling he most coveted in the world. He liked to try to communicate this view to his son, or to pretend that they shared it.

You know, he said, you should let your mother know which commercials you're singing on so she can tape them. She has a lot of them already.

I don't know why. Most of them, you can't pick out my voice anyway. Julian looked at his father. But okay, he said. I'll try to remember.

They sat in the living room and talked; in a few minutes his mother came out of the kitchen and motioned for his father to take her place. Maureen, she whispered to him. This was the first of many phone calls that would come that day from friends and distant family members. Julian's parents spent most of the afternoon talking to them, and to him, in turn. These individual interviews seemed right to him, emblematic of their ingenious and comfortable marriage. The way in which they lived together—shared, in a sense, one life—was intricate, though they would never have been able to explain it, or rather, would have denied the very idea of its complexity. They had found a way to rely on each other, completely, in spite of all the disappointing things they had learned about each other over the course of more than three decades. To Julian—who could not imagine for himself any relationship with a woman which did not follow the same arc of desire, faith, weakness, and destruction—if their feat was not completely admirable, it was nonetheless amazing. It was not a skill he wanted to acquire, necessarily; still, he felt that at the center of this complicated, placid life, there was a secret, which could perhaps be helpful to him.

The sun moved behind the house, and the light turned into the soft, low, uniform light that Julian associated with home, a light in which the city was never cast. The living room looked over a sloping lawn, which had seemed vast to him in the days when he'd had to mow it in order to collect his allowance; at the bottom of the slope was a split-rail fence, the road, and another white house, sitting opposite atop its own man-made rise. He did not know who lived there anymore. Behind the house were woods, or the illusion of woods, since in this part of the state, everything was property. A sense of solitude was expensively maintained; true solitude was certainly within the means of most of the people who lived in the area, but true solitude would most likely have been terrible to them. They took comfort in the sense of one another's presence.

The light was perfect; the blinds were open, no lamps were necessary. Julian's mother poured them each a glass of wine. The phone stopped ringing. Across the street, a boy and a girl emerged from the white house and began shooting at one another with expensive new toy guns. Julian had seen the guns advertised; they used lasers, and each child had to hang a large white target around his or her neck.

At last they opened their gifts. Julian, as he had done since he was three, gathered up the boxes from beneath the tree and redistributed them, stacking them beside his mother's chair, his father's, and his own. It did not take long to open everything, though they made it take as long as they could. The days when Julian would be surrounded by presents, when the exchange would evolve into a long, rapturous ceremony of his pleasure, were long gone — not because his parents no longer had the desire to do so, but because it was no longer possible to know of that many things Julian would want, or would be interested in.

He received a sweater, and a new watch, though his old one worked fine, and a new coffee maker, since he had mentioned pointedly in November that his old one had melted. His father also got a sweater, and a book about the America's Cup; his mother got a pair of earrings, a pair of theater tickets, and, extravagantly, from Julian's father, a fur coat. There was a strong, if obscure, pressure for gratitude as the boxes were torn open. Everyone reacted to everything — their own presents and the others' — as if it were the ideal marriage of utility and beauty; the giver of each gift would watch shyly, expectantly, even anxiously, for this show of delight. The pressure to be believable had nothing to do, really, with the gift itself, whether it was in fact perfect or some strange manifestation of the giver's image of the recipient. There was, inevitably, a slight sense of discomfort about the re-enactment of the Christmas ritual. It was not a lie, though in its feigned naturalness, it was the very opposite of spontaneity; still, they put up with it because within it, they knew, was an expression of love, no matter how lost or obscured.

At around sundown, his parents went to church. They knew he would not want to go, and they asked again only out of politeness, not to reproach. They themselves went only three or four times a year. For them, church served as a symbol of a serious intent. Julian stood and watched them as they bundled up in the front hall, looking older with each layer; his mother pulled her scarf away from her face to give him some instructions about dinner and kiss him goodbye, and in a short blast of cold air they were gone. He made himself a cup of hot chocolate — something he could not remember ever having a craving for outside of home — sat down in the living room, and flipped through some recent magazines. After a while, he stood at the window, hands in his pockets, and watched the empty road. As the sun went down, the view of the lawn and the house beyond gave way to his own reflection. The television rested on its cabinet against the wall. For reasons that were easily explained away, there seemed some shame attached to watching television on Christmas day. But the solemnity of Christmas, he thought, at its core, was nothing more substantial than peer pressure. There was no telling what was on. He went back to his chair, picked up the remote control, and turned on the set. It had the power to stop him from thinking.

Kendall and he had had their Christmas the previous night in her apartment. Warner, taking advantage of the school's long holiday, was away with his family, in Minneapolis, or near there. Kendall had seemed so festive and happy that Julian was taken aback. She turned out the lights and lit candles. Neither of them could cook very well. Kendall had wanted to try a turkey, but she was nervous and had second thoughts; so Julian let her off the hook by telling her that he would be getting one the following night anyway. They made spaghetti, something more within their range. She cleared off the big table and opened a bottle of wine. Traffic whispered outside. The whole thing seemed to Julian like a genuine attempt to recreate the kind of ritual that he would be going through the next day, and, even stranger, that she had no doubt gone through as a child in the home she was now so loath to visit. It surprised him and made him slightly ill at ease, not because the attempt seemed unsuccessful but because he would never have guessed that Kendall considered those formal aspects of home something worth imitating. There was no tree in the apartment, no decorations of any kind. A few cards were arranged on the small table by the couch, including one from her brother. She looked sleepy and beautiful. They spoke softly. When they were finished eating, Kendall got up, carrying her wine glass, and retrieved her gift to him from its hiding place in the back of her bedroom closet. He pulled his out from under the couch, where he had hurriedly stashed it when he walked in. In candlelight, they knelt in the middle of the floor and opened their presents. He looked for some sign that her happiness in this domestic situation was some effort of will; but it seemed genuine, natural, not a mood but a force, one that might have pleased him had he been more prepared for it. Her skin glowed, her eyes shone; she looked into his eyes as he fumbled uncomfortably with the wrapping paper. It was still early. They kissed, and kissed again, and then they made love, because there seemed, really, little else to do.

From the television came music that called forth a visual memory for Julian, the memory of a printed score. He looked up and saw it was a Chevrolet commercial. He had sung that song about the Chevrolet some fifteen times in a row in a windowless studio, but this was the first time he had ever seen the actual commercial, or, for that matter, to his knowledge anyway, the actual car. The Chevrolet drove through the desert, past great rock formations, places he had never seen. Even now that he knew this was a commercial he had sung, he could not pick out his own voice. By the time he thought to record it for his parents, the thirty seconds were up, and it had vanished.

Julian got up when he heard the front door bang open, earlier than expected, and exclamations of relief at the warmth inside. In the front hall, his father stood with his back to him, slowly taking off his coat. His mother headed straight for the kitchen to check on dinner; he could hear her lifting the lids of pots on the stove and noisily replacing them.

He took one step forward but suppressed an urge to help his father out of his coat. It seemed to be taking him a long time.

Aren't you home early? Julian said.

His father abruptly turned his head; apparently he had not realized that his son was there. He frowned.

Those pews in that church, it's like they're made of marble. I don't know how anybody can stand it. I don't know why everyone in town isn't walking around bent double.

Your back acting up again? Julian said.

A little. But really, that god damn church, it's enough to cripple you. I've tried to get them to do something about it.

His mother walked in. I picked up some more medicine for you last weekend, she said. It's by the sink—

I know where it is. He started up the stairs.

Do you need a hand? she said.

No, he said angrily, not stopping. I do not need a hand.

Julian turned to his mother, wanting to ask what was going on. It seemed to him she was trying to provoke his father somehow. She waited until they heard muffled footsteps on the bedroom carpet above their heads.

Your father has arthritis, you know.

Well, I know that.

Well, it's gotten worse lately. To him it's such an old people's thing, you know? The worse it gets, the stricter the prohibition against even saying the word at all. Does he think it will go away if he doesn't say the name? It's like dealing with a child. We went through the same thing with the false teeth a few years ago.

Julian smiled. Look. I know he's being a little childish, but it's sort of understandable. Is it so hard just to play along? I don't think we need to bait him about it. Do not go gentle, and all that.

A buzzer went off on the stove. She shook her head and started back toward the kitchen. The two of you, she said. The men in this family.

At dinner, all the serving dishes were full, and there was barely room for Julian's mother to fit them on the table as he maneuvered around her to pour the wine. The atmosphere of plenty seemed in obeisance to some idea of family happiness. His mother lit the candles and turned off the lights. His father lifted his glass for a brief, grateful, secular toast. They began to pass the dishes and then to eat. Though the table was small, the fact that there were only three of them, that there was one unoccupied side of the rectangle, gave the gathering a sense of imbalance; perhaps it was this that led Julian's father to ask after Kendall, whom he had never met—how she was, how things were, where she was today.

Julian winced as he realized that he had forgotten a promise to call her. She was working at the station today, a lucrative assignment with the overtime, but he did not tell his parents that. He knew that the truth would lead to a well-meaning but still intolerable scolding for his not having done something to prevent this. They would have asked him why he had not invited her to spend Christmas with them, and they would then have waited for his answer. No one should be alone on Christmas day, his mother would have said. Ever since he was a teenager, such pieties from his parents had pushed him close to losing his temper. Never was the fragility, the received character of their relationships to one another more inescapable than at such moments. So he lied. He told them that Kendall was in Illinois with her family for the holidays, and that she sent her best, and that she hoped to meet them soon; he consoled himself by reflecting that this last was actually the truth. His parents seemed pleased. His father asked as well about his landlords, the Camps, whom he had met and been impressed by on a trip to the city, and whom he seemed to have settled upon as an icon of un-complicated happiness and good fortune. He was pleased to hear of Liz's pregnancy.

They overate, and, licking sugar from their fingers and carrying coffee cups, they adjourned to the living room. To Julian's great relief, his mother left the dishes scattered messily on the table. His father went to the breakfront and, with a smile, brought out three enormous brandy snifters. His fondness for the snifters was about as great as for the brandy; Julian had seen these produced only on holidays and special occasions. I'll get it, his mother said, and went to the kitchen, stopping on her way to pick up a stack of cold serving dishes.

Julian and his father sat down heavily on the couch. It was night; the curtains were drawn behind them. The fire had burned down; off to the right of the grate, a bright piece of wrapping paper that had rolled away from the flames sat gaily in the ash. On the sideboard stood a row of anonymous-looking Christmas cards. The glass coffee table in front of them was covered with current magazines; Julian's coffee cup stood on top of the lean Christmas day edition of the newspaper. His eyes ran over the headlines on the front page and on the magazines. All were about the war. A holiday truce had been declared and then violated, though only one person had died. The weekly magazines did not report this yet; their more pensive headlines were outdated. Julian glanced over and saw that his father had followed his gaze. After a moment, they looked at each other.

I spent one Christmas in France near the end of the war, his father said. We actually had to camp out. I never knew how cold it was, but I don't remember ever being that cold again in my life, and that was after drinking two or three bottles of wine. It was too cold for the wine to taste very good, but we drank it anyway. It just seemed like one of those five or six nights in one's life where it's very important to get drunk. I shared a tent with a guy named Manthous, a Greek guy, from New York in fact. We both knew our families would be sending us presents, but obviously at that time of year there was a huge strain on the army's mail delivery, and so naturally the presents hadn't arrived yet.

His mother walked in with the bottles of liqueur on a tray, which she put down on the coffee table.

So we lay there and drank and smoked, Julian's father said, and we talked about all the Christmas presents we could remember getting in the past, all the favorites and all the least favorites too. Starting with the last year we were home, then going back, sixteen, ten, six, air rifles, bicycles, baseball gloves. We kept getting drunker and drunker and going back further and further until finally one of us passed out, or maybe both of us, I can't really remember.

Well, what about the current situation? Julian's mother said. He could have sworn he saw his father glare quickly at her. Do you see many of these protests they keep showing on TV? she said.

Not really, Julian said. I think it's a little bit exaggerated, or maybe it's just that it always looks like more people on TV than in real life. It's mostly on the campuses, I think, and I don't live near any of them. So I don't see much.

Julian's mother leaned over and touched his father's arm. Why don't you pour, she said. He did, and they drank to one another's good health and safety.

Later, when it was time for Julian to leave, his mother, who was staying behind to start cleaning up, stamped her feet to keep warm as she waved goodbye to Julian from the porch. His father was driving him back to the train station. They backed out of the driveway; Julian waved, his father bounced his hand twice off the horn, and they started up the street. On the way to the station Julian felt each curve in his body as he watched the road turning in the wash of the headlights. The heater, turned up all the way, sounded like a second engine. Outside, all was quiet. Lights burned in every house. One renegade neighbor had strung lights along the eaves of his house, and a reinforced plastic Santa Claus and reindeer were somehow fastened to his roof. There were few streetlights, and the trees disappeared into darkness.

You aren't bored when I talk about the war, his father said, not taking his eyes from the road. Are you?

No, Julian said quickly. When his father spoke about the war, he referred, one understood, to World War II; but sometimes it seemed just the opposite, as if he were speaking in a general way about war itself, a male rite of passage, the same everywhere in the world and in every era, divorced from its causes or its larger consequences. He spoke about it as if he were speaking about a dream landscape, a place where he had found himself in dire circumstances without knowing how he had gotten there or why, a place he could never get back to.

Oh, he said. Your mother says you are. He paused for a minute, as they came into town. You warm enough?

Fine.

His father lit a cigarette. It's not that I have any great nostalgia for it, you know. It was about ninety-five percent horrible. But when all's said and done, in that kind of life and death circumstance, there's a lot that you find out about yourself.

Well, Julian said, all the same, I'm glad I'll never have to go through that. Find those things out.

His father nodded. Yes and no, he said. On the one hand, I wouldn't wish it on anyone's son, least of all my own. On the other hand, I'd hate to think that there was anything about myself I'd go through my whole life never knowing.

At the station, his father got out of the car to say goodbye. They were a few minutes early. After they hugged each other, they stood in the parking lot with their hands under their arms. A few people waited under the lights up on the platform, holding bright shopping bags. There was the sound of wind and of traffic beyond the trees.

Everything's okay? his father said.

Pretty much.

You're doing all right?

Yeah, I'm doing fine.

Your mother and I would love to meet Kendall some time.

Well, some time, sure. It just seems like a big thing, I know it shouldn't, but it does.

No rush. You're able to take her out sometimes?

Julian laughed. Yes. Sometimes she takes me out too.

Finally his father reached into his pocket and pulled out a check, folded in half. Here, he said. For doing something nice with her some time, something lavish. Or just for things.

Julian smiled, took the check, and put it in his pocket. Thank you, he said. You don't have to do this, though, you know.

For Christmas.

Okay, for Christmas. But I don't want you to think that I'm not doing okay. I'm really fine.

You can use it?

Of course I can use it, anyone could use it, that's not what I—

Then use it, his father said. What would I do with it, anyway? What did I get it for if not to give to you?

Julian smiled.

Think of it as an advance on your inheritance, his father said.

Oh, cut that out.

Seriously. What fun is it to leave someone money if you're not around to bug him and see how he spends it?

The train horn sounded, and they both turned to look at its one powerful light, just visible through the trees.

So that's my goal, his father said, I'm giving it all away, little by little, and the object is, on the day before I die, to give you the very last of it.

The train stopped along the platform, hissing tiredly. Cars all around them, which had looked to be empty, opened up to discharge people who shouted goodbyes and trotted awkwardly under the weight of their bags toward the platform steps.

Besides, his father said, laughing, I hear it's easier to get into heaven that way.

The January afternoon was bitter, windless, and already growing dark. In a little while—before five o'clock, these days—

the streetlights would come on, dimly, at half power, flickering slightly. Lights were snapped on behind the windows of the townhouses; the snowless stoops were abandoned. A doorman looked out from behind polished glass. No one walked on the side street; the parked cars sat dully beneath the signs and the streetlights, freezing to the touch, looking as if they might never move again. In the third-floor classroom, the heat was not broken, but it was not working either. A few of the girls, those most prone to the theatrical, took notes with their gloves on. Warner leaned back against the front of his desk in line with the draft from the uninsulated window; he was not warm, but he could feel two strange circles of sweat chilling the skin beneath his shirt and jacket. The radiator banged angrily.

That's close, but that's not it, he said. Let's see, how can we do this. Taylor, would you read the passage on page one sixty-two? Starting with the ways he finds.

Taylor ran his index finger down page 162 of Jacob Riis's *How the Other Half Lives. The ways he finds of "collecting" under the cloak of undeserved poverty are numberless, and often reflect credit on the man's ingenuity, if not on the man himself. I remember the shock with which my first experience with his kind — her kind, rather, in this case: the beggar was a woman — came home to me. On my way to and from the office I had been giving charity regularly, as I fondly believed, to an old woman who sat in Chatham Square with a baby done up in a bundle of rags, moaning piteously in sunshine and rain, "Please, help the poor." It was the baby I pitied and thought I was doing my little to help, until one night I was just in time to rescue it from rolling out of her lap, and found the bundle I had been wasting my pennies upon just rags and nothing more, and the old hag dead drunk. Since then I have encountered bogus babies, borrowed babies, and drugged babies in the streets, and fought shy of them all. Most of them, I am glad to say, have been banished from the street since; but they are still occasionally to be found.*

Okay, stop there, Warner said. Taylor mimed being out of

breath and smiled. Now, this book is important historically for a number of reasons, which we've discussed — as a major chapter in the growth of the form of journalism called muckraking, as a kind of demythologizing of the immigrant experience in America, as a discussion of the effects of the rise of the city. Et cetera.

Outside, a streetlight flashed on. About half the students' heads turned to see it. Their attention was that unfixed, that unable to differentiate. Warner slid off the desk and began to pace.

But of all the people who still read this book today, he said, a full century after it was published, you are in a unique position. We can see the results of Riis's call for reform, we can check out his predictions, because we're here in the same city he's describing. Some of us are living in, or near, some of the very neighborhoods he wrote about. So, what has changed here since Riis's day? And all the things that haven't changed, do you think that they could, or are they eternal somehow?

He was at the window. The moon was clearly visible even as some daylight remained. The sky was one color. Teachers and students without a late afternoon class were trickling out the main entrance two floors below him. He turned to look at his class. No hands were in the air. Two girls in the back moved their heads suddenly and looked straight at him, as if they had just been caught whispering.

Come on, he said. The chapter about gangs and gang warfare. The chapter about the color line in some neighborhoods. Overcrowding — he flipped the pages — thousands of poor children are crowded out of the schools year by year for want of room, Riis says. All this is still part of our lives here. What about it? Take the beggar woman, with the phony baby. How many of you were stopped on your way to or from school today, or this week, by someone asking for change?

The students livened up noticeably, as the subject — as they saw it — swung around to themselves. Almost all of them raised their hands. One boy named Ned, who was still tan from his

Christmas vacation, spoke without being called on. So what you're saying is that even though Riis called for all these reforms, things are still the same?

Do you think that's true? Warner said. And what things?

The two girls in the back row were flipping through the back of the book, looking at the pages of photographs of the destitute. One put her finger on a page and turned to her friend, who laughed and put her hand over her mouth. The man in the photograph had been dead for a hundred years.

There will always be poor people, Sarah said confidently.

Well, maybe you're right, Sarah. But God doesn't make poor people, you know? When you see people on the street today, like the beggar woman with the baby, what do you think?

I'm glad I'm not one of them? Taylor said.

Well, no, that's not the point, Warner said.

I don't give them change, Natalie said, because they don't learn to help themselves that way. If they get enough money begging, then they'll just be out there again the next day, which doesn't do anybody any good.

Come on! Warner said. I'm not trying to teach you that these people exist. I'm trying to get you to see yourselves in relation to them. You're in the heart of a city, for God's sake. Everything is spelled out for you here if you just open your eyes. Can't anybody tell me the difference between rich and poor? Can't anyone tell me the difference between you and the people outside your window?

About six figures a year, a voice said, and they all laughed, not derisively, but easily, as they would laugh if someone merely repeated the punch line of a joke they had all heard. Warner stared at each row, in turn, his nostrils flaring. The bolder ones made faces, but all of them gradually returned their gazes to their books. Warner waited until his anger had caused an uneasy silence in the room. He wanted their discomfort.

I am not laughing, he said. You know, this city was not born the instant you were. You people are seventeen, almost eighteen, years old. I expect you to know your place in the city, if not in the world. I expect you to be able to discuss all this in terms of social injustice and its causes. So. What has changed, and what, in your opinions, will never change?

He could feel his color rising. While he spoke, his voice loud in his ears, a rare yet recognizable transformation had occurred in the room's atmosphere. The students were sullen and defensive. They felt they were being scolded unfairly; they looked doggedly at random pages of their books, scowling, even sighing. This was the kind of injustice to which they were sensitive. Warner felt their resentment.

Come on, he said. I even picked a book with pictures, to make it easy on you.

This time it was they who did not laugh. He often teased them like that, to goad them to think harder. But now it was too late, he had already lost them, and so with his joking he had only insulted them further, made them feel stupid. But it was too late to turn back. He had confronted them; he had to go all the way with it, or disavow everything he'd already said, and thus increase their advantage, encourage them to believe they'd been wronged. He had nothing, as he saw it, to apologize for. He checked to see what time it was.

Ned, he said. Would you read the passage beginning on page one seventy-eight?

It is easy enough to convince a man that he ought not to harbor the thief who steals people's property; but to make him see that he has no right to slowly kill his neighbors, or his tenants, by making a deathtrap of his house, seems to be the hardest of all tasks. It is apparently the slowness of the process that obscures his mental sight. The man who will fight an order to repair the plumbing in his house through every court he can reach, would suffer tortures rather than shed the blood of a fellow-man by actual violence. Clearly, it is a matter of education on the part of the landlord no less than the tenant. In spite—

That's fine, Warner said. He stood up from the desk and went back to sit in his chair. Are any of your parents in real estate? he said.

The radiator whistled, wavering between two notes.

I think you're being really unfair, Taylor said.

How so? I mean, maybe you're right, maybe I am. You're allowed to defend yourselves. How so?

Why should I have to defend myself at all? Taylor said.

I think what he's saying, a girl named Paige said, is the Riis book is really well written, but we've come a long way since then. He was writing about a hundred years ago, and you're asking us about it like it was today.

All the people in these pictures are dead, Warner said. Others have taken their place. I think these pictures are affecting precisely because they haven't lost their timeliness. Don't you?

Here's another thing I don't like about this book, Sarah said. What about this shit here? She began reading. *Thrift is the watchword of Jewtown, as of its people the world over. . . . Money is their God. Life itself is of little value compared with even the leanest bank account.* I don't know, she said. How am I supposed to take what this guy has to say seriously?

Warner closed his eyes. I never suggested that this was the Bible, he said. Casual ethnic stereotyping by journalists was rather common at the time. It is one of the things that has changed, I think, in the century since Riis. Mercifully.

He looked around the room. All of their eyes met his now. The air was heavy with resentment. One of the fluorescent lights had burned out, leaving the faces on one side of the room in shadow. He leaned forward onto the desk. Any more questions? he said. Paige raised her hand. Who's making up the twelfth-grade history final? she said.

She asked it with a trace of defiance, her eyes flashing. She was one of the better-looking students in the class. He felt a spasm of anger. I am, he said.

There were exhalations of disappointment, and disbelief at the way the odds were stacked against them.

What kind of thing are we supposed to know from this? Paige said, tapping the book. What should we study? Will there be questions on the individual cases?

No, Warner said. Jesus. I don't care about the individual cases. History isn't just names and dates and memorization. I don't know what kind of classes you've had before this. What existed then is a part of what exists now. I expect you to be able to discuss your own lives in terms of the lives of these people. To look at this city and see that city. Right? He looked around. Some of them were already closing their books. Others, having given up taking notes, were drawing pictures in the margins of the Riis book. Okay, maybe this will be a help, he said. This is the kind of thing I'm talking about. If you want a sort of sample section to study, try this. He flipped to the back of the book.

The sea of a mighty population, he read, *held in galling fetters, heaves uneasily in the tenements. Once already our city, to which have come the duties and responsibilities of metropolitan greatness before it was able to fairly measure its task, has felt the swell of its resistless flood. If it rises once more, no human power may avail to check it.*

The bell rang. The students clapped their books shut; chairs moaned against the linoleum floor.

The gap between the classes in which it surges, he continued in a louder voice as they stood up and began to walk out, *unseen, unsuspected by the thoughtless, is widening day by day. No tardy enactment of law, no political expedient, can close it. Against all other dangers our system of government may offer defence and shelter; against this not. . . . Think ye that building shall endure, which shelters the noble and crushes the poor?*

He looked up. Ned had stopped at the desk for a moment on his way out. Why are you mad at us? he said.

In Colozan the fighting had slowed to occasional, if steady, outbreaks of bombing and cease-fire violations; these seemed almost like eruptions of bad temper rather than something proceeding out of a social cause. Still, soldiers and civilians killed and were killed. Over the course of the winter months, four funerals for dead servicemen were conducted around New York.

They were celebrations of the most violent emotions. Supporters of the occupation seized upon them with a righteous fervor; the closer one got to these events, the less complicated they seemed. The fact of a dead son was an eloquent one, and awakened feelings simpler and darker than patriotism. Citizens crowded the churches and synagogues; loudspeakers were erected on the sidewalks so that the overflow, and passersby, could hear.

Since there were so few of these services, the local media further transformed them into general catharses. When they were allowed inside, television cameras aimed at the eulogizers; when they were not, they waited patiently on the sidewalk, recording the fanciful reports of correspondents, and, over their shoulders, the huddled, dark-coated mourners, the husky, uniformed pallbearers, the mothers who wailed and the fathers who were shocked into impassivity, the steaming breath of the crowds on the cold sidewalk.

When the bodies had disappeared from sight, the mourners dispersed and the reports were filed. News is at its most effective when it can adapt itself to a particular, fictional structure; the handsome young man struck down in defense of his country was a venerable dramatic form, older than news itself. The correspondents wrung out of it all the considerable emotion it contained. Coverage of the funerals was always publicized in advance; people tuned in to the news that night precisely because they knew what was being televised. They wanted a share of the communal participation in, the common creation of, a work of tragedy. Everything about these four stories — the diction, the various camera angles, the suggestion that the guard of the reporters was about, involuntarily, to crumble, to give way to the need to join in the collective desire for revenge — was deliciously familiar to them.

One report, expertly done but of course without the matchless potency of a visual image, was broadcast on the radio station where Kendall worked. She sat and listened over the monitor, not in her own office but in that of a coworker named Felicia Sykes, a newswriter. They didn't know each other very well, but Kendall had felt the urge to seek out company at work lately;

and Felicia, for whatever reason, had been glad to see her. Felicia's office was not much different from Kendall's; it was hard to understand why it was assigned to her, since the metal shelves stood empty and the expensive tape equipment was never used. The office did have a few more personal touches than Kendall's — cartoons and humorous articles stuck to the wall, an elaborate pencil holder, one photograph of her parents and one of a husband who wasn't hers. She was a year younger than Kendall but had worked at the station for three years.

When the story was over, Felicia whistled. She and Kendall were both impressed, not so much by the highly charged, somewhat hysterical tone of the report but by the speed with which it had been filed. The funeral had ended at six-thirty that evening; what they were hearing, at a minute or two past ten, was already a rebroadcast.

It's not that tough to do those, Felicia said. She was short, with spiky black hair, and given to abrupt bursts of energy; while waiting for the story to come on she had been spinning herself around in her desk chair, like a child at a soda fountain.

He can't have done many like that before, Kendall said.

Yeah, but he's seen stories like that before. Everyone has. There's a formula, a model, for big dramatic stories like that; I couldn't tell you what it is exactly, but every writer knows it. Everyone born after TV was invented knows it. I'll bet you could crank out a story on a tragic funeral in half an hour yourself. You don't even know you know how.

Kendall wanted to be offended by such cynicism but was also intrigued by the thought. An advertisement blasted from the monitor. Felicia, in her wheeled chair, kicked herself across the carpet to the back wall and reached up to lower the volume. The knob gave her a static shock, which Kendall could hear. Fuck! Felicia yelled. She swiveled around, pushed off the wall with her feet, and rolled back to her desk.

Well, why should there be formulas? Kendall said. I mean, wouldn't you get more satisfaction out of doing something a little tougher, a little more original?

Maybe, maybe not. There are formulas for stories because

there's competition to be first on the air, time pressure, and there's competition because the formulas can always be refined. If I took a day to reflect on a story like that, I could turn in a nice classy think piece, but I'd wind up reading it to myself because the new writer the station had hired to replace me would have written a story which had already aired five times.

Sports scores, like a buzzing in the ear, flew faintly out of the monitor.

Besides, Felicia said, and this is going to sound cynical but it's really a consideration, people tune in here to get these stories immediately, and if they don't hear it they'll just go up the dial. If they want some artsy piece on the country's current wahoo state of mind, they'll turn on National Public Radio. I'm serious.

But then there's nothing to differentiate between these stories, Kendall said. Every one's like every other one. I know that people want the drama in these stories to be played up, but if everything is played up equally, how are we supposed to know if one story is really more significant than another?

Well, there are all sorts of little signifiers for that, Felicia said. She patted her hair. For instance, if one story is on at the top of the hour and another is on at four minutes past.

The winter sky was black. The wind blew hard outside, though they could not hear it.

It doesn't seem right to me, Kendall said.

Felicia straightened some folders on her desk. There was a knock on the door, and a teenage boy came in trailing a long sheet of paper torn off the wire. As he backed out, he was unable to suppress an admiring look at Kendall.

Should I go and let you work? Kendall said.

Felicia ran her eyes quickly over the thin paper, moving it in her hands as if she were climbing a rope. No, she said. No big deal. She folded it and dropped it on her desk. She looked back up at Kendall and smiled; for a moment there was silence.

And so let's face it, Felicia said, people tune in hoping to hear something new, something they didn't hear last time they listened. Ergo, the more important stories are the more recent ones.

But don't the bigger stories defy that? Like the war?

No, the bigger the story is, the slower the process. But it's still the same. Everything moves further and further from the top of the hour until it disappears. Nothing new has happened in Colozan for a while, right? Just the same statistics, the same sporadic fighting. What was the lead story last night, did you catch it?

The cold weather, Kendall said.

The cold weather. Under five degrees. Cold weather and the homeless. Cold weather and cars. Cold weather and buildings with heating problems. Cold weather and tollbooth collectors. I wrote that story, by the way, she said. Thank you very much.

But why are there these rules? Kendall said. She felt herself turning red. Why is there this formula? Doesn't it ultimately just confuse things? Doesn't it just encourage people to forget?

She could tell from Felicia's face that she had spoken too loudly.

Hey, Felicia said. I thought we were talking about the way things are. If you want to talk about what I think is right or wrong, that's a whole different thing.

There was a tension in the still room. The two women were not close enough friends for exposure of this sort. Kendall could not think of anyone, actually, with whom she could have a discussion of the kind she and Felicia seemed on the border of. Looking away from each other, they could feel themselves backing away from any intimate accusations; and that backing away was the sign of the beginning of their friendship.

I mean, I'm no different from anyone else when it comes to the war, Kendall said. I'm like a baby. You know how you can hold something up in front of a baby's face, then if you put it behind your back he supposedly forgets that it exists? That's sort of the way I am about this invasion or whatever it is.

What, Felicia said, smiling, are you getting all political all of a sudden?

No, Kendall said. I don't think of myself as a political person at all. No, it's much more personal than that, much more selfish. I'm just taking an interest in what it is I do, you know. What my job is.

Well, good. I'll tell you this. I know you have a technical talent which is pretty rare, and pretty lucrative, I guess, but you're smarter than a lot of the people on the news side here. Seriously.

Well, thanks. But anyway, no, it's not some big political awakening. Kendall was getting upset again, she could feel it, but this time it was as if she were taking up an argument within herself. It's just, I've always been an honest person, I think. At least I've never been habitually dishonest. But suddenly other people's dishonesty just infuriates me. In my personal life, in my working life. Any relationship that's allowed to go unexamined is a lie, or turns into one. So I sense the lie in all of this, and lies just make me mad lately.

Felicia smiled wickedly and raised her eyebrows. I see, she said. And how is the love life going, if I might ask?

Kendall never would have suspected that this connection, which even in her mind was not fully formed, could have been clear to another person, even if she had tried to explain it. She felt at once excited and caught out; she would have to explain herself now, to go on, as it were, before she was ready. That someone else could have guessed at such an oblique relationship only strengthened the idea of it in her own mind.

I don't know how it's going, she said, I've told you, haven't I, that I'm seeing this guy.

Yeah, What's his name again? Justin?

Julian.

Julian, that's right. Felicia assumed a sly look. I hear he's a babe.

Kendall's eyes widened. Julian had never been to the station; she had never introduced him to Felicia, or, as far as she could remember, to anyone she worked with.

Meriwether told me, Felicia said. It seems he was out on the street one day and saw the two of you, or he assumed it was the two of you. He said the two of you were kissing, and you were more or less flattened up against a mailbox. So he thought he'd just as well not go over.

Kendall shook her head. Yeah, she said. That sounds like us.

So Meriwether said that, even though his face was sort of mashed, he could see that this Julian was a good-looking guy.

He is that, Kendall said, god damn him.

About broke Meriwether's heart, I'll bet.

Who did, me or Julian?

Well, you with Julian.

Kendall stared. I thought he was gay.

Felicia held her palms up. No one seems to know. Either way, he's got a thing for you. Anyone could see it. So, your boyfriend is hot; it's not clear to me yet what's wrong here. You don't have a picture of him, by the way?

Kendall shook her head. He hates pictures of himself. Anyway, he's just another one of those difficult types. He's moody, he's reticent, he'll get mad and not tell me why and get mad at me for asking. He won't call for a few days and thinks I'm being clingy when I point it out.

Classic, Felicia said. The bad boyfriend. We always think ours is different somehow.

So I used to think that this was just the way he was. I would simply have to cope with it, and besides, let's face it, in our stupider moments we think that bullshit is sort of attractive, right? We think it's sort of mysterious. But lately I've been thinking that it's not just him; it's him and me. You know? That he's like this in relation to me. Not that I could change him; but there's an equation here of which I am one side. Am I making any sense?

Sure.

I used to think it had to do with personalities. But now it feels more like a power thing.

It's always a power thing, Felicia said.

You think so?

Absolutely. In love, as opposed to politics, nature abhors a balance of power. Someone always has the upper hand. Think of everyone you've ever gone out with. Think of your parents, for God's sake.

Jesus, that's depressing, Kendall said.

I went out with this guy once. I'd been seeing him for a while, a couple of months. He was the mysterious type too, the you-can-never-figure-me-out type. I went for it completely. One day he calls me and says he has an ex-girlfriend who's coming to town; his apartment is small, he doesn't want me to get jealous or anything, so is it okay if she stays with me. I actually agreed to it. I gave her her own key, so that I'd be free to go out with this guy and stay at his place if I wanted. I stayed away from her as much as I could, but still, we saw each other a little bit. She seemed great; we sort of got along. She was there for a week. The night she left, this guy comes over to my place to celebrate. I make him dinner, like a moron; we have some wine, things start to get a little steamy. So we're half undressed, doing this sort of waltz step back toward my bedroom, and suddenly, out of nowhere, I ask him when was the last time he slept with this ex-girlfriend. Yesterday afternoon, he says. I always told you you could ask me anything.

Kendall laughed, then put her hand over her mouth. Sorry, she said. What a line. So what did you do?

What did I do? I did what any simpering coward would do. I fucked him. Then, the next morning, I told him I never wanted to see him again. That's the thing about these power relationships. The imbalance just keeps growing until somebody reaches their own personal humiliation threshold. And you can never, never forgive someone for showing you where that low point is in you. So, if I may ask, and I'm not necessarily talking about specific practices here, does this power struggle translate itself into the sexual, ah, arena?

She was trying to be light about it, but Kendall wasn't laughing. She looked at her hands. I wonder about that, she said.

That's the last refuge, you know, that's the last part of our relationship that I ever would have questioned. In some ways — well, in all the ways you'd normally think of — this is the best sex I've ever had.

Yes? Felicia said.

He's one of those guys who's completely attentive. He's only interested in my pleasure. He enjoys himself, too, of course, but that's always his second thought. He wants me to go crazy. That's why he's there.

Have we gotten to the bad part yet? Felicia said.

I used to think it was like that between us because he was so good at it. Then I wanted to think it was because we loved each other; that was closer, at least on the right track. Now, though, I think what happens to me when I'm having sex with him is just an expression, a particularly clear, simple, harsh, violent expression, of what happens between us when we're not in bed.

No, Felicia said. It sounds to me like he's just good at it.

Well, you see? That's how I used to feel about it. I thought I had found the one unselfish guy. But it is selfish, in its way. He doesn't just want me to come. He wants me to come over and over again. I think if I actually lost consciousness, that would really make him happy. Is that love? It's control. He's trying to extend his power over me. And it works, I hate to say it, but it works. I can talk like this to you now, but when Julian and I are together, I can't really hold on to reason that long.

Well, you've lost me there, Felicia said. The guy is so good in bed that you hold it against him. You've lost me.

They looked at each other.

Did I ask you, Felicia said, if you have any pictures of him?

A week or so later, Kendall was called in to her supervisor's office at the beginning of her shift. She was told that her increased dedication in the office lately had not gone unnoticed and that everyone was pleased. On Felicia's particular recommendation, they were assigning her to produce some of the smaller news features. She would have the final edit on these segments, though she would still be doing much of the technical work on them as well. It amounted to a promotion. Most significantly, perhaps, it meant that she would be moved to a day shift, from ten to six, something that she had long hoped for. Conscious of good form, Kendall was as grateful as she could rouse herself to be. Still, she was troubled when she returned to her own office afterward, and when she went home that morning. It's fine, she said to herself, there's nothing wrong with this. Still, she felt as though someone had missed the point. Perhaps it was her fault. She had been feeling negligent about her job, almost guilty; the idea had not been for her to profit personally by that feeling. No, she wanted to say; that's not what I meant.

Lewis was single, and what's more seemed entrenched in his particular rhythm of life; over the course of the school year, he and Warner had discovered one another to be sympathetic spirits. Their schedules differed slightly in the winter term. Generally, they would run into each other in the school's loud hallways just long enough to make some plan to meet at the end of the day. Together, out of boredom and some vague impulse toward self-abasement, they began, at night, to explore the world of bars.

These were not dangerous places even by the most conservative standard. The patrons were mostly young professional people; many of them belonged to what Warner thought of as the murky, indistinct world of finance. No matter how sober, he listened to their explanations of what it was they did all day in utter incomprehension. Nor did these bars carry any strong suggestion of a sexual danger, moral or viral. In fact, the bars were the grounds for a kind of tense war game of the sexes. They were not singles bars in the conventional sense. Any time two people met and went home together in one night — Warner overheard groups of young men talking about such nights — it was a rare victory, for the man, of quickly legendary proportion. Still, though seldom achieved, this kind of unbounded sex was their object. The women's object — and women, against expectation, came to the places in equal numbers—was harder to discern. Once the initial engagement—a beer bought by a stranger, a teasing remark from behind—was made, their goal would be to make the man desire them so heatedly that he would renounce his own objective; that is, he would agree, in effect, to pay heavier, more traditional dues for sex—an exchange of phone numbers, a promised date, a kiss goodbye which embodied longer-term intentions. The women acted as if they were looking for a serious relationship. Though there were exceptions—people who met in the bars sometimes did become involved, for a while at least—for the most part this was only a role the women played, just as the role of predator was assumed by young men who would never act this way anywhere else. The object was to win the engagement, and the engagement, on both sides, was born of bitterness. Predictably, there were mostly stalemates; standing outside any of these bars at closing time were men and women in overcoats and gloves kissing hungrily in doorways, or staring with promise at each other beside open cab doors, or describing drunkenly to a stranger the vanished friend with whom they had arrived.

Since most of these night spots, as well as St. Albert's itself, were on the Upper East Side, Warner would usually first go to Lewis's cramped apartment; there the two of them would sit and talk, have dinner, watch television, while waiting for a more seemly hour for the night to get under way. After a month or two of this, when Lewis complained that he still had not seen Warner's apartment and suggested that they find some place to go out downtown, Warner felt slightly put out, but agreed. He knew of a place near New York University which, he said, looked worth a shot.

They ate first and arrived at the apartment around nine. Warner, with both his gloves in one hand, opened the door and listened. Kendall? he called. He removed the key, pushed open the door with his foot, and walked in, followed by Lewis, who carried a six-pack of beer in a white plastic bag.

Not here? Lewis said.

Warner shook his head. At work, I guess. Who knows. He showed Lewis where to throw his coat and scarf, took the white bag from him, and went into the kitchen. He came back out with two cans of beer, handed one to Lewis, and motioned him toward a chair.

Make yourself comfortable, he said. Cheers.

They touched their cans together and sat down. Lewis looked around the small living room; Warner reached over and turned on the radio.

Too bad, Lewis said. I was kind of looking forward to meeting her.

Yeah, well, she's still got the boyfriend, so take it easy. She's not that pleasant to be around lately anyway. He's not a bad guy. Better you should meet him.

It's just I've heard so much about her, Lewis said.

The radio was tuned to an all-news station. Warner flipped the dial until he found some music. They drank their beer and sat through the slow, impatient limbo between night and night-life. Midway through their second can they began to brighten. A song neither of them had heard for years came on the radio; Warner turned the volume up and left it up. They compared notes, as they had done before when alcohol and their own company made them feel less susceptible to shame, on a certain senior girl at St. Albert's whom they both currently had in class. She was tall and remote, with long brown hair and a long face that ended in a mouth of indescribable promise. Neither of them, they agreed, had ever seen such a creature haunting the halls of their own high schools. They challenged each other's memory as to what she had recently worn. They laughed over scenes they had observed in which boys her own age attempted to win her attention. At a sufficient distance from all this, they felt free to let their own feelings out for a run.

Restless, Lewis got up and looked out the window, down toward the West Village. Talk turned to real estate; Lewis mentioned that having a roommate seemed a fair price to pay for such a comfortable apartment in such a good location. Warner stood up.

Well, where, he said, are my manners? I haven't even given you the tour yet.

Drinks in hand, they went down the short hallway. Warner slapped the light switch. Here, he said, is my bedroom. Note the window. And here is Kendall's bedroom. Lewis took a step inside the dark room. Listen for the echoes, Warner said, and laughed. He slid by to turn on the lamp, then moved behind him again, to give him an unobstructed look.

And here, he said with mock solemnity, is the wall between our bedrooms.

The telephone rang. One sec, Warner said. Lewis heard him run past the phone, turn the music down, then run back to pick up the receiver. He looked into Kendall's bedroom and experienced a small, illicit thrill, as if he had broken in. The closet door stood open; inside, the blouses and skirts hung too tightly packed together to be distinguishable other than by color. At the bottom of the closet sat an electric fan, put away for the winter. A shiny tangle of earrings, brittle and colorful, sat in an old cigar box on the dresser. Kendall apparently was not a conservative dresser. It was as if a wild woman had come in and taken over his mother's bedroom; childhood, in fact, was where he remembered this sight from, with its concomitant thrill of punishment. Various bottles of makeup and moisturizer and prescription medicine were scattered on the dresser and on the bedside table around the base of the lamp. The bed, fat with blankets and comforters, was unmade. He saw Kendall — though he had in fact never seen her — getting out of this bed that morning, pushing the blankets with her foot to just this position. In the mirror he could see, on the wall behind the open door, a framed Van Gogh poster from the Museum of Modern Art. He could see it only in the mirror, since the door hid it from him; the image seemed ghostly, ungraspable. This was where a woman lived. The close scent of her days and nights here filled his imagination. It was not such a novelty for him to see a woman's bedroom; but he was always present as a visitor, there was always an awkwardness to it, even when he slept over, which made it unreal. He felt those rooms had been prepared for him. This place was untouched; he was violating it somehow. That he had idealized this Kendall, the more so as the bitterness with which Warner spoke of her increased, made him especially alive to the secret quality of this room.

He heard Warner behind him and turned around, embarrassed. But Warner was not looking at him. He seemed to be thinking of something else, not upset but distracted. After a few moments, he in turn noticed Lewis standing there.

Ready to go? he said. Lewis nodded.

They went to the living room and put their coats on in silence. Warner turned off the lights and the stereo, and found his keys. They looked at each other.

Anything wrong? Lewis said.

Warner wound his scarf loosely around his neck. That was Kendall's brother on the phone, he said. He's looking for her. He says to tell her he wants to come to the city this spring and visit. Wonders what would be a good time, when he could come and stay here.

Is that bad? Lewis said.

I suppose not.

Have you ever met the guy?

Warner shook his head. His confusion now seemed to be giving way to anger. I didn't even know she had a brother, he said. I've known her for about two years. She never told me.

Trying to keep things light, Lewis said, Well, you probably never asked.

That's the thing, Warner said. I'm not positive, but I'm pretty sure I have asked.

He picked up his gloves. Lewis went to the door and held it open, waiting. Warner turned off the last light, got out his keys, and took the doorknob from Lewis's hand.

Fuck her, he said. God damn her.

The door closed, and the locks turned.

A friend of Holly's, a dancer, was performing as part of an ad hoc company in a converted third-floor loft near Chinatown.

Holly, as a general rule, never went out anywhere unaccompanied; the thought of attending this performance, with its air of poverty, by herself was particularly chilling. She asked Julian, and she did not ask if he wanted to bring anyone. But then, she had noted as she played his acceptance on her answering machine, he didn't ask, either.

To Julian, the dance they saw performed seemed embarrassing by virtue of its very sincerity; he was not miserable, but he was glad he would not have to talk afterward to anyone involved. Holly enjoyed it more, but then she seemed to have decided to disregard the piece as a whole. When her friend was onstage, she watched only him, intently, anxiously, as if worried he would trip; when he was off, she behaved as though it were intermission. After the final bows, she bounded up the aisle and through the thin curtain — there was no other way backstage — to offer her congratulations. Julian stood by his seat, near the back, amid the black plastic and chrome chairs, kicked out of alignment by the crowd filing past him out the door. It was cold inside the loft, even with all the people there. At times like this he wished he still smoked. He blew into his hands to warm them.

Holly was back sooner than other evenings he had spent with her led him to expect. She stepped through the curtain and stood onstage for a moment, enjoying herself. I've never seen him so happy, she called to Julian. They were alone in the loft now. He would have felt strange speaking that loudly, so he made a drinking gesture with his hand and raised his eyebrows. Holly nodded, skipped up the aisle, and took his arm.

Outside it was colder but manageable, and they decided to walk west until they found some place that appealed. The cold air neutralized the ripe smell of garbage he normally associated with this area. He was proud to know his way through these streets; a good many were laid out in unlikely directions, some curving back on themselves, some so short you could shine a flashlight from one end to the other. The dark iron buildings looked like machines from another century; anything could have gone on inside them, or in their shadows. Holly kept her arm through his; they walked mostly in silence.

They found a bar that looked satisfactory, just quiet enough to be private but not so quiet as to be without diversions. Holly made a halfhearted suggestion that they go to a club and make a longer night of it, but Julian didn't feel up to it, or so he said. Holly smiled and said, Another time. Inside the door was a sign asking them to please wait to be seated; the bar was full, and they preferred a table anyway, so they stood there. Each of them knew that together they made a glamorous couple. No one stared, but almost every eye caught and admired one or both of them for a moment. The two of them could never discuss this phenomenon — there was no way to bring up the subject without sounding insufferable — but they were very much aware of it, and subtly acted out their imaginary roles. No one would have believed they were not lovers.

When they were seated, Julian ordered a vodka, Holly a glass of wine. She asked him if there was anything new.

Not a lot, Julian said. I'm working. Oh, well my upstairs neighbors, my landlords, the Camps, had their baby.

Baby? Holly said.

Julian smiled. You've heard of them? he said. Yeah, a little boy. Liz just came home from the hospital a week ago. You've never met them, have you?

I've never even heard of them.

They're both bankers, but they're real people, he said. She'll obviously be taking some time off. The baby is incredibly cute.

Every baby is cute, Holly said. Is there an uncute baby?

Bill took this big walk-in closet they had next to their bedroom and widened it, don't ask me how, for the baby's room. He's extremely handy. I don't know how you get that way. It's impressive, though. I mean, I'd never change lives with the guy; but he seems in control, you know? In their lives, things seem to change, things progress.

Holly nodded solemnly. You know, you're wigging me out with this kind of talk, she said. Babies? Bankers?

Julian laughed.

It wouldn't be nearly so scary, she said, if you didn't sound so envious. And the awful thing is to think that maybe you're pointed in this direction, a young, fabulous guy like yourself, ready to start making home improvements and become a Camp.

Julian stirred his vodka with his finger. If I'm not mistaken, he said, this will be leading us to some remarks on the subject of Kendall?

If you insist, then okay.

I know what you think, but no, she is not pointing me in that direction, there's no pressure from her to—

Well, I could differ with you there, but the important thing is that you seem to be the one longing for it. The whole domestic gig seems very appealing to you.

That's not necessarily true. That kind of life has some appeal to everyone, I'm sure even to you at times, but I'm not thinking about that with Kendall at all.

So you're not really serious about her. In the long run.

Julian frowned. What constitutes a long run? I don't know. For now, things seem okay. There's no reason to end it. I guess I feel committed to her. Maybe not as committed as she'd like me to be, but she has a right to think that.

Gosh, Holly said. The words every woman dreams of hearing.

Julian had observed that while Holly had few qualms about saying anything, she seemed to feel particularly free to bait him in this way. It amounted to a kind of sarcastic pass at him. He thought that all the irony might conceal a true attraction to him; but it was only a guess, and the nature of that attraction —predatory, hypothetical, playful, sincere—was something upon which he could never decide. He knew her well enough to suspect that her interest in seducing him might be a fleeting, even a sporting, one. And the less inclined he seemed to call her on it, the further she pushed the joking. He concealed his reluctance to act on this tension with a show of sly distance. By answering questions with questions, he tried to mask his desire to avoid taking responsibility for whatever might happen and turn it into something sexy, something alluring, a show of noncommittal.

How about you? he said. Seeing anyone lately?

Not as a regular thing. There are so many boring men, aren't there? But they're so good at concealing it. All men look the same, they really do; I don't mean their features, obviously, but the way their faces show, or rather don't show, personality. So some stranger asks you out. With five minutes' research you can find out if he's actually interesting, but unfortunately those are usually the first five of ninety minutes worth of dinner. They call this dating. Sometimes I think I'm holding down a second job, diminishing men's expectations.

But you do find the occasional one who can stay interesting for a whole night.

Well, we all have our needs, she said.

She was about to go on; but she looked at Julian's face, smiled, and drank some wine. There was music, on tape, playing at a refreshingly low volume throughout the bar; a song had come on which Julian apparently thought particularly well sung. She had seen this look on his face before. He heard nuances in delivery, she supposed, to which she was not sensitive. In any case, even though he didn't realize it, he was concentrating deeply, and she thought it would be rude to break in. She looked around the room — it was a good-looking gathering — until the song ended.

Realizing she had caught him, Julian looked embarrassed. Carla Thomas, he said. Sorry.

So anyway, Holly said. Maybe it has something to do with my being around, some catty thing, but Kendall seems very clingy to me. Very possessive, very dependent. Which is fine for some people; but I would have thought that was exactly the kind of thing that would drive you crazy.

I think it does have something to do with you, Julian said. She's very independent, very strong-willed — that's what I liked about her from the start — but she's also possessive, in a way.

What way is that?

She feels — Julian scratched his nose — she feels that if we're together, we ought to be together. I'm a fairly private person, and I can see the way the idea that I have any secrets from her just tears her up. She can do her own thinking. She just wants to know what I'm thinking, too, that's all. She doesn't like mystery. She always wants to know where I am.

Does she know where you are now? Holly said.

He knew she was only being provocative. He smiled; then his smile disappeared.

No, he said.

He stayed over that night with Kendall. When he went home the next day, there was a registered letter for him — Bill Camp had signed for it — from Selective Service; it informed him that he was required by law to register for any possible future draft. The deadline had passed eight months ago, the letter said, without his compliance. His failure to cooperate could lead to heavy fines or a possible prison term. Julian sat down and wrote a letter addressed to the man whose signature was photographically reproduced at the bottom of the letter. In it, he pointed out that he had been born more than thirty years ago, and so he was, as he understood it, too old to be subject to the fairly recent registration law. Two weeks later, he received another letter in which the government apologized for its error.

On May 4, 1886, Warner said, a group of anarchists held a meeting near Haymarket Square in Chicago. We all know what anarchists are, yes? The meeting, more of a rally, was held to protest the events of the previous afternoon, May 3, when, at the McCormick Reaper Works, the Chicago police had fired their revolvers into a crowd of workers striking for what was then considered a bit of creeping socialism, the eight-hour workday. Several people were killed. At the May 4 meeting, there was a lot of fiery rhetoric, but everything proceeded peacefully. The last speaker of the evening, Samuel Fielden — Warner spelled it for them — started to turn it up a little bit. *There is no security for the working classes under the present social system*, he said;

and, *You have nothing more to do with the law except to lay hands on it and throttle it until it makes its last kick. Keep your eye upon it, throttle it, kill it, stab it, do everything you can to wound it.*

Two police spies were in that crowd, and when they heard those words they ran to the police station nearby and reported to an Inspector Bonfield that the meeting was becoming violent and unruly. Bonfield called out his men and marched them over to Haymarket. He got there just in time to hear the end of the last speech.

A police captain ordered Fielden to break up the meeting. Fielden, dumbfounded, said it was about to break up anyway. The captain just repeated his order. All right, we'll go then, Fielden said.

And then as if out of nowhere—in fact, truly out of nowhere—came the event which assigned Haymarket its place in American history. A bomb whistled over the heads of the crowd and exploded in the middle of the ranks of policemen. No one has ever discovered who threw it. Sixty-seven policemen were hurt; eight of them later died. Well, the enraged police simply opened fire on the crowd. Forty or fifty civilians were killed or wounded, by some estimates. There was never any official record kept of those casualties. The police were in such a panic that quite a few of them shot one another by accident. The whole thing was over in about five minutes.

This incident produced what is generally regarded as the first, and one of the most hysterical, red scares in history. And in order to satisfy the common desire for revenge, eight leaders of the anarchist movement, including Samuel Fielden, were subsequently arrested and charged with murder. None of them, by the way, was ever accused or even suspected of having thrown the actual bomb.

Well, perhaps you can guess what happened. The judge, a conservative man anyway who was out to make a name for himself, started out by refusing to disqualify jurors who stated that they had already made up their minds that the eight were guilty; and it was downhill from there. They were all convicted. Their appeals were all rejected; the United States Supreme Court ruled that it had no jurisdiction in the matter. It was an American show trial. You think those things don't happen here? It would be one thing if we could simply cast Judge Gary as a villain. But everyone, everyone, wanted these men to die. In fact, four of them were hanged. A fifth committed suicide in his cell the night before execution. The other three were pardoned by the governor of Illinois in 1893.

The names of the dead men were Adolphe Fischer, Carl Engel, Auguste Spies, Albert Parsons, and Louis Lingg. I expect you to know them.

Warner stood and came around to the front of his desk.

Well, there's little enough to talk about here. There's little in the way of ambiguity. It's simply a stain on our national record, a kind of touchstone in the history of American infamy. So it's important to know it. Everything I've just told you was in last night's assignment, and anything you missed just now you can get there. I realize a lot of you probably haven't done it. I know the workload has been a little heavier lately.

But what I want to know is this: What about the bomb thrower? Where did he or she come from? Why did he do it? History is full of figures like this. Think of the person who shot our secretary of state in Colozan back in October. No one knows who it was. Some people are suggesting now it was an agent of some other government. I suppose we'll never know. But look what that person has set into motion. It doesn't matter, really, that we don't know his name, his identity. His identity, as far as history is concerned, simply consists in that one act.

Got your pens? Here is the topic for your final paper for the winter term. It's due two weeks from this Friday, and it will count for thirty percent of your grade. I want you to imagine yourself the bomb thrower at Haymarket on that day in 1886. Anarchist, Pinkerton, psycho, it's up to you. Whomever you choose, it's up to you to explain your reasons for bringing that bomb to the demonstration that day, for throwing it when you did, and for remaining anonymous afterward. I want you to tell me why you did what you did, how you feel about it now. Would you do it again. I want you to justify yourselves, your role, your actions, to history, and to me. You're dismissed.

Julian, after knocking and getting no answer, used his own key to enter Kendall's apartment. As he waited for her he paced the living room, lifting magazines he had already read and putting them down again; his lips moved as he began putting an edge on his anger. Then he remembered that Kendall now worked a normal, ten-to-six shift. It was just after six-thirty. She hadn't been late, or forgotten her arrangement to meet him, as he had begun to imagine; she was simply on her way home from work. He sat down to wait. She had worked a night shift almost all the time he had known her; it was the reason she had given him his own key—a rushed intimacy, born of practical considerations—in the first place.

Kendall arrived a few minutes after seven. Hi, sorry, she said, and headed straight toward the bathroom, taking her coat off as she went. He stood up; she came back out to him a minute later and put her arms around him. They stayed like that for a while, moving their hands slowly up and down each other's back; he held her a little tighter, and she made a sound of relaxation.

It's so cold out there, she said.

I know. You didn't walk back, did you?

No, God. I never would have made it. I took a cab cause I knew I was late.

You worked late? He felt her nodding against his neck. What a pro.

She laughed, and lifted her face. They kissed luxuriantly, until they began to lose their balance. He stopped to look at her, and traced her cheekbone.

So you still want to go to this thing? he said.

She nodded again. Do you?

He didn't at all, but he felt that he was under pressure; this was one of those tests that came up in a relationship, which for some reason took on an importance all out of proportion with —in fact, bearing little relation to—the matter at hand. Moments like this maddened him. He did not like being given little tests to pass. If you do, he said, trying to smile convincingly, desperate to avoid a fight. Absolutely. That's why I came over.

She had mentioned to him, several days ago, to his astonishment, that there was that night, on the second floor of the Greene Street Café, a public symposium on the war in Colozan. She thought it would be interesting and wanted to go. He could think, off the top of his head, of nothing in the world less interesting; he had tried to draw her out, asking her what particularly made her want to go. It seems very nonpartisan, she had answered; not a lot of chanting and shouting, just a bunch of journalists and professors, that's all, just an informational thing. Informational? Julian had said. You work at an all-news station. What kind of information wouldn't already be available to you? Well, she said, if I knew the answer to that, then I wouldn't have to go. But I feel sure there's something I'm not getting from there. There's a lot I don't understand.

She had seemed happy, though almost unsettlingly so, when he had agreed finally to go with her; it had seemed worthwhile at the time for that reason alone. But now, as the boredom of the evening loomed larger, he felt himself battling his own petulance. He wondered if something could still happen, with the whole thing less than an hour away, to get him out of it.

He started kissing her again. She kissed him happily, excitedly, making noises that turned into a laugh; she pushed away from him, smiling.

We'd better not get into it, she said. Otherwise we won't have time to eat beforehand.

She squeezed his hand, turned, and walked toward the kitchen.

I ate, he said.

The blinds were open. He could see, if he focused beyond his reflection, a small stretch of Sixteenth Street below. There was no traffic. It was March; the sky was a deep, uniform blue, but down below, in the light of the street, things looked colorless and bitter. A delivery man on a bicycle, his hood pulled over his head, pedaled slowly in the wrong direction on the one-way street. Julian let his eyes refocus on his face in the window. He felt angered by the evening he had let himself in for; he felt unfairly accused.

She came back into the living room, full of energy. She carried a sandwich, a diet soda, and a piece of cake. You sure you don't want anything? she said.

He shook his head.

Did you see Warner when you came in?

No, he said. I let myself in.

I haven't seen him in like a week. He has this friend he hangs out with.

Female?

We wish. A guy, another teacher.

He sat down and watched her eat. She smiled at him while chewing, and at this moment when he felt so confused and put off by her, she seemed most happy to be with him.

So, he said, you've really gotten into this sort of current events thing lately, huh? I think it's great. It's like we're seeing political Kendall all of a sudden.

She swallowed. Not really, she said. You make it sound like it's cute. Like it's a phase I'm going through.

Well, I don't know what it is. I haven't had any chance to figure it out, it's happened so fast. All of a sudden there's this great interest in politics.

Politics? Kendall said. Even though he had been in the mood to provoke her, he didn't know what he had done to touch a nerve. You say it with such contempt. Anything that doesn't have to do directly with you belongs to the realm of politics, is that it?

Hey, relax. I didn't say there was anything wrong with it.

Well, you make it sound like there is. You make it sound like it's at your expense.

She finished her sandwich in silence and immediately started in on the cake.

But I just wonder, he said, and I'm not trying to belittle it, I just wonder if there's some particular thing that's brought this on.

She thought for a moment. It's not really about the war, or anyway about being for it or against it. It's work. I'm putting together a lot of these features now, public-opinion stories, stories about the way the local media are handling the news. It's important stuff to a lot of people. And I just feel like I should take an interest, like I should know what I'm talking about. Like I should have a responsibility. Otherwise, what kind of job am I doing? I feel a little more responsible for the work I do, you know? Otherwise, what does my life have going for it?

She looked at Julian earnestly. Do you know what I'm talking about?

He was unused to such seriousness, and felt the need to defuse it somehow. Well, I wouldn't put too much pressure on yourself, he said. If you didn't like it before, you can't just make yourself like it now. It's just a job.

It was as if some bridge she had been walking across with careful steps had given way beneath her. Feelings she normally wouldn't permit herself, fearing the damage they might cause, flooded through her. She felt a kind of urgency, even an exhilaration, knowing that she had very little time because in a short while the moment would be gone, she would no longer want it, the permission she was giving herself would be revoked, and her best intentions would replace her honesty.

Yes, it's just a job, she said. Coming from you, I guess I could have called that one.

What?

I mean with the relationship you have to your own job, if that's the right word for it. Yes, it is the right word, I guess.

He was shocked at the idea that she could be provoked to attack him like this, especially in a discussion about politics. What are you saying?

You don't even seem to acknowledge the fact that you have any relationship to the work that you do, other than financial. And that it's singing, too, that it's art that you're so cavalier with. It's infuriating.

Relationship to it? What are you talking about?

Who you do it for.

I do it for myself.

No, I mean who do you work for?

I don't work for anybody. You're the one with —

When you sing, you serve somebody. Every time. You don't even know who, and you don't care. It could be any words you're singing. It doesn't matter to you. That's what I mean by relationship.

Listen, he said. Do you think you've stumbled onto something original here? I've heard this same bit, this same kind of bogus agonizing, at ten or fifteen dates I've done. Everybody talks about it between takes, or in bars afterward, about how we're whoring ourselves or whatever. And everyone goes right ahead and does it. It was a bullshit argument then, and it's a bullshit argument now.

Well, if it's such bullshit, when someone says it to you, what's your answer?

My answer is that singing well is its own end. Singing well affords its own satisfaction. I don't care what happens afterward. I don't even care that there's a tape recorder going. The fact that checks come in the mail for this is just a piece of great luck, as far as I'm concerned.

That money comes from somewhere. It doesn't just appear in your mailbox. It's not like your father's money.

Excuse me? Julian said.

No, look, I'm sorry. That has nothing to do with it anyway. I know you have to make money at this somehow. It's just that it seems like you don't even have any hope for any sort of serious career, any interest in one, even. I never hear you talk about it.

Julian felt himself turning red. Of course I have hopes. I

guess I just don't always want to share them with you. But they're realistic ones. I know how hard it is to really make it. I know that a lot better than you do, Kendall. I also know a lot better than you the hopes that I had for myself when I started. Some days I'm incredibly disappointed with how things have gone. But it doesn't do any good. And even leaving aside for a moment the question of whether a recording career is somehow less commercial than what I do now, I'm just happy I can make a living singing at all. That's not such an easy thing, you know. In any case, it doesn't change anything to feel bad about it.

See, Kendall said, that's the thing. I don't believe you really do feel bad about it.

She was scared, suddenly, by the look on his face. He himself looked frightened; he was looking at her as if she were a stranger, an impostor. All the intimacy was gone from his face. He looked not so much threatened as shocked.

Why do you want me to feel bad? he asked.

The moment was passing now; she was beginning to feel sorry for what she had said. I don't, she said. I don't want you to feel bad. I'm sorry the whole thing came up. Come on. We can take a cab and still make the beginning of this thing.

He was much more willing to go now, not only in the interest of making things right with her but of putting some physical distance between them and this entire conversation. They stood up to go.

Kendall seemed nervous now as she put her coat on; she worried that she had gone too far. Normally, any sort of criticism caused Julian to withdraw into himself; he might never come out again after this, he might never forgive her, even — or especially — if she was right. Julian saw this in her averted face, saw her verging on regret, and knew that he held the advantage again. He had been on the defensive a moment before, but now she was waiting to see what he would do. He turned her around by the shoulder and kissed her as gently, as tenderly, as he could. It was a good tactic. When he stopped, she could not keep from laughing in surprise.

I don't understand you, she said. I can't figure you out at all.

And with those words, he felt that everything was all right, back to normal again. These were the words that meant the most to him. Every man wants to be a mystery. He believes his appeal must surely be based on the promise of the unknown. And when, in spite of all his efforts, he feels himself completely comprehended, naked as it were, that is when he finds himself falling most obsessively and most helplessly in love. Julian felt safest when he was least understood.

As they got ready to go, Kendall noticed a new stack of mail on the table; Warner must have been home today after all. She sorted through the bills and flyers, and stopped at a hand-addressed envelope; there was no return address, but she knew from the postmark it was from her brother. She didn't want to throw the letter out in front of Julian, who would ask about it, but she didn't want to read it, either. She slipped it back, unopened, into the pile of mail and dropped it all on the table.

As they waited for the elevator, they checked all their buttons and turned up their collars. It was brutally cold outside. They walked to Sixth Avenue; Julian saw a cab and ran the last few steps to the corner to intercept it. Inside, with the doors closed, as he leaned forward to give the driver directions, Kendall started to shiver. Julian put his arm around her — she could barely feel it through all she wore — and gradually they both warmed up.

With the windows rolled up tight and the radio on, the streets rolled by like a movie badly matched to its soundtrack. The dark sidewalks were empty. Lights burned behind windows that were cold to the touch. In the frozen air, white car exhaust billowed like a sign of fury. From the cab radio, salsa music played to them in its endless groove. The moon seeped through clouds as thin as gauze.

The café was dimly lit, its windows laced with steam. They hurried in and closed the door as quickly as they could, exhaling loudly, hugging themselves. A waiter came up and smiled sympathetically. Two? he said. Julian shook his head and said they were looking for the symposium. The waiter pointed out the stairs and walked away.

The long room on the second floor was noisy and bright; a formless collection of folding chairs faced two long tables on which Julian saw microphones and pitchers of water. Somehow, even with all his doubts about the utility of the event, he had assumed it would be packed. It was hard to tell, with so many people milling around, but he guessed that about a third of the chairs would stay empty. Paintings, with price stickers in the corners of their frames, were hung on the walls and spotlit expertly from the ceiling. A lot of people were loitering by the head tables, but there was no telling how many of them were panelists. Julian wondered how long all this would go on; he looked around on the chairs for some sort of program but didn't see one, nor did he see anyone holding one. Kendall hung her coat over the back of a chair that was, he gratefully noted, not far from the exit.

A minute or two later, someone closed the door to the stairway and the meeting came to order. The men and women took their seats and seemed, to Julian, remarkably quiet and well behaved, as if they were in some advanced-study seminar at college. The coordinator for the evening was a writer for the Village Voice, a tall woman with very short black hair streaked with gray. She began by making some welcoming remarks, congratulating all the people who had come for their persistence and their un-willingness to take part in the general campaign of forgetfulness spearheaded by the larger media.

Far across the room, through a temporary lane among the heads, Julian was certain he spotted Warner. Warner apparently did not see him; and since chances were it would only make Kendall self-conscious to know that he was there, Julian sat back and said nothing.

It was not a debate, which stood to reason since everyone present, at least on the panel, was on the same side. Instead, each speaker delivered a kind of progress report on the area of his or her expertise; the speaker then took a few questions from the audience and from the other members of the panel. A leader of a local protest organization described a series of passive re-sistance demonstrations staged outside government buildings recently; he said the numbers in his group had dropped off for a while but now seemed to be holding steady. Only the most fiercely dedicated remained. He bemoaned the lack of media attention given to theirs and other demonstrations in the area.

A New York University professor briefly addressed the question of draft registration. Refusal to comply was turning out to be an ineffective form of protest, he said; the government was simply declining to prosecute. As for the reinstitution of the draft itself, he said that, in spite of the fact that the fighting had dragged on longer than anyone had expected, it remained extremely unlikely.

A local magazine writer detailed the general drop-off, with the aid of a few large color charts, in national media coverage of the war. He tried to demonstrate the ways in which television and the newspapers, which had at first assumed a kind of opposition role — he attributed this to their initial pique at being barred from Colozan — had gradually swung around to the right, until their own views of the war's progress were almost exactly in line with those of the government. The justification for the U.S. presence seemed, increasingly, to go without saying.

A young woman reported briefly on the resistance efforts inside Colozan itself. She did not have much positive news; but she gave the names, addresses, and phone numbers of several organizations in and near the city which would take donations for the opposition forces. Those interested could specify, she said, whether they wanted their contributions earmarked for humanitarian aid. She urged those present to act now while support of such resistance efforts was still legal.

The last speaker was an author, a middle-aged man who had made a career as a partisan of the left. Other than the professor, he was the oldest person in the room; but beyond that he had a dignity, a lack of excitability, that was commanding. He had listened to everything with great interest, but had not offered a word of his own. The woman from the Voice could not keep pride from shaking her voice as she introduced him. When he heard his name, he ran his fingers nervously over his beard. He would be speaking, the woman said, on the subject of The War in Colozan and the Nuclear Threat. Somewhat awkwardly, given that title, the silence after the introduction was filled with applause. The author sat forward. Folding his hands on the table in front of him, he ran his eyes over the faces in the room.

Well, he said, this is the question that occupies all our imaginations, isn't it. Maybe none of you here is old enough to know what it was like not to know about it. In our time, it is like a cartoon balloon hanging over the head of every small conflict, like a common dream it took the power of the collective unconscious of the planet to produce. I don't need to recapitulate this dream, you see, because you all know what I'm talking about.

I have to say that the title of this little address—well, I wouldn't have titled it at all if they hadn't asked me to—is somewhat misleading. I should apologize; and I should say straight out that the chances of the Colozan campaign escalating into the kind of warfare where nuclear weapons are involved are extremely remote. I'd go so far as to say that there is absolutely no chance of it. The threat that I wanted to talk about, that the title refers to, is of a very different nature. It would be ridiculous, of course, to say that it is more dangerous; but it is less apparent, less obvious, stealthier, and therefore perhaps a more present threat, one more deserving of our attention.

The more observant have noticed how very little there is at stake in the Colozan war. There has been talk from government sources about the importance of maintaining a government in Colozan with which we can have friendly relations—the irony escapes them there, of course, as it always seems to do—because of the country's important location in terms of military strategy. Such ideas, of course, are rendered long out of date by our own weaponry. Colozan is of no economic importance; it imports almost nothing from us and exports less, its economy was rubble even before the fighting started. Though obviously there was some internal dissent which occasionally spilled over into violence, their government, in point of fact, in most ways took our own as its model.

The question, then, is what are we fighting for?

We have seen over these last few months — and I think future generations will see it in this episode as well — that, truly, it is no longer the idea which binds us together, but the image. The image's power to unite is terrible to behold. It, too, is a weapon which other centuries, other warriors, could never have dreamed of. The widely broadcast image is enough to send a nation to war. Think of it. Wars are fought over symbols. And, more to the point, wars can acquire and make use of a symbolic value of their own.

Wars in our time stand for the triumph of order. They are never fought unless the outcome is certain. It's no trick to think of examples of this phenomenon in our own lifetime. Grenada, the Falkland Islands, Panama. This is the face of war now. The battle is not between ideologies but between the forces of order and those of disorder — or, as it is most commonly called in our day, terrorism. The major powers are secure and have no reason, no need, to fight one another. They need to fight only to maintain their own dominion, and those fights — though many thousands of people have died in them and will continue to die — are less for territory or for doctrine than they are simply for victory, the idea of victory, the idea of ascendancy in the minds of the world, not least in the minds of their own citizens.

We have seen, I think, the last war ever fought for justice. Why? Because the stakes have obviated justice. When any pitched battle can end in mutual annihilation, no idea has any moral character except the idea of peace. Therein lies the true nature of the nuclear threat, the hidden nature; our beliefs are devalued, our own morals are superseded. Fewer and fewer principles can accurately be described as worth fighting for. For all the horrible injustice that exists in the world, as a practical consideration the very idea of right and wrong in the social sphere finds itself imperiled.

In short, it is the end of justice, that is to say justice on any kind of ambitious, global scale. Perhaps such ideas were overly ambitious to begin with, though I think not, personally. Our plans have been thrown in our faces. The world grew smaller and smaller, and now it has grown large again. What we see is not an end but a return. Do not be overly ambitious in your own lives, then. Return to the more immediate world, the world of your own verifiable experience. You must start again, start small. Justice is, once again, a neighborhood affair.

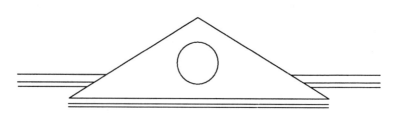

THE distance between Warner and his students, particularly the seniors, continued to grow. Everyone habitually arrived in his classroom with a hardened expression. The final papers he had asked for on Haymarket were a disappointment, if not a surprise; his students' failure had a petulant, willful quality. They weren't even trying. Warner took this as a personal attack, which in many respects it was. He gave out the lowest grades he could remember giving. Though he didn't hand the papers back until after the bell on the last day of the trimester, he was not spared some response—colorful language, not addressed to him but designed to be overheard, and furtive, withering glances in the direction of his desk.

When drawing up the history final, he backed down from asking the kind of challenging questions he would have liked; the other classes were not used to it, and he expected they or their teachers, more likely the latter, would get him into trouble over it. After filling the exam with short-answer and ID questions that would, he thought, satisfy everyone's requirements for the simple, temporary retention of disjointed facts, he wrote a few sample essay questions. One had to do with the gold standard.

One had to do with Reconstruction. He had gotten both of them from four- or five-year-old exams, on file in the history department office. As soon as he had copied out the questions, though, they seemed to him cold and insulting. They were remote from the lives of the students who would be asked to answer them in such dead earnest; what was galling to him was the knowledge that that was precisely the way the students seemed to like it, feigning interest rather than displaying the genuine article. He tore out the piece of paper on which he had written those questions, and in the center of a new page wrote: 1) Identify four main effects of racism in nineteenth-century America as discussed in W.E.B. Du Bois's The Souls of Black Folk, and 2) discuss the ways in which these effects either are or are not prevalent, in your experience, in contemporary urban society.

He deliberately avoided delivering the exam to the department chairman himself; instead he typed up the proposed final and dropped it off in the chairman's mailbox with a note. He half expected some sort of battle over the appropriateness of the final question, but he heard nothing for five days. Then, just two days before the exam was scheduled, he saw a heavy stack of papers, rolled into a half-circle, jammed inside his mailbox in the faculty room: sixty-seven copies of the final, exactly as he had written it, retyped by the department secretary.

On the appointed day, with the exams in a manila envelope in his bookbag, Warner went straight to the gymnasium, where the history final would be given. It was quarter to nine in the morning; the light on the sidewalks was still wintry and unclear, but in the underground gym it was as bright as an operating room, and every anxious whisper echoed. A blue rug had been laid beneath the rows of desks to protect the finish of the polished basketball court. The strong echoes enforced the quiet. At their desks, some students went through nervous rituals involving precise numbers of pens and pencils and the mumbling of secret exhortations; others, in observance of some obscure law of mental energy, refused to sit down until the last possible second.

Few of them, for once, seemed to have any urge to talk. They could never be sure, Warner guessed, when some irretrievable pearl of historical knowledge might tumble out of their open mouths. It was surprising how seriously they chose to take these exams, and their grades in general, when, in truth, so little was at stake for them.

Instructions for exam conduct were posted on cardboard signs along the walls; it would have been impossible to shout them out in the cavernous gym and be understood. Since exams were being administered in several different disciplines, the teachers could not give spoken directions of any kind beforehand. If the written directions on the tests themselves were at all unclear, students could raise their hands. There were five teachers in the gym. At two minutes to nine, at a signal from Mr. Cannon, a chemistry teacher and the senior faculty member present, they began passing out the blue composition books and exams. A taut silence spread over the ranks of children. The teachers returned to their own seats, facing the rows of desks. The clock in the gym office, where he and Lewis had watched the tapes of the assassination, was visible through the Plexiglas window. At nine o'clock exactly, Mr. Cannon said, in a loud, practiced voice, Begin.

Warner had brought a book, Edmund Wilson's The American Earthquake; he planned to skim through it to see if there was anything in it he might be able to make use of next term. He took the book out of his bag and opened it. But he could not stop himself from looking up to catch the reactions of the seniors sitting in the history section as they read through the exam questions for the first time. They kept their heads down in frantic concentration, but he thought he could see some surprised expressions, some rapid breathing, among the history students who were not in his class. Then he felt himself being watched; off to his left, about ten seats back, Paige was staring at him, her nostrils flaring, trying to lock in his gaze. He looked back down at his own book, feeling himself blush.

The exam period was ninety minutes long. Though he tried

to read, the extreme, tense quiet, in a room filled with more than a hundred people, made it difficult to concentrate. He wished he had brought a newspaper. He thought briefly about his own nervousness the first time he had administered an exam — much more stressful, he thought at the time, than simply taking one — about two and a half years before, when he had been teaching for only a few months. It felt like the end of an audition. He wanted so badly for his own students to do beautifully; he felt that this would reflect well on him not so much in the eyes of his superiors as in those of the students themselves. He wanted their approval, wanted them, in fact, to be proud of him; and they had seemed to be.

The teachers were instructed to stay seated as much as possible; standing and stretching, walking around, and especially talking to other teachers was an unfair distraction to the students. There was no one Warner would have particularly enjoyed a conversation with anyway. Besides Mr. Cannon, there were Mr. Carpenter, the biology teacher; Ms. Erikson; and Mr. Morrissey, the math department head, a truly frightening creature he had heard his own students joking about. The one closest to his age was Ms. Erikson; Jane was her first name, he remembered. She was in her early thirties and taught English, but the few times he had spoken to her, she seemed pale and lifeless. Now she caught him staring idly at her; he looked away, through the window into the office, with its refrigerator and empty desk and blank television.

For some reason, it made him think of Kendall. They saw each other more often lately, now that she worked traditional hours. She seemed both nicer and more distant. He was at a loss as to how to interpret it. She was kind and polite and solicitous and yet seemed in a great hurry, whenever they talked, to get away from him. She would go out at night and not come back for hours, or, more often, just spend a whole evening in her room. She had to leave her door open because there was so little air in there; but Warner heard nothing that gave her away, though he couldn't have said what it was he listened so hard for. And then, a few nights ago, she had sat down in the living room with him and asked if they could talk. What she wanted to talk about, it turned out, was the lease on their apartment, which ran out in July; she was looking for a new place of her own and did not want to renew the current lease, she said, although he was free to take it over and find a new roommate if he liked. Stunned, he said he would think it over. He didn't feel a sense of loss, exactly; but the matter-of-fact way she proposed this brought home to him how perverse their living arrangement had become, how there was no longer anything at all left of their friendship and so they were free to be this cordial, and he felt sad and somehow ashamed. He had never asked her about her brother.

It was only about ten minutes after ten when the first student collected his materials, stood up, and walked to the front of the gym. He came from the row just to Warner's left—a history student, though not one from his class. A few others took an instant away from their writing to look up at the boy in hatred. He approached Warner's desk. Warner smiled at the boy as he laid his blue book down, but the boy did not smile back; in fact, he looked distraught, as if he couldn't get out of there fast enough. He walked quickly through the double doors into the hallway; the doors clicked shut behind him.

Warner looked back at the ranks of students. Those who were writing, which was the majority, did so at an improbable speed. There was always a great concern with length on the essays, a concern that Warner's repeated admonitions had failed to discourage. Their heads were very close to the page. Some looked off at the wall for a moment, to relax or order their thoughts, and some shook their hands furiously to uncramp them. With only a couple of exceptions they looked to be under great strain. A second student got up to leave, again from the history section. It was Ned, from Warner's class. He, too, did not smile, and he made a great show of tossing the blue book defiantly in front of Warner and walking out. Warner noticed Mr. Morrissey and Ms. Erikson looking at him. After the doors shut behind Ned,

Warner opened the blue book and flipped backward through the pages until he found the end of Ned's main essay. The essay was only two pages long. Warner fought down the urge to read it. He felt sure it would upset him; he was feeling uneasy enough as it was.

Another history student got up to leave; then, to Warner's great relief, a girl from across the room; then two more boys from Warner's class. They looked at each other significantly as they headed for the door, but did not speak. When they were out of the room, but before the heavy doors could close, one of them said to the other, Well, that was a blowjob. It was said in a normal tone of voice and probably not meant to be overheard; but in the churchlike quiet it could not have been clearer. The students in the gym laughed, looked up at one another from their blue books, and laughed more; they were hushed loudly by Mr. Morrissey. Ms. Erikson had her hand over her mouth. Warner could not look up. He told himself that if he relaxed, his face would not turn red.

Sarah appeared before him in sneakers and gray sweatpants, a fashion code for serious labor, and set her exam down. Eager to be occupied with something other than his thoughts, he did not even wait until she was out of the room to open her blue book. On the last page, there was a curious, one-line space between the end of the penultimate paragraph and the beginning of the final one, which turned out to be a message to him.

Mr. Warner, it read, *I know this is a bad time to complain because you're probably grading this now, but I don't think it's fair the sort of questions you've been giving us. I know I'm not the only one who thinks this. I tried to take this essay question seriously because I had to, for my grade, but I think you're putting us in an unfair position. I don't want you to take this the wrong way, but we're really not learning anything in class anymore. It's like we're being tested not on what we know but on the way we think, and not only that, the object is for us to think as much like you as possible. The more we show our opinions are the ones you think we should have, the righter we are, the better we do. I don't think it's right, and some others don't think so either. I'm sorry to say all this to you, because I like you, but I just had to say something. Have a good vacation. —Sarah Vollmer.*

Warner closed the book and put it back on the pile. He said to himself that she was missing the point, that the idea was not to parrot his thinking but to show that they were capable of thinking from some point of view other than their own—to show that as children of privilege they were entitled to that privilege, or at least were not abusing it, by virtue of their understanding of their place, their ability to relate other circumstances to their own. But it was all right; seventeen-year-old girls would occasionally miss the point. As more students came at him, he assumed a stern expression, combative now for the same reason he was combative in the classroom. He was scared of these self-confident children, of their disapproval. They seemed to know that their subjection to him and to those like him was a temporary thing. Suddenly he was seized with fear at the idea of going through all this again, of having to confront them for another three months. The faces of the girls especially loomed before him. To take his mind off this, he thought instead of the material they would be covering in the spring. They would go through the twentieth century and come quite close to the present. It would very likely be more interesting for them, the causal chain would be more apparent. In that, he tried to find some cause for optimism.

She had seen the same obscure book cited in two different magazine articles in the space of two weeks; still, it was the weather as much as curiosity that prompted Kendall to seek it out. As the days warmed and grew longer, she found herself appreciating the look of things when she left the station at her new, still unaccustomed time. If it was still barely light now when she walked out onto Times Square, before it had been the light of dawn, gray and underpopulated. Now the sunset was visible down the narrow shaft of buildings facing the Hudson

River. She felt herself newly in tune with the city, and with the faces of the thousands of other people, also ending their work-day, who made the sidewalks so difficult to negotiate.

So on a particularly fair night in April, instead of heading straight for the subway, she walked up Broadway to a bookstore she knew. The book in question, Raymond Williams's Key-words, was more pretext for the trip than purpose. A strong spring wind played roughly with hair and hats and newspapers. The sky was a wonder. Almost violet in the east, it lightened as Kendall craned her neck slowly to her left, until she found herself looking into the muted sun over the water. It seemed an element separate from the air of the city, like a picture projected on the sky. The clouds sped by so fast she lost her balance if she looked up for too long.

The bookstore was thrillingly crowded. A long line of people stood patiently by the two cash registers, sneaking looks at the books displayed there, or turning their heads to take in the other customers. Kendall went at once to the shelves of hardcover nonfiction. A man idling there sensed her behind him and took a hurried step out of her way, as if in her urgency she might knock him down. She smiled at him and ran her gaze over the alphabetically arranged books, patiently, skipping nothing on her way to the letter W.

Once she saw that the Williams book she wanted was not there—she had no idea, really, when it had been published —she relaxed and allowed her eyes to be distracted by colors and sonorous titles. People searching the shelves in an orderly manner came up on her left, stepped around, and moved on, slowly, steadily. In no hurry, she went to the paperback shelves and checked under Britain, sociology, and media, with no luck. As she searched, she often followed with her gaze the other customers as they walked past, some of them with a seeming sense of purpose that was both daunting and funny. More people were coming in now, men with their ties loosened and women who had slipped their running shoes on. A bored-looking guard sat on a stool by the door and took for safekeeping every manner of thing—shopping bags, briefcases, a tennis racket—from those who did not come in empty-handed. It all reminded Kendall, briefly, of being in college, the sense of anticipation and temporary distress of buying one's books for the semester. There had been a sense of mission then, though the mission was of course all spelled out for her.

She went over to look at the new hardcover display, a four-sided structure built of books, shaped something like a crypt. She recognized more of the authors than she thought she would; when she came across an unfamiliar name, she picked up the book and searched it for a photograph. All these people, particularly those unknown to her, seemed to her to have impressive faces—serious, unfashionable, faces of integrity. She was pleased at the sight of the collected products of such imaginations. Though she knew that she was going through a kind of false revelation, she was enjoying herself thoroughly and silently, dreaming of change, all on her own.

See something you like?

She looked up. Across the stack from her was an older man with a round face and a neat beard, smiling at her. He did not move. He must, she thought, have been wondering how he could have startled her so. She said nothing.

Because, he said, you've been standing there for like minutes with that big smile on your face.

She didn't know how to respond.

It's gone now, though, he said. Too bad. The smile.

I'm sorry, she said. I was just distracted. I don't know. Thinking of something else. She had the idea that she was in some kind of trouble, having loitered so long in the bookstore without buying anything.

Were you looking for something specific? the man said. Maybe I could help you find it.

Kendall regarded him. She was starting to regain her bearings. I was, she said. I'm sorry, but do you work here?

The man laughed and walked around the stacks to stand next to her. No. But I spend so much time in here, maybe I should. So what were you looking for? What's the author's name?

She looked him over. No one else noticed them. He dressed like a student, though he seemed a good ten years older than she was. Maybe it was the beard. Raymond Williams, she said.

He seemed thrown. Don't know him, he said with a frustrated look. Is it a novel?

No. Listen, I can —

Well, then you're in the wrong place to begin with, no wonder. The nonfiction is over there, come on, I'll —

I've looked. It's not there.

Oh. Well, in that case, you could try Papyrus, they have a lot of the more obscure stuff. You know where it is? It's up by Columbia. I live up there, so I'm headed in that direction anyway if you want to split a cab.

She stared at him, unable to say what she should have. Her heart pounded, surprising her, as she realized what was going on. He was not an attractive man.

He leaned closer, no doubt misinterpreting her intent look. Or, he said, we could just go have a cup of coffee, if you like.

She looked down for a second. What's your name? She said.

Don, he said. He put out his hand. She kept her arms folded. What's yours?

Kendall.

Kendall what?

Listen, Don. Does this kind of stuff go on here all the time?

His face fell. What kind of stuff? he said. Hey, I don't want to —

No, I'm not trying to be insulting, I'm just curious, that's all. Just surprised. Because I had no idea. I mean, this pickup stuff, is it a regular thing here?

He looked uneasy now, but he had not lost control of his smooth demeanor. I don't know, he said. I'm not trying to pick you up. You just looked like a nice person, smart, and very pretty if it's all right for me to say so.

Of course you're trying to pick me up, she said. It's okay, I mean I'm not putting you down for it. There's nothing wrong with that kind of thing. You just don't see it that much anymore.

Don seemed to brighten at this; he smiled again through his

dark beard. They had gravitated to the far corner of the long room and were speaking in a near-whisper.

You seem like a nice guy, she said.

Then let's forget all this and go get—

I'm seriously involved. That's it. I mean, I'm sorry, though I can't imagine it's a great disappointment to you, since you don't even know me.

She continued to look at him intently. She was fascinated. She could not keep herself from imagining all sorts of intimate details of this man's life. They flashed through her mind as he spoke.

Well, I am disappointed, actually, he said. How long have you been involved with this person?

A little more than a year.

What does he do?

He's a singer.

Oh, well, who could compete with that.

What do you do? Kendall said.

I work for the city government. So you and this guy are really in love?

Yes, she said. Only in saying it did she realize how untrue it was. There was the same race of her blood and shallowness of breath that she had felt when she lied as a child. It was a fiction, useful in this case for keeping the Dons of the world away; but it was also useful for her in an emotional sense. She saw what security this fiction gave her in every social and even private situation. She saw how her happiness was dependent on its fixed place in her self-image. She could answer a question such as Don's instantly; thus the lie was deep within her. She could not see it but could always refer to it. She was shocked at herself.

He's in love with you?

Yes.

Well, he's a lucky guy. You both are. It's hard to find some-body you can feel that way about. So, you think you'll marry him?

Well, we've talked about it. But not right away. He's a little older than me so naturally he's a little more anxious to start a family. But I'm not really ready.

They went on in this vein a while longer; he would look for some opening, and she would quickly spin some fantasy to close him out. She said she had to go home—the singer was waiting for her—and Don went outside with her, saying he was on his way home, too. He tried once more to get her phone number; she refused as nicely and as clearly as she could, and they went off in separate directions.

Only after she had walked a block toward the subway did her heartbeat slow; she smiled helplessly the way someone getting over some small excitement smiles. Then she began to laugh quietly. She thought about what she had done, the way she had humiliated the unfortunate man without really meaning to, by befriending him, and the way she had lied about her own life in order to drive him away. In review, these lies seemed so ludicrous, she didn't know how anyone could have believed all that about her. The life she had imagined for herself was so funny. Giggling, she began to recreate it, Then to embroider on it. Yes, she said to herself, I have a boyfriend named Julian. He's devoted to me. It's nice, yes, but in practice devotion is so boring, isn't it? He's asked me to marry him. I haven't made up my mind. Sometimes he's sweet about it, but sometimes my uncertainty drives him into terrible fits of temper. He threatens to break it off. He calls me late at night and tells me that he can't sleep, that he's in agony. But he always comes back. He has a bad temper, that's all. He's very protective of me. He's very jealous. If he saw us kissing like this, he'd kill us both.

When Stephen Honeywell was first appointed the headmaster of St. Albert's, sixteen years earlier, he was chosen over three other candidates, friends of his, who were neither less nor more qualified than he, and who had, like him, attended the school as boys before returning there to teach. Perhaps even then it had been possible for the selection committee to see how easily and how perfectly he would age into the role of the headmaster of an exclusive school. Now, having passed sixty, he had thick white hair and a body as straight as a flagpole. He could summon the demeanor of an older man when he needed it; but in general, there was very little of the middle-aged about him. He was as at home in an academic robe as he was throwing a football to some of the boys down the street in Central Park, with his tie loosened and his sleeves rolled. The trustees used to joke, when they were alone, that it didn't much matter that Honeywell was not a riveting public speaker; they could probably have raised the necessary funds for the school with just a photograph of him.

His desk, clear and well organized, stood at one end of a long, narrow office. A smudged sheet of glass sat heavily over the blotter. There were a few framed photographs, all of school occasions, and two expensive pen holders with engraved plaques at their base. A faded rug reached from under the desk almost all the way to the door. Along the borders of the rug were four leather chairs, positioned strictly for decoration, and two standing flags, one for the country and one for the school.

There was a light knock at the door, and Honeywell started; he took a second to compose himself, to assume his administrator's face, before calling out, Come in. The door was pushed open by his secretary, and Warner entered, empty-handed. Neither man smiled. Warner walked down the rug and leaned over the desk to shake hands. It was the sort of thing which made a good impression on Honeywell. He pointed to a leather chair; after Warner had dragged it forward to face the desk, both men sat down.

Honeywell leaned back and scratched the top of one hand. He looked at Warner; he, too, was leaning back, but he did not seem relaxed. One of his hands was in a fist. Do you know why you're here? Honeywell said.

I have an idea, Warner said.

I've been receiving complaints from the parents of some of

your students for the last six weeks or so. Do you know anything
about that? Have any of them tried to contact you directly?

No. Do you have any of their letters? I'd be interested to see
them.

They don't write letters, Honeywell said. They only write
letters when they have something good to say or a favor to ask.
When they're angry, they call me up, or they demand to make
an appointment to see me, and I'm not really in a position to
turn them down. You can understand what I dislike about this?

I think I can. What did they complain about?

Warner was not quite insolent, but he seemed to want to
engage the headmaster's temper. Honeywell was determined to
keep the upper hand. They complain about the amount of work
you assign, about the nature of particular assignments, about
the general atmosphere in your classes—

I appreciate that you're beholden to the parents in many ways,
because of the nature of your job. I really do. But I hope you
appreciate that the only relationship I'm concerned with is the
one between me and my students. It's an equation into which
the parents do not enter. I don't really consider what they have
to say to be germane. Besides, it's not them I'm assigning work
to, though believe me, I'd—

Well, if you can keep a secret, in terms of the classrooms I
don't really put a lot of stock in what the parents have to say
either. The thing is, in this case it's obvious that they're only
repeating the complaints that their children are bringing home.

I know you still teach yourself. You can't tell me that when
a high school student complains he or she has too much home-
work that that's a serious charge.

Honeywell frowned. Robert, he said, it's not just the amount
of work they object to. You must know that, and the stance
you obviously take toward them more or less bears out what
they have to say. I've had several students of yours in here this
semester, a couple of them nearly in tears, complaining that
you browbeat them, that you're insulting to them and to their
parents in class, that they do more and more work but their

grades just seem to go down. One girl wanted to know if I knew what it was they had done to make you hate them so much. I hoped at the time it was something that could just work itself out, but now I'm much less sure.

Warner snorted. They're just acting when they do that. Don't you see it? They're wonderful actors. Surely you've had enough experience with them to realize that. They know how to put on an act to get what they want, or get out of what they don't want. Especially the girls. Which one of them was it that said that to you?

They also say that in general you seem to have it in for them, and I have to say you're not helping your own cause with your remarks here. These are just children, for Pete's sake. I know you and I haven't spent much time together, but from what I'm told, your belligerence extends itself outside the classroom as well, to your dealings with other teachers, particularly the older ones.

And is that a standard of my performance? How well I get along with the senior faculty?

The headmaster paused. Not really, no, he said. And it's not as though the other history teachers particularly care about it, either. They generally go their own way and are happy to do so. They don't much care about what goes on in your classes, and they were willing to let all the complaints go, I'm sure. But after the stunt you pulled with the seniors' exam question, I tell you frankly that they're calling for your head. They feel that a lot of their own work with their own students was just wasted.

I object, Warner said, to the use of the word stunt. Ted Albrecht read that exam and approved it personally —

Ted Albrecht has admitted to me that he didn't ever read it. He just gave it to the department secretary to type up. He was behind in his own work and just assumed it would be okay. Ted's been teaching here for a quarter of a century, and there's not much I can really do other than reprimand him, which I've done. I'm not excusing him, but to make him the culprit here is to miss the point.

The point being?

The point being that this is not an isolated incident—

Incident? Have I committed—

Call it what you like. It's not the first time your methods have been called into question. For instance, am I to understand that you once assigned these children to justify throwing bombs?

Warner closed his eyes. That's a great oversimplification of one assignment, but yes.

For the first time, Honeywell looked taken aback. Clearly he had expected a different answer, some denial. He sat forward, eyes wide. Are you crazy? he said. Do you realize what a position you've put this school in? Put me in personally?

So much of the history they learn is one-sided, Warner said. I'm not urging them to go out and throw bombs, for Christ's sake. They wouldn't do it anyway. The assignment called upon their imagination. It required an act of sympathy on their part. That's all.

Honeywell looked as though he were trying to understand. He crossed his legs and spoke slowly. I know, he said, that the attitude of these kids toward the world at large can be exasperating. I know that they bring with them a lot of lazy opinions, whether from home or from the street. But we cannot be all things to them. Some disciplines they have to learn by themselves. Remember how young they are. You can't assign them acts of sympathy. You can't grade them on imagination. Your job is to instill the facts. The facts will speak for themselves. If not now, then maybe years from now. Or maybe not at all.

Warner looked down at his fingers interlaced in his lap. From whom, he said, do you derive your idea of what our job is?

There was a long silence. Honeywell's expression did not change; he waited to reply until Warner looked up again. I have an idea, he said, what you think of me. What you think, I'm afraid, of this whole school. I recommend that we steer clear of personal attacks. We'd both regret it later, I'm sure. But the thing is, I'm not the one called upon to justify myself. You, Robert, are the one in some trouble right now. Why don't you tell me, then, just what it is you think you've been trying to do here. What our job is.

In fact, Warner had sat at home nervously the night before, having been summoned to this unscheduled meeting by the headmaster's secretary. In his imaginings, several scenarios had included this question, and he had silently honed his answer so many times that he found himself surprised to hear it actually asked, as if an image from a dream had suddenly confronted him in his waking hours.

These children are born into every advantage, he said. They are wealthy and they are surrounded with their own kind. They even have beauty on their side, for the most part, and that's not insignificant — believe me, at their age especially, there is nothing as tyrannical as good looks. Now they're still too young, I suppose, for all that to be held against them. But they're part of a self-perpetuating order, and by the time they come to us, most of the work, the educational work, the conditioning, has been done, in their home and in their social life. They are taught the lesson of their own aristocracy, of their own natural entitlement to everything they have and will come to have. Their vision has been narrowed. Privilege is something they have; it doesn't come from anywhere. It's not at anyone's expense. They see themselves as the world. All that work has already been done. Our job is to undo it. It falls to us only because this is the last chance to do it. I'm not suggesting holding the kids responsible for everything that brought them to where they are. I'm suggesting that we have to make them know just that — that there are forces that brought them to where they are, forces of history and class. We have to show them that history — their own history — is the record not only of the advantaged but of the disadvantaged. One does not exist without the other. If I ask them to put themselves in the place of a black man or woman in this city, or of a frustrated working man in another century, it's only toward that end, to make them see the other side of the coin, to make them know that there is another side at all.

When he stopped himself and looked at the headmaster, he

knew he had finished everything. Honeywell's face was red, a combination of perplexity and fright. Warner had never seen this face on him before; in fact, there were only a few expressions of his, all public, with which most people in the school were familiar at all. Suddenly he realized who he had been talking to—or rather, who had been listening, since in essence he had been talking to himself. This could never be a sympathetic ear. Honeywell was a product of this place. Warner found his mind filling with the easily imagined details of Honeywell's own life and past, what sort of upbringing he had had, what form of service he had chosen to devote his life to. His heart sank. He had traveled here, into foreign territory, on a hopeless mission.

Honeywell composed himself as best he could; some hint of fear persisted in his face. He touched his fingertips together. It's obvious to me, he said, that no one who holds these young people, or any young people, in such contempt for something that is an accident of their birth can be placed in any position of authority over them. Clearly I have endangered them by doing so. Maybe I had no way of knowing what you were feeling, or maybe I should have made it my business to talk to you more frequently. In any case, I have no excuse now. I'm informing you officially that your contract here is terminated. I think you've already picked up your last paycheck for this term. If not, it's on its way to your home. Good luck to you.

He stood up and held out his hand. His expression had now hardened completely. Warner swallowed. He could keep his own countenance steady, but he felt the blood firing through his temples. Here was the end, he thought. The logical end. Though he had not wanted this exactly, he had all along been courting it nonetheless. A steely exit was all that was left to him. He stood and shook the headmaster's hand.

It's for the best, he said. I don't think our views could ever be reconciled. I'm sorry it had to end this way.

So am I, Honeywell said. Sorrier, I'm sure, than you suspect. All of us here considered you very promising. He let go of Warner's hand.

The words took Warner by surprise and moved past his defenses to wound him. He did not like to disappoint, to be disapproved of. No matter how tainted or inauthentic the source of Honeywell's authority, Warner was overrun by guilt and regret, by a sense of having failed to live up to expectations. He could still remember how promising it had all seemed to him, his own excitement and the esteem in which he was held. Now he saw what it had led to. To his great consternation, he could not think what to say. He merely nodded, smiled feebly, and walked stiffly, with muffled steps, out of the office.

Classes were over for the term, and the hallways were empty and unusually clean. But the bells, which operated electrically, would continue to ring out at programmed intervals—on the hour, and at ten minutes of—all week long. Warner had forgotten to wear his watch; he hoped the bells were not about to go off. The lockers shone. He saw no one as he left the building. He was glad that this had happened when it had—that he would not have to face his classes again and acknowledge their victory over him. They would, he knew, have been merciless. Beyond the heavy front doors, the sun was bright.

He was numb as he walked to the subway, and found to his slight relief that, in his state, any distraction was enough to occupy his thoughts. He saw a small child, barely old enough to talk, dressed in a miniature Yankees uniform. A breeze blew a withered green leaf over his feet. A young woman, her hair a mass of oily curls, sat in the ticket booth of a movie theater, reading a book. A display window full of television sets of all sizes, tuned to two different stations, showed two different soap operas. The sets and the faces of the actors were very similar, and the images jumped in a strange syncopation. Warner watched from across the street for several minutes before entering the subway station.

There were a few empty seats on the train, but he felt like standing. As they left the station, he read, with numb fascination, all the cautionary advertisements over the passengers' heads—what Lewis liked to call the Paranoia Train. Foot Pain? they said. Roaches Spoil Your Party? Pregnant? Can't Get Off

Drugs? Had An Accident? Need A Lawyer? There was a roar at one end of the speeding car as an indigent black man opened the door and struggled through; one leg of his pants was rolled up to reveal his swollen, scabbed calf. He said nothing as he limped past, but rattled a waxy take-out coffee cup filled with a shallow layer of change. Two passengers dropped coins into the cup. The man seemed not to notice; he was wrapped up in the journey from this car to the next. It was odd, Warner thought, how people who probably spent much of their lives apologizing for one thing or another resolutely refused to apologize, or even look apologetic, for not giving any money. The other passengers tried quite unconvincingly to look like the most uncaring people in the world. They were afraid, perhaps, of their own capacity for pity; once you gave into it, it could take you over. Across the car from Warner stood a tall black man in an expensive-looking suit. He was reading something inside a manila folder; he held a briefcase between his feet. Without looking up, he replaced the piece of paper, closed the folder, stuck it under his arm, reached into his pocket, withdrew some money, and dropped it into the beggar's cup just as he passed obliviously by. Then the process was repeated in reverse, until he had picked up where he had left off in his reading. His face could have been made from iron. Only when he noticed Warner staring at him did his expression change, to a glare so hateful Warner thought for a moment he would have to change cars.

He arrived home to an empty apartment. It was late in the afternoon. He read through the newspaper, but before he had come to the end he realized that more than anything else in the world, what he felt like doing was sleeping. He went to his room, opened the window all the way, and lay down on his bed with his clothes on. When he woke, the light outside was softer; he had pulled the blanket around him in his sleep. His head was clearing now, and he was able to give fuller attention to his plight. The prospect of the evening ahead, with nothing in it to occupy him, began to seem terrible. He went to the phone and called Lewis, who was not home; he found that it was easy to explain the day's events to an answering machine, which did not interrupt him with any sympathetic questions. He suggested that it might be a good night to get drunk, if Lewis was free. Then he hung up and sat staring at nothing in the kitchen. Stuck between the phone and the wall were several business cards and notes on torn pieces of paper. In no state to question his impulses, he took down the note with Julian's number on it—Kendall knew it by heart, of course, but had left it there for Warner in case of emergency—and called him.

He was home, and to Warner's mild disappointment did not seem very surprised to hear from him, as if they spoke to each other on the phone all the time. As calmly as he could—he felt he could stand Julian's pity least of all—he explained that he had been fired that day, was consequently in the mood for a few drinks, and wondered if Julian might be interested in joining him.

Of course, Julian said. I'm really kind of shocked to hear it. I never would have expected this to happen to you. Sure, I can go out. You're sure you're okay?

I'm fine.

Well, fine then. Only, let me suggest that we not go out to one of those hellholes that you and your friend hang out at. Totally inappropriate. Not good places for an introspective binge. Let me pick the place, okay?

Anywhere is fine.

I think I've got just the spot, actually.

You don't have any plans with Kendall? Warner said.

No. Should I invite her?

I don't think so. If you don't mind, that is.

I don't mind at all. It's your call.

She's not there now, then?

No. I don't know where she is. On her way to work, maybe.

I thought she didn't get any more night shifts.

Oh, yeah, yeah, that's right. You're right.

The bar was on the ground floor of an old three-story brick building on an asymmetrical block near the Holland Tunnel. When he and Julian got there, Warner left Lewis a second message with the bar's address, and wished him luck finding it. It was the kind of place Warner would have been terrified to enter on his own, though to the sullen, hard-looking people inside, Julian must have looked even more foreign. But Julian had an instinctive skill for maintaining both self-confidence and respect for the general custom of a place and could make himself accepted anywhere. Warner felt comfortable being there with him.

The place was brick on the inside as well, with dusty, unlit corners. There was a long bar with an elegant, filthy mirror behind it, and half a dozen tables with uneven chairs. Space that could have held three or four more tables was taken up instead by a modified shuffleboard game, scaled down but still enormous. It stood about waist-high and was covered in sawdust. Four fat men were playing with a precision no one looking at them could have predicted. There was also a dartboard, though no one was using it. Warner and Julian took seats at the end of the bar. There were twelve or fourteen other people there altogether, none of them women. There was no television and no music.

Warner asked Julian if he knew any of these people, and he said no; but the bartender walked over and nodded familiarly to him. Julian ordered a vodka, and Warner, not wanting to ask what beers were available and thus mark himself as a rube, asked for a Budweiser. When the drinks came, they looked at each other, unsure of what to say; they touched glasses silently and drank.

So what are you going to do now? Julian asked. Or you haven't really thought about it.

Not really, no. I don't know. I expected to take the summer off as it was, so maybe I'll still do that. I think I feel like a vacation. Maybe I'll go back to London for a while.

Back? When were you there?

Seven years ago.

Oh. Well, it might be a good time to go someplace new, too, you know. Somewhere you've never been.

I suppose. I'll think about it. He finished his beer and ordered another. A few minutes later, as Julian was lifting his own glass to order again, the door opened and Lewis came in. Julian saw everyone's head turn at the sound of Lewis's voice. Short and stocky, with short brown hair and his hands in his pockets, Lewis looked like the product of some second-tier fraternity. His blue oxford shirt was untucked, with the sleeves rolled. It was possible, Julian thought, to guess which three stores these and all his other clothes were purchased from. Lewis smiled when he saw them, then the smile quickly slipped from his face. Not sure what else to do, he put out his hand for Warner to shake.

God, I'm so sorry, he said. Unbelievable.

Lewis had never met Julian; Warner introduced them, and they too shook hands. Lewis took a seat on the other side of Warner. He signaled to the bartender; as he was walking over, Lewis said to Julian, Do they do pitchers here?

They did, and Lewis bought one for Warner and himself. Julian, in spite of himself, was pleased that he had not taken these two to some place where he was better known. He listened as Warner related the story of his firing; it was hard to stay involved since he referred, taking time out for disparaging comments, to so many places and people Julian did not recognize, but he stayed politely attentive. Lewis loudly condemned Honeywell and the whole school. They drank to that. He ordered a second pitcher.

There was a lull while they waited. Lewis looked at Julian, and was afraid to look away again without saying anything lest he seem unfriendly. They hadn't yet exchanged a word. So, he said finally. You're the one who goes out with the famous Kendall.

Warner looked slightly embarrassed.

I think so, Julian said, smiling.

Warner's eyebrows went up. What are you talking about? Are you guys having problems?

I guess that's what we're having. I don't know, I haven't talked to her lately. You must have noticed I haven't been around your place very much.

Yeah, but neither has Kendall. I know she's out looking at apartments, but I figured she was with you.

No, Julian said. I don't know who she's out with. I guess she just goes out on her own. It's funny, I was sure she was spending a lot of time with you. Because suddenly she's trying to become Ms. Politically Correct.

Yeah, Warner said, laughing, I've noticed a little of that, too. I don't know what brought it on. Certainly not her desire to spend more time with me, though, I can tell you that. But suddenly I'm finding books of mine in her room, stuff like that.

They both made sounds of mild, bored surprise.

Well, Warner said. Personally, I think it's bogus. It won't last.

As they drank they lost their sense of discomfort in the place, though the place did not lose its uneasiness over them. Julian had resolved to stay in control of his drinking and not to match Warner's own desperation just out of sympathy for him. But as he grew embarrassed at their loudness, and bored as they traded mean-spirited stories about the other teachers at St. Albert's, his pace picked up without his noticing it. Warner began to feel that downing beer out of a pitcher was too collegiate an image for Julian to be associated with, so he decided to switch over to vodka, and persuaded Lewis to join them.

You know, Warner said to Julian with a serious face, what I can't figure out about you. Holly wants you so badly. She practically told me so as she was blowing me off forever. Why don't you just do it? She is only perhaps the most fabulous animal I've ever seen.

What? Lewis said. Who's Holly? Wait—

She said that? Julian said.

Warner feigned a look of shock. You didn't know?

Well, I guessed it. I'm just surprised she would say anything to you. It's occurred to me. But I just don't want it. I don't think it would be a good idea, that's all. She's a good friend, and once you introduce sex into a friendship, it's over. You can never go back. Besides, she doesn't really want me, she just wants to have gotten me. I'm a challenge for her. I don't think it would be good for me, I wouldn't get anything good out of it. It'd just be sex.

Just sex, Warner said, frowning sarcastically. He turned to Lewis. Yeah, just sex. No big deal, who needs it? Just sex with a wild stunning she-wolf who thinks I'm an insect.

Oh yeah, Lewis said. I went out with a girl like that once. It got really boring, you know?

And besides, Julian said, what about Kendall?

Well, what about her? She wouldn't have to know.

Hey, Julian said. I'm surprised at you. I would have thought you'd have been squarely on the side of monogamy.

Well, Warner said, for us, yeah, sure. That's our only possible appeal to women. Virtuousness and devotion. It's our only chance, so we grab it. But you, man, I would think you would just slash your way through them like Sherman on his way to the sea, and they wouldn't care. They'd want you anyway. And it's my opinion that if you can do it, then you must do it. God smiles on it.

That's right, Lewis said. So take advantage of it, for our sake. Will someone tell me what this Holly looks like?

So you've never cheated on her? Warner said.

Julian shook his head and smiled. Not for lack of desire, he said. But I shall continue to act as if I had faith in fidelity, in the hope that faith will be given to me.

He excused himself to go to the bathroom. Warner looked at Lewis and saw that his friend was drunk, with a heavy head and earnest, confused eyes. He had matched Lewis drink for drink, and so must, he realized, have looked about the same. The bar was a little more full than it had been when they arrived; everyone who came here, it seemed, came for the night. The two of them watched the shuffleboard game for a minute, and when one older man made an especially delicate shot they made sounds of admiration that were louder than they intended. The two players stopped the game for a moment to send them a hard, unfriendly stare. There was an awkward few seconds, which Lewis tried to defuse by giving the men a sly, almost feminine wave. In spite of himself, Warner laughed, and turned away to try to avoid any hint of confrontation. Julian came back in time to get them to restore order. Warner clapped him heavily on the back, for no real reason, as he sat down. Three more, Lewis said to the bartender.

So, Julian said. You think you're going to want to look for another teaching job, or what?

Maybe, Warner said. I think I'd still like to teach. I just need some different kids, a different kind of school. A public school, or at least a place outside the city.

How come?

Warner took another sip and rested his head on his hand. The kids in that school, he said. They just wear me down. They don't know anything at all and yet they're so fucking sophisticated. How is that possible? You wouldn't think it.

It is, though, Lewis said.

They feel very superior to you, they feel like you're the servant, which is pretty much the way they feel about the world. And it's not just that they're young, it's not that simple. They sense what it will be like for them when they're older. They will be superior.

And the girls, Lewis said, nodding.

The girls are worst of all, because they have a whole other way, a whole other sphere in which to lord it over you. They're gorgeous and grown up, sure, but still, they're teenagers. It's infuriating that they flirt with you to try to get what they want. Where do they learn that? Where do they get the nerve? I tell you, the only way to cure them of it would be to take them up on it, you know, to let them know that their little kitten acts have consequences.

I'll bet you wish you had done something about it, Lewis said, now that you know you were going to get fired anyway.

Warner didn't answer.

But what about the boys? Julian said. What kind of interaction do the girls have with them? They must be equals to some—

No, at that age the girls are still a little ahead of the boys.

But they'll even it up. Actually, it's the one endearing thing about the girls, that they're the one force the boys can't cope with. They're the one thing that can humble the boys. It's fun to watch.

Lewis snorted.

You know how I used to amuse myself sometimes? Warner said. Just a little fantasy? I used to think, what if the war got a little hotter. What if they started up the draft, with no college exemption? I liked to imagine one of these guys, out of his beret and three-hundred-dollar overcoat, lying on his belly in Colozan with bullets whizzing over his head, shitting in his pants trying to figure out how his gun works.

Warner and Lewis laughed.

Couldn't you just see it? Warner said. He and Lewis clicked glasses. Julian was looking away, down to the other end of the bar. There was a loud conversation down there which Warner could not quite make out.

What? Warner said to Julian, who did not turn around.

He shrugged and turned back to Lewis.

Maybe you're right, he said. Maybe I should have tried one of them. So who do you think would have been the most likely —

Fuck, Julian hissed. Oh, Christ. Shut up a minute. Just be quiet.

What? Warner said. What is it?

He squinted down at the other end of the bar.

Buddy, someone said behind him, and he felt a hand against his shoulder. He turned around. Even before he was sure what was happening, his blood began to beat.

You talk a little loud, the man said. He was bald, with a large, tight belly, and looked to be at least thirty years Warner's senior. Somehow he seemed all the more threatening for it.

Warner was aware of the danger now, but still too drunk to think for the long term, or even to know what specifically the man was talking about. Julian stood up. Warner felt everyone's eyes on him.

Sorry? he said, and had the impression that this only aggravated things.

The man looked angry but not agitated; he seemed quite comfortable in his rage, at home in it. His fingers for some reason were spread as far apart as they could go. Lewis was silent but would not close his mouth.

I heard you talking about the fighting, the man said. Have a good laugh over it?

He's just drunk, Julian said. He got fired today.

The bartender walked over, quietly.

Every couple of days I have a laugh over it, Warner said. Why?

He heard Lewis sigh.

The man said, My son is over there now. Been there for a couple of months. He's defending you three faggots. He has a couple of friends got killed doing it. You think that's funny?

Listen, Julian said. He's sorry. Why don't you let us set you and your friends up, and then we'll just get out of here.

It was just talk, Lewis said.

How old is your son? Warner said.

The lights became brighter, and the walls moved away. All sounds traveled away from them, out of hearing. The soundlessness was a roar. Warner caught a fleeting but powerful scent.

Nineteen.

Then I forgive him, Warner said.

And then it was decided. There was a hot sensation in his chest without his ever seeing the hand. Chairs were scraping; Julian was talking fast, with both hands out beside him like Samson. Outside, the bartender said. Outside! Warner got to his feet. The door seemed to be coming closer to him. Someone pushed him through it, but it did not hurt.

Outside, the air was cool, and there was considerable traffic waiting to enter the tunnel. He heard the sound of idling motors. He caught himself worrying that all the strangers in their cars were going to see him. Bracing himself against a parked car, he turned himself around. Nearly everyone in the bar had followed them outside. He wondered why the bartender was not there. He saw that some of the men were holding Julian and Lewis by the arms, gently, almost protectively. They were all under a streetlight, though the crooked streets behind them were mostly dark. It seemed like a strange, exciting scene from a walk of life he had never before gotten to see and that he could watch undetected; but then he took a step forward, and with the first blow to his face, it all changed. The pain blasted away his drunkenness, and he was alive to every sound, every hammer blow of his heart; the rough touch of the pavement was like a lover's touch. With an effort, he stood up. He had never been in a fight in his adult life, and he was not prepared for the rage that one punch could produce; but once it came over him, nothing else was as important. This instinct, this euphoria, this love of violence, was what lay invisibly, menacingly, at the floor of every conflict, no matter how large or intricate. Nothing compared to it. Now it was all he knew. Only for as long as it lasted did he have a place here; he did not want it to pass, because once it had passed, he felt, there would be nowhere he could go, no type of place that would accept him. Here it is, he thought. Here I am. It was a fact to which there was no reply; it was the force that marshaled all his other, meager forces. He gave himself over to it and moved forward again, stumbling under the light.

Below street level in the Whitney Museum, there is a small coffee shop. The furnishings are spindly and white and modern, and you look through large picture windows into, essentially, a large concrete well; the torsos of pedestrians are barely visible outside if you lean over in your chair to pick up a napkin or a pen. In spite of its location, at certain hours of the day the café and the inhospitable well outside are filled with sunlight. Large-scale paintings are hung on the white walls, and sculptures peer out from beneath the stairs.

Kendall waited restlessly for Julian at a table near the back. He was not late. It was a Saturday, and the café was fairly crowded, though it was not noisy and in fact had never been so in the half dozen or so times she had been here. Perhaps it was the art that inspired restraint. Twice before, she had been here with Julian, once for an opening, once when they were out walking in the neighborhood and passed by. Are you thirsty? he had said. She wanted to pick someplace that held no memories when she called him this morning; but he had suggested the Whitney, and if she had said no, it would have meant explaining why.

He must know, she thought, he must know why we're meeting. Even so, she was surprised by the somber cast of his face when he finally appeared at the top of the stairs. He saw her and smiled tightly, trying to look more relaxed; then he started down. She thought that he had never looked more attractive. When he sat across from her at the small round table, he seemed out of breath. His leg started to bounce. She felt as if his body were an extension of her own. She held her hands together and hoped he did not see her shaking.

How are you? he said.

Fine.

At a loss, he signaled to the waitress across the room. She came over and took out her pad. You already know? she said. He looked at Kendall, suddenly polite, and suggested that she go first. She couldn't speak at first; she was angry at him for the way he was behaving, for his cowardice. She wanted the occasion to have some dignity, though she wasn't sure why it mattered, and he was not cooperating. You go ahead, she said.

His eye caught the small, laminated menu cards standing at the center of the table. He grabbed one and ran his finger down it. I'll have a green pepper omelet, he said, that comes with bread, right, and that's it. And coffee. He put the menu back in its holder. The waitress looked at Kendall.

Just iced tea for me, she said.

What? Julian said. The waitress nodded and started away. Hold it, he said. I'm sorry, forget that. Just the coffee. Forget everything else.

You don't want anything? the waitress said.

Nope. I'm not really hungry, actually. Just coffee. He looked back at Kendall, a trace of anger showing in his own face now. It was such a little thing, Kendall thought sadly.

He tried to smile again. How's Warner look? he said.

He looks like somebody who lost a fight, what else can you say. His face is still a little swollen, and he still has a black eye. He says that it doesn't hurt, that the only part of him that really hurts is his ribs. I'm not sure why you think that it's funny. You should know better than to take him to a place like that.

I don't think it's funny, he said. And I also don't think it's my fault. He got himself into it. I tried my best to get him out.

When was the last time we talked to each other? she said.

He stared at her for a long moment. Twelve days ago, he said, which to her surprise was exactly right. Did you not know the answer to that yourself?

Yes, I know it.

This is a quiz, then?

She sighed. I'm not testing you.

Of course you are.

No. I just wonder, she said. If I hadn't done something, if I hadn't called, you would have just let it go, wouldn't you? You could just have never seen me again, and that wouldn't have bothered you. It means that little to you.

Of course it would have bothered me, he said.

But that's what you would have done.

His nostrils flared. Do I have to defend myself? he said. Do I have to apologize for something I haven't actually done? Don't tell me what I would have done. Don't tell me what I think.

Two people at the table next to them stood up to leave, and Julian used the opportunity to break his gaze away from hers, following them as they walked past.

All right, she said. Would you never have called me again?

I don't know. Possibly.

What do you mean, possibly? What kind of thing is that to say?

All I—

Even yes would be better than that. Yes would imply that you'd at least given any thought to it at all.

All I meant was I don't appreciate being given these little tests to pass. I knew that's what was going on, that you were counting days, to measure me somehow. I hadn't made up my mind how I was going to respond, that's all.

I can't believe you, she said. I can't believe the way you talk. Am I your enemy? Is that the way you think of it?

Don't get righteous about it. You know that's the way you treat me. I always have to prove myself to you. It's always been that way.

He was glaring at her. She felt sure this could not have been the same look she was giving him. Surely her own face had something left in it of the confusion of love. Still, she had drawn this out of him somehow. She had suspected that this was what the afternoon would engender—coldness, contempt, accusation. She didn't want him to see that it scared her a little. She didn't want any of this to be a part of her life.

I don't think, she said softly, that we're seeing each other anymore.

He did not look away, though he turned a little red and waited a while before he spoke. All right, he said.

All right, she repeated. It's okay with you. It's okay either way. Whatever I say.

What do you want from me?

The waitress brought the coffee and iced tea. Thank you, Julian said. She smiled and wandered off to another table.

Do you think she's cute? Kendall said.

What?

Nothing.

She took a sip of her iced tea. It was cold, not too strong, with lemon and no sugar. She thought she was going to gag on it. She swallowed with difficulty and put the glass down on the table.

It's such a waste, she said. It's not just the time, the year or so of my life that I spent with you. That's not all that much time. There's lots left. It's just such a waste of my own hopefulness. I had such hopes for us at the beginning. They were so strong, it took me this long to give up on them. And for what? Would it have made me happy? It never would have. And even if it did, why should such a little thing as happiness with you — approval from you — take up all my hopes?

Julian was staring at his coffee cup, pressing all ten fingertips against it at the same time.

And it's a waste of everything that's good in you, Kendall said. You have a lot to offer, I think, but you put all these conditions on it. I think you're only interested in women you can dominate.

Julian's face seemed made of stone. Any expression, it seemed, would afford her too much satisfaction.

Do you think that's true? she said.

He lifted his face. I think, he said, that if you'd like to talk about what an asshole you think I am, that's fine, that's your right. But do you expect me to take part in this conversation? Talk about it with somebody else.

No good, she said. All my friends already know what an asshole you are.

You left some things in my apartment, he said. When would you like to come get them?

It was like the furious fighting just before a cease-fire was scheduled to take effect; she would not give him the satisfaction of crying, though it was what she most felt like doing.

Do you have to be so smug? she said. I can't tell if you're being honest or if you're doing it to hurt me, and I don't know which is worse.

His face softened slightly. I don't feel smug. I know I haven't acted as well as I should have. We had a lot of fun and I'm sorry it's ending this way. I'm sorry that I hurt you.

Yeah, well, bully for you, but it's not enough to know that you acted badly. You knew it all along. You liked it, it was the way you wanted it. I'm the one who's just getting hip to it now, I'm the sorry one, not you.

Fine, he said. Okay. Look, I'd love to stay here and listen to
you run me down for a while longer—

You know what's really illuminating to me? And scary? The
more things deteriorated between us, the more our whole relationship got to rely on sex. It was like sex wasn't a way to get
closer but a way to avoid closeness at all. And the more that
happened—the more we corrupted the whole idea of what we
were doing with our bodies—the better the sex got. Isn't that
evil? I can't believe I went along with it. When I think now
about the way I was when we were making love—when I think
about how much was going on that I ignored—I'm ashamed.
Ashamed.

He closed his eyes. If you want to make up thoughts for me,
he said, in order to cast me, and our time together, in the worst
possible light, then there's nothing I can do to stop you. Am I
supposed to answer to your fantasies about me?

Don't give me that. You just don't consider your own actions
important enough to have to answer to. They don't mean anything to you. That you have no commitment to me, and never
had one, is the least of your problems. You're not even committed to anything you say and do, to the idea that these things
have any weight at all. Not to how you treat people, not to the
work you do, nothing.

Commitment, he said. You think you've discovered what this
word means. Frankly, I think your whole grasp of this idea of
commitment is a shaky one. It's a fashion for you. You like to
think that these lofty things matter more to you than they actually do because it helps you feel great about yourself. It's so
simpleminded. I've had the feeling all along that your whole
dissatisfaction with me is connected somehow, in your mind,
with political things, with the war. It's childish.

She spoke slowly. There is a way, she said, of thinking, a
way of thinking which can be applied equally to a far-off war
in which I am complicit, and to a love affair in which I allow
myself to be overpowered, court it in fact. There is a way of
thinking about a corrupt, about an unexamined relationship.

And what is it?

I'm trying to learn it, she said. I know it's there.

Terrific. I'm very impressed.

She had, a little selfishly, wanted to make him stay and listen until she had said everything she had imagined she would say. Now she felt the last of her energy drain away. She no longer had the illusion that she was not talking to herself. Suddenly her anger was spent and an age within her life seemed over. Julian's face across the table was already strange to her. He was rather handsome, she thought. She ran her fingers over the sweating glass of iced tea. She touched her moist fingers to her lips.

Do you want to stay and finish the rest of your coffee? she said. He had more than half of it left.

I've never wanted anything less in my life.

He reached into his wallet for a five-dollar bill and dropped it on the table. She was already standing up. They both were in a hurry now.

One more thing, she said. I shouldn't ask this, but otherwise I'll always wonder. Have you been seeing somebody else? Holly?

No. Less because of you than because of Holly. She and I are friends. I know what she wants out of a man, and it's not a role I could play for her. She wants someone she can enslave, someone she can cheat on, run out on, be forgiven by. It's all a thrill for her. I don't play that, and she knows it, so we get along fine.

They walked to the stairs in single file, Kendall in front. For the last time, he looked at her back, her shoulders, the fall of her hair. She was one step above him; it was all very close and available, and it struck him that this was an angle one normally saw only in bed. The stairs seemed endless and loud. His legs were stiff. They reached the busy lobby. She did not stop but headed straight for the front door, and he followed close behind. He could certainly, he thought, match her eagerness to be away from there. They cut past the line of ticket buyers, the sleepy security men, the arrangements of bright posters and note cards. He saw in the sunlit street, as they pushed through the glass door, an end to his discomfort. Nervously, involuntarily, he smiled. They crossed the concrete bridge outside and reached the sidewalk. A part of their lives was ending, and at the last minute he found himself wanting it to end well. He did not want her to remember him badly. It occurred to him that they were both heading downtown now, and the absurdity of it, the way things like this could undercut their efforts at drama, again made him smile. Quickly, congratulating himself, he devised an excuse for heading over to the West Side.

Well, he said, I'm —

She turned around and his voice caught. Her eyes were filled with tears, and her beautiful face was contorted. He felt his own mouth open. She had come within just a minute of keeping him from seeing this, the hurt he had inflicted. But now it was right there for him. Her lips, her sensuous mouth, was stretched taut by crying. Her eyes seemed to swim. He felt an adrenaline surge of fear, the kind that came from stepping out into the street just before seeing a car coming. All these things were connected, but he couldn't see how. He searched himself for something to say.

Goodbye, she said, and turned away. Her voice was like a pane of glass falling from a great height. He didn't understand. He wanted to call her back and argue with her; he wanted to prove to her that all the time they had spent together couldn't have justified that face, that voice. She must have been lying to him. There must have been something else going on. He leaned out toward the street to watch her, but she was already out of sight. People coming in and out of the museum bumped against him and apologized as he stood at the entrance. Their touch was unbearable to him. He took it as a challenge and was afraid of what he might do. He spun around quickly and folded his arms over the concrete wall beside the bridge; he looked down into the well and listened in astonishment to the rhythm of his own distressed breathing.

They had met fourteen months before, when Kendall was still doing freelance work at a recording studio in Brooklyn. It was unusual to work with a woman engineer. He had come in for a television commercial for the tourism board of North Carolina. The session had been booked beginning at one in the morning, an inconvenient hour reserved for first-time clients. Julian generally preferred working late, though, to working early in the morning. Her hair was much longer then.

There were several others in the booth with her, but all the male singers noticed her right away. When they had reason to believe that the intercom was turned off, they traded speculations about her; they knew not to point or gesture, and to maintain the most innocent faces. Julian was careful to ignore these remarks, or at least, when they were addressed to him directly, to smile and say nothing. He was involved with one of the other singers; she was standing right in back of him. No one else—certainly, as was apparent from their conversation, none of the men—knew of their affair. The woman's name was Julie, and she was a jealous sort; in the short time they had been together he had given her no reason to be, but she must, he reasoned, have heard stories about him. The door to the booth opened, and a bald man with a southern accent stepped out, clutching some papers. There had been a minor change in the words to the jingle, he reported. The two lines that originally ended in dapple and apple had been junked and replaced with something a little less frivolous. He passed out copies of the revised lyrics. Everyone was looking them over, laughing openly, and so Julian did, too. The words meant nothing to him. Without thinking, he lifted his head and looked into the booth. The engineer was staring at him. At the same moment, Julie, her own head down, took advantage of everyone else's efforts at memorization to run her index finger quickly, lightly down the small of his back. He looked back down at the lyric sheet. A small, nervous smile was tightening his mouth. I'm in trouble, he thought. Strangely, he felt very much alive.

After the first two takes, something unusual happened to him. He began to wonder how he sounded to the people in the booth—that is, to everyone other than the bald representative of the North Carolina tourism board, who couldn't have distinguished good singing from bad. He listened to the words he was singing, and in his mind it was as if he were alone there, reciting before strangers, and the words were his. He had never been to North Carolina; what was more, it had never occurred to him that it was a place people aspired to visit. Such thoughts were distracting; in the fifth take he made so egregious a mistake that they had to stop immediately. He heard groans around him, though as was the etiquette, no one tipped off the people in the booth by looking his way. Angry at himself, he closed his eyes and tried to recover his concentration. When he opened them again, the engineer was again looking right at him, expressionless. His first thought was that she had heard him blow the last take; but there was no way she could have told. She would have had to know his voice as well, as intimately, as he knew it himself.

At the end of the twenty-second take, two hours or so later, the bald man got on the intercom and said, I think we've got it. I want to thank you all very much. There was a halfhearted cheer, and just like that, the session was over. This was a development Julian was unprepared for. The ranks broke up, and the singers went for their coats. Julie stood near the door, talking to someone, waiting for him. He looked up at the window separating him from the booth. The engineer had her back to him; the bald man was giving her some sort of instruction. Julian couldn't just stand alone in the middle of the room, among the dead microphones. He went to where his own coat hung across an empty riser. His mind was racing. Before, it seemed to him, he had even thought of it, he pulled his gloves out of his coat pocket and dropped them on the floor behind the riser, out of sight. He took a few steps toward the door; Julie saw him and brought an artfully abrupt end to her conversation. They walked out into the hallway together, not looking at each other.

Before they came to the front door, he stopped and buttoned his coat slowly, looking down. Almost everyone had left, but there were still a few people by the door, gossiping, afraid to face the cold. Julie walked up close to him, then closer. He thought she was about to risk some intimacy, which would have surprised him. He looked down into her eyes. She was smiling.

Didn't you forget your gloves? she whispered.

It was perfect. He put his hands into his pockets. Oh my God, he said. He touched her arm in thanks, turned, and hurried back toward the studio.

The door was still open. He was careful, for the sake of drawing out the moment and for verisimilitude, not to glance toward the booth until he had gotten what he came for. He bent to retrieve his gloves, and only when he had straightened up and turned around did he allow himself to look through the window. She was there, by herself, watching him, with the same attentiveness and lack of emotion. It was quarter to four in the morning. He smiled; she did not smile back. He stood there a moment, in the middle of the room, with his gloves in his hand. Then he put them in his pocket and, as slowly as if he were about to receive some punishment, he walked across the tile and opened the door to the booth.

Hello, he said. How are you?

Fine.

Did you just start here? I've worked a few times here, and I've never seen you.

No. I've been here a while.

I guess we just must have missed each other, then.

I guess so, she said.

She wore a loose sweater, black jeans, and short boots. She sat at her ease among the panels, the rows of dials and knobs, many of them bordered by bits of fraying white adhesive tape marked with enigmatic initials. She did not move.

He sighed, smiled, and held up his hand. I forgot my gloves before.

No you didn't, she said.

His mouth opened. She continued to stare at him. Then he saw — and everything he saw in her he would later see come true — that her impassive, perfect face, her lack of movement, her economy with words, were deliberate, were measures she was taking to hold herself back. She could not give way to what she was feeling because she could not trust herself against the power those feelings could wield. Somehow her very restraint now gave him a clear picture of her potential for abandon. It would, he thought, be something to see.

You're right, I didn't, he said. How did you know that?

Because I was watching you.

Why were you watching me?

She did not answer.

I'm Julian Fraser, he said.

I'm Kendall.

Neither of them could move. He worried that Julie, in her impatience or concern, might come back into the studio at any moment. Kendall, he said, next week I was thinking of going to hear Betty Carter at the Vanguard. I'd love it if you would come with me. Is that something you'd be able to do?

What do you mean, able? she said.

Julian pursed his lips. I mean, he said, is there another person whose existence would make something like this difficult for you to do.

No, she said. No such person exists. And you?

If there were, he said, I wouldn't have asked. I'll call you here.

I'm in and out.

I'll keep calling till I get you. He smiled. She still had not stirred or taken her eyes from him. Bye then, he said, and backed out of the booth. As he walked back through the halls he felt his muscles jumping to the time of a familiar thrill; but he had only a minute to let the excitement wash through him before, out of consideration for Julie, he had to act as if nothing had happened.

Like all such moments, though, it proved impossible to renew; and so the following week when they went out, it proved difficult to get past how little he and Kendall knew about each other. It threatened to become too much like any first date.

There were plenty of questions to ask, all of the most banal sort. It brought an ordinariness to things. They were nowhere near through with these questions by the time the music started. It was loud enough to postpone conversation. Between songs they could lean over and shout remarks to one another over the applause, but that was all. Before long, in any case, he was lost in the music itself.

When the show was over, he wasn't sure what to do; when she said, Shall we go? he didn't understand what was meant, but to ask, or to say, Where to? would force the issue. Outside, they walked quickly to stay warm. They said little about the music; he wasn't sure how much she knew about it and didn't want to seem as if he was showing off. There was little enough to say about it anyway. Their conversation became more general. They talked about work; they talked about their school years. They talked about people in the business whom they both knew. Julian noticed they were walking in the direction of her apartment; he had picked her up there earlier in the evening. No mention was made of this, and no invitation was extended; still, they passed several subway stops and she did not slow down or interrupt their talk. He felt this was a spell that could easily be broken, and so he controlled his curiosity. Her apartment was exactly where he wanted to be.

When they found themselves at the front door of her building, she said, rather politely, Would you like to come up? He said he would. He stood just behind her in the elevator and they rode up in silence. When she unlocked the door, she stuck her head inside and listened before entering; she explained that she had a roommate, but he was apparently already in bed. Julian was struck by the use of the word he, but didn't say anything. This night was moving like one long flight of an arrow, and he was not going to do anything to disturb it. She made him a drink, poured a soda for herself, and they sat down on the couch. The glow from the street cast shadows on their faces. She had not turned on any lights.

She asked him where he had grown up. He asked her if she

knew a recording engineer whose first name was Burton. She asked what sort of singing he would do if he could do anything he wanted. He asked her how long she had had this apartment. She asked him how to spell his last name. He asked her if she had any brothers or sisters.

He felt the heat of her eyes on his. One brother, she said. They were holding hands, and he could not stop the stroking movements of his fingers. His name is Sam. He's eight years older. He's in prison, she said. He dropped out of school when he was seventeen and my parents threw him out of the house. He was living in an apartment on a friend's couch, less than a mile away. He lost two jobs and asked if he could come home for a while and my father said no. So he decided he needed to leave town and get a fresh start somewhere far away from my parents. He was very young, and had nothing. He and a friend were trying to steal a car, and the man who owned it came back. He ran up and grabbed them and started yelling for the police, and my brother hit him in the head with a crowbar, three times, the last time when he was already down. The man almost died. He was from our town but he was nobody we knew. I was nine when that happened.

Julian sat up straighter to look into her face. She was leaning back into the couch. She looked down at his leg and ran her fingers along it. She seemed grateful that he did not say anything, try to comfort her or sympathize with her in any way. It encouraged her to go on, softly.

He used to call me up after he got thrown out of the house, to talk to me, about school or whatever, and my parents would sort of look the other way, but after that the calls stopped, too. He called from jail and they hung up on him. It was okay with me. I didn't want to talk to him. He'd upset my parents terribly. I didn't really understand what was going on beyond that. My parents might have bailed him out, but luckily for them in a way, they never had to make a decision about it because it was way more than they could ever have raised anyway. They did go to the trial. They got a babysitter for me because they said

I was too young to go, and they didn't want him seeing me anyway. I remember I would be sitting in the living room watching TV, and the babysitter would come in right at six o'clock and turn it off and take me outside to play. She was afraid the news would come on. In any case, his lawyer got the charges down to assault and grand theft, and he agreed to plead guilty to both. He's been in jail ever since. Things were never really the same in my family, in my home, after that. We're not all as close as we used to be. I haven't spoken to him. My mother is sometimes in touch with him, I think. She keeps it a secret from my father. I've never gotten a letter from him, though sometimes I think he may have tried to write me and my parents intercepted it. I'd probably just throw it away myself anyway.

Her fingers grazed back and forth over the length of his thigh. He was almost looking down at her now. His hand lightly squeezed the muscle near her neck. He could feel how relaxed she was. Her eyes were half closed, and he imagined that this was what she looked like when she was beginning to make love.

So I've just told you the single most intimate thing in my life, she said. My most secret detail. The thing that the fewest of my friends know about me. What are you going to do now?

He drew his head back slightly. His mouth opened as if he had just been accused of something; it was a joking expression, one of mock ingenuousness, but the truth was he could not think of what to say. He tried to come up with something he could offer her in return, but his mind was not clear; he wanted to make love to her so desperately that his imagination would admit nothing else. He was worried about moving too quickly. He wanted to be cautious, respectful. Her fingers felt hot to him. She smiled as she watched his face, and, behind it, his discomfort. She had accomplished what she wanted.

Slowly, in the near darkness, she reached out her hand; then, as it came close to his face, she extended her forefinger. The tip of it passed into his open mouth, not touching him. Gently, she crooked the finger at the first joint, over his bottom teeth. Her head leaned back slightly over the couch; her neck was exposed. Her hair ran smoothly over her shoulders and his hand. He put his other hand on her ribs, just beneath her breast. It was the moment that doomed their relationship, the moment he would forever try to regain, the surrender that could not be recreated. They would never relive it. She pulled lightly with her finger, to bring his mouth to hers. It was a journey that seemed to last for hours and to cover all the space he had traveled in his short life. Her face tilted, just perceptibly, to one side; her lips made a sound as they parted. She was smiling. Her eyes began to close. He felt the need to live forever.

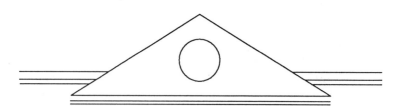

I N April, more than five months after the initial invasion, the armed forces declared the island of Colozan secured, and the press was allowed to return. There was a brief upsurge in news coverage; the attention, though, was more reflective of the novelty of the televised images and photographs than of any shift in the situation, or in attitudes toward it. In fact, the pictures and interviews that legions of journalists were able to obtain on their own did not prove substantially more revealing than those the government's information agencies had provided and continued to provide. Citizens of Colozan, hailed on the street by American camera crews, crowded the frame to express their gratitude. Only an occasional lone sniper, unwilling to let go of his purpose, kept the casualty count from dwindling to zero; still, American troops stayed on, ostensibly to prevent the natives from looting one another. Before long, as the novelty wore off, war coverage thinned out again, and the true news consisted more in the release of official figures than in the suffering that those figures, in their various ways, quantified.

An increased sense of desperation had begun to manifest itself among those still committed to protesting the American involvement in Colozan. Their numbers had continued to dwindle, but what remained was a dedicated and bitter cadre. As they were forced to confront their own inconsequence, their goals, and thus their tactics, changed. Their dissent had long been evident, their arguments ignored; their battles now were born of hatred, and they were themselves more violent. Organized campaigns targeted government officials and executives of companies that manufactured weapons. Chalk outlines of bodies were drawn on the sidewalks outside their fortified homes. Cars were damaged, and bags of fake blood were thrown at press conferences and other public appearances. Sometimes, the attacks became more literally violent. One chief executive officer had his jaw fractured by a gaunt young man who shouted too quickly to be understood as bodyguards dragged him away. Such actions were disavowed by the organizations themselves, conscious of their suffering public image, but the feelings that were thus made manifest could not be disowned. The president managed to avoid any potentially embarrassing confrontation by hiding out in the White House. His spokesmen said that he had decided that all public appearances would have to be canceled, regrettably, until the time of national emergency was past. In New York, packs of protesters dressed in black filled various, randomly targeted blocks, at three or four in the morning, with bursts of noisy mock gunfire.

News reporters had been fascinated from the beginning with the street-theater quality of the demonstrations; the activists, in turn, had courted them by tipping them off to protests and concentrating, in the planning stages, on succinct visual impact. But as the protesters became more insistent, more agitated, angrier, less passive and polite, the stories began to focus on the near-total erosion of popular sympathy for them (one of these stories was put together, with reluctance and some distaste, by Kendall herself). Citizens were tired of hearing about the war — it quite literally bored them; they hated having their roads blocked, they hated having their sleep interrupted by the explosions of blanks in the street, and they hated those who would not let them sleep. In the beginning, the protesters had been out to win people to their cause. Their aim was to ingratiate through the sincerity of their outrage. They believed themselves protected and admired, and never lost their trust in their own rightness or in the essential good faith of those who declined to join them. Now their dissent was joyless, and their demeanor was bitter. They understood what it meant to live in opposition.

Summer had arrived early, and the heat was like a net thrown over the city. It was too hot to walk. Kendall gave an audible whimper as she looked out through the glass doors of the air-conditioned lobby of her office building. Beyond the glass, people walked as if through flood water; shirts and dresses were mottled, hair clung to heads. A man waiting in the lobby overheard and turned to look at her, surprised; then he followed her gaze out onto the street and smiled sympathetically. It was six o'clock. She was standing with one hand on the glass, gathering her courage, when a sweaty man, rude and frowning, barreled through the door from the sidewalk. The blast hit Kendall like an open oven. He did not stop to savor the cool air but walked quickly, exerting himself, toward the elevator as if worried that his discomfort still pursued him.

Mercifully, she did not have to wait long outside before a bus arrived. It, too, was air-conditioned; but the postures of the men and women who sat or stood all around her showed the general physical toll. Some leaned back against the sticky plastic seats in the attitude of one about to be sacrificed; others, without room enough to lean back, rested their arms on their knees and regarded the littered floor, their heads bouncing helplessly as the bus shouldered through traffic. Those who stood hung onto the straps as if it were all that kept them from giving in to a desire to lie down in the aisle; some used two hands. The driver also seemed affected; he held the wheel tightly and drove with a furious concentration, as if struggling with his temper. Even the newspapers and shopping bags were dark with sweat. Through the windows of the bus, the storefronts scrolled by, their giant metal shutters shimmering dangerously in the sun.

The pressing need to find a place to live weighed on Kendall; she had just over three weeks to be out of the apartment. She was making a little more money now, but that advantage would be erased by the extra expense of living alone. In the last two months she had looked at an awful lot of unlivable places. It was a wonder such spaces could even be set aside for human habitation. That was the thing about New York, she thought; the simplest, most basic needs wound up occupying the lion's share of your time and attention. She was sure, for instance, that in other places it was possible to take for granted the notion that if you needed a place to live you could find one. It didn't help her any to know that the dismally practical Warner, who was leaving tonight on vacation, had already packed up all his belongings and put them into suitcases or in storage.

The apartment was the one thing left that could keep her from feeling that she'd set her life pretty well in order. Though she was not always pleased with the programs she or her colleagues produced—and though, to her frustration, that displeasure with others' work was almost always misinterpreted as ambition—she felt engaged by what she was doing at the station. Even when she was unhappy there now, she was unhappy for reasons that had to do with the work itself and not with her alienation from it. She could see how she had hurt Warner by refusing to live with him anymore, but did not regret it. She was too old, she told herself, not to have a home she wanted to return to. There was something adolescent and false about their living together, and she was glad it was over. They just were not friends anymore; that happened all the time to people their age, it was perfectly natural. She didn't want to go on ignoring the sexual imbalance between them; she thought it was cruel of her, somehow.

And she had not seen or spoken to Julian since their breakup. She was proudest of herself for this because it matched her against some of her strongest impulses. In spite of her high-mindedness, sexual satisfaction, no matter how tainted, was harder to do without than she had guessed. She had started to rationalize, to spin fantasies about Julian's capacity for change.

But always she stopped herself before she picked up the phone. The closest she had come was when she had walked up the block where he lived while on an errand in midtown one day. The scene she played out for herself then, as she watched his windows, was enormously appealing; but she realized in time that none of the sources of its drama could be found in real life.

On good days she enjoyed her single life and looked forward to a new apartment and nights at home alone. Of her friends in the office, only Felicia knew what had happened to Julian, and Kendall made her promise not to pass the story around the station because she did not want to be asked out just now.

Two blocks from the apartment she pushed open the back door of the bus and stepped out. She could feel the heat of the sidewalk through the soles of her shoes. She was struck by the bus's exhaust as it pulled away, and she swore in a whisper. She couldn't make it home without stopping at a deli for something to drink. Just as she got to the front of the fast-moving line to pay for her soda she remembered that she had left her newspaper, with its real estate listings carefully annotated, in the office. She would have to do it all again. She made a face and tossed a new Times on the counter next to her soda; the Korean woman behind the cash register looked at her in undisguised amusement.

In her lobby she threw out the soda can and the unnecessary sections of the paper. She found the apartment listings, folded them over, and began to look through them as she rode up in the elevator. The listings started downtown and moved north, in the fashion of the pioneers. She took her eye off the page to fit her key in the lock, and opened her door, and there, sitting in the chair by the window, was her brother, Sam.

For a moment it was as if she had stumbled on an old photograph; she stared at him unself-consciously, as if he could not see her. She recognized him instantly, but it was only after examining him that she saw how much he had changed. His hair was still long, as she remembered it, but darker now; in places it had gone quite gray. His belly stuck out a bit, but otherwise he was dangerously thin. He must have been on some kind of eating or drinking binge since getting out of jail, she thought, to acquire that stomach. His face was all hollows and angles. The eyes seemed brighter than she recalled. He wore, in this heat, a thin flannel shirt and jeans, and though he didn't seem uncomfortable — the window was wide open just behind him — his attire contributed to her sense that he had the look of a man who was not ready to make his own way in the world.

He, too, stared curiously at her for a few seconds as she stood in the door. Then, abruptly, a wide smile took over his face, and he stood up from the chair. The smile was clearly willed and unspontaneous; its intensity was frightening. He walked over to the door, put his hand gently on her arm, and pulled her into the room until the door could swing closed behind her. Then he put his arms around her.

Diane, he said.

Uneasily, afraid of angering him, she put the hand without the newspaper briefly on the center of his back and removed it again.

He took his chin off her shoulder and looked into her eyes. He was choosing not to see what was in them. Don't you recognize me? he said.

Yes, she said, of course.

My God, he said. I dreamed about how beautiful you'd grow up to be. My dreams didn't go far enough.

How did you get in here? she said.

He smiled, touched her arm, and stepped back into the living room, beckoning her to sit down, as if she were his guest. Your roommate, he said. He was on his way out right when I got here. He let me in.

He put his hands demurely behind his back. Why, he said. Did you think I broke in?

No, of course not.

He your boyfriend?

Rob? No, no he's not. She was holding the newspaper so tightly the apartment listings were smudging beneath her fingers.

Just as well, Sam said. Because I was going to give you some bad news if he was, because he walked out of here carrying a bunch of suitcases.

What? Oh, no, we're just friends.

I thought maybe he and you had had a fight, some lovers' spat or something. Maybe I'd come at a bad time.

No. He's just going on vacation. It's nothing like that.

You do have a boyfriend, though?

No, I don't.

She felt compelled to politeness. It had less to do with any sense of obligation than with simple shock. Politeness was a wall she put up, to give herself time to gather her forces behind it. She had known for months that this might happen, and yet she could not have been less prepared.

You look upset, he said. I'm sorry to ask all these questions right away. I know this is a big surprise for you. But there's so little I know about you anymore. There's not even any good place to begin, you know? I can't help it.

When he smiled this time it looked sincere but uncomfortable; it looked like a smile a man practices in front of a mirror. Kendall could feel the strands of her hair pasted by sweat to her forehead. She shook her arms as if trying to rouse herself. Would, she said, would you like anything?

The form of her question, the familiar, even rote quality of it, seemed to please him. He was back in the world of manners, and questions like that meant more to him than any unexpected or unique display of affection. Yes, please, anything, he said. Anything to drink.

It was such a relief to stick her head in the refrigerator that she would have stayed like that for ten minutes if she could. She reached for the beer; when she took her hand away from it, wondering quickly if it might not have some dangerous effect on him, she realized that she might be going too far. She closed her eyes and took a deep breath; she brought two beer bottles into the living room.

As they sat down, Sam pointed to the phone machine; the red light was blinking. That's Mom, he said. I was here when she called. I felt funny about picking it up, so I didn't. She was calling to warn you I might be coming.

Kendall drank from the bottle and tried not to look as if she needed it too desperately.

You know what? Sam said. Until I got out four months ago, I'd never seen an answering machine. They're really ingenious, aren't they?

Kendall made a noncommittal sound. They watched one another. An intermittent breeze was blowing out the curtain behind his head. He still had the look of delight impressed on his face, but it appeared to be waning, as if the power were running out on it. He was expecting her to say something, to make the same kind of effort he was making. So, she said. What brings you here, to New York I mean?

Sorry?

I mean why did you make such a long trip? Do you have a job lined up here, or did you just want a little vacation, to enjoy your freedom, or what?

He laughed. What are you talking about? he said. I came here to see you.

The sense of threat that hung in the room was, she realized, distinctly sexual. She could not easily think of him as a brother, and so none of those rules seemed, at first, to apply. She felt his strength like a shadow behind his pale skin.

You didn't answer any of my letters or my phone calls, he said. If I wanted to talk to my own sister I had to come and see her, that's all.

His anger was beginning to show through. It was daunting but less scary to her than the freakish display of family love he had been making.

What are you doing now? she said. Have you found a job?

Not yet. I'm living in Chicago, actually. About four miles from the jail, if you can believe it. I still get up to see Mom and Dad every so often.

Kendall was so surprised she could not disguise it. How are

things between you and Dad? she said. I mean, he was so furious with you, it's hard to believe.

We're okay, Sam said. I was furious with him, too, don't forget. But it was a long time ago. And we're family, you know. That never changes. That's where you go when you want forgiveness, right? That's what families do. I don't have any other loved ones, you know. No one who knows me. I mean, I'm not worried about making a fresh start. Making a fresh start is easy. What I worried about when I got out of prison was there'd be no one in the world who knew me. But as long as there's family, that will never happen. Plus, you know, Mom and Dad are getting older, and I guess they figure there's too little time left to worry about pride or being bitter or whatever.

Moved by his own thoughts, he drank from the bottle of beer.

It hurts them, you know, that you never call them, or come home, he said.

When she had finished her beer, she stood up and walked toward the kitchen. Everything about this moment in her life seemed as though it couldn't possibly be real. His voice followed her. Mom's very proud of you, you know. She's told me all about what you're doing. That you're working at an all-news radio station, that you're a producer or something. And she told me you were seriously involved with this guy named Julian something. I was looking forward to meeting him. It was like some kind of spy mission. I was going to report back to Mom all about him, because she's never met him. But now you say you have no boyfriend, so I guess you've broken up. Mom doesn't even know that yet.

She dragged the fan from her bedroom, set it up in the entrance to the living room, and turned it on. She went to the kitchen and returned with two new beers. She sat down.

What I want to know, she said, and I'm not trying to make you mad because I'm not angry myself, just sort of, I don't know, aghast, is how on earth is it that you think you can talk to me that way. How can you, of all the people in the world, scold me for neglecting my family?

He gave her a smile intended to reflect the difference in their ages.

I'm your brother, he said.

I mean, how can you even talk like that? How can you even use those words? In what sense are you my brother?

In what sense? He laughed. You're confusing yourself, he said.

I haven't seen you in almost eighteen years. And I was so young when it happened, I don't even experience it as a loss, you know? I missed you, but too much time has passed. I just don't feel close to you anymore. Why would I?

His smile was dimming again. Let me ask you something I've been wondering, he said. When your friends would ask you about your brother, or if you had any brothers or sisters, what would you tell them?

She was surprised. Actually, I lied about it most of the time. A few people know about you. But mostly I say I don't have a brother, and it's only a lie in the most technical sense, because like I was—

Oh my God, he said. How could you do that?

He looked devastated. The bottle seemed about to fall from his hand; Kendall stopped herself from reaching forward to take it from him.

How could you do that? he said again. I could understand your being a little ashamed of me. I mean, I'm not an idiot. But just to deny me. Really, that was evil. As evil as anything I've ever done.

I guess I can understand, she said, why it's so important to you. The family thing. I know, I mean I don't know but I can imagine, how hard your life must have been, and still is. You must have been terribly alone, from a very young age, and so I can understand why you would cling to that ideal about the bonds of family or whatever. But I've had a very different kind of life. You don't really know me either. Think about how different you and I are. Think about all the things that separate us. Being related is just not a lot to have in common with someone. It's not enough.

He finished his second beer and stuffed the empty bottle between the cushion and the arm of the chair. He looked around him, wide-eyed, as if disoriented. It's not important to me, he said. It's important period. You've got to have someplace to look back to. You've got to have some kind of anchor. Family is the beginning of everything. If you renounce it, then you're just lost. You have no past, no history. Maybe this all explains why you strike me as such an unhappy person.

She began peeling the label of her beer bottle with her fingernail.

Do you remember, he said, when you were about five, and we used to sit out on the porch and watch the sun go down in the lake? I used to tell you that the sun was like a big match going out in the water, and every morning God struck a new one.

She recrossed her legs. Questions were occurring to her now, about him, about their parents, simple, almost technical questions about the details of their well-being that nonetheless took her by surprise; it had never really struck her how resolutely she had dismissed them. She had a sudden image of Sam as he used to be; it gave way quickly to a more powerful image of herself as she was then. She was so different now. No one could have predicted her. She had come so far, she felt, in such a short time, against such odds. She felt suddenly that everything she believed about herself was very new and very fragile. She was determined to preserve it. It was up to her; she did not have to include all this in her notion of who she was. He was a sympathetic figure, but he was also a near-stranger; she was not obliged to him. It was too much to give in to. It was too much to think about, for now.

No, she said, I don't remember that.

She could see him sag. She had to go to the bathroom but was afraid to take her eye off him now. He seemed sad enough to do anything.

Well, he said finally, you were pretty young then, I guess.

The room was growing darker, and with the fan blowing on the sweat of her arms she was even a little cold. She went to get the last two beers. He accepted his without a word. She noticed how half-hearted the apartment itself appeared now, with all of Warner's belongings gone, how temporary, how unlike a home.

She leaned forward. Do you have someplace you can stay tonight? she said.

No, he said, but I can find one. No great trick.

She saw how dispirited he was, and was overcome with wonder that it could have anything to do with her, with someone he did not even know.

I'm sorry that this has all gone so badly, she said. I honestly am. I just, I was very surprised. It's a long way to come, and I'm just not sure I understand what you expected from me.

He lifted his head.

Well, he said, I'll tell you one of the reasons I came. Believe it or not. Somehow, you know, I had the idea that you would be happy to see me. How about that? That you wondered what had happened to me, how I was doing, what stories I had to tell. What I looked like now. That the way you ignored me, my letters and calls, for so long, was just some mistake, some misunderstanding, or maybe you were just nervous.

Kendall was getting a little drunk; she rubbed her eyes. She wondered how he could find a place to stay at this hour, how he could afford a hotel, whether he had friends here, what he could do; but she thought it best not to ask. I'm sorry, she said. I feel very badly for you. I'm not an unfeeling person, really. But this was all so long ago. It just doesn't seem like a part of my life now. I just don't feel any real connection to you, that's all. You can understand that.

You won't let yourself feel it, he said. But it's there. It's there whether you like it or not. You make it sound like all this is my original idea, like I made it all up. Like there's no one else in the world who feels the way I do about this. It's just the opposite. This idea that you think is so weird, that there are bonds in your life other than the ones you choose, is not mine. It's the way of the world. It has been forever. You're the one who's refusing to acknowledge what's true. You hurt your mother, you hurt your father, by ignoring them, by declining to let them in or pay them respect. If you thought about it at all, you'd see it. You hurt me. Those bonds are unbreakable and they have to be honored. You don't get to choose them. You don't get to invent yourself. I came a long way to try to respect those bonds, and I guess my little trip here has been a failure. But I did the right thing. I'm sure of it. Believe me, I know what can be escaped and what can't. I failed, but so what.

She crossed her arms and caressed her shoulders. They were six feet apart. The darkness gave his face an appearance of great dignity and age. He had traveled all the way from her childhood to accuse her.

At least I tried, he said. At least I made the effort. What did you do?

Warner left for the airport hours before his flight; he knew he would be nervous and unhappy in those hours no matter what, but he would rather spend them in the airport than in his apartment, surrounded by his bags. He was so unmoored, so ready for anything, that even meeting Kendall's ghostlike brother at the door of the apartment hadn't particularly unsettled him. He'd let him in, told him to help himself to anything in the refrigerator while he waited, and that was that; he'd just picked up his bags again, gone out into the street, and hailed a taxi.

He hadn't realized that he was just in time to catch the evening rush hour. When the cabbie apologized, with a strong dose of obscenity, Warner nodded and made sympathetic sounds of suffering; but in truth, he didn't mind. It was a way to kill some of the time before his plane boarded. The night was hot, and the air in the cab was difficult to breathe but cool. There was no hurry. He watched the other drivers on the expressway, some calm, some agitated, some with sweat visible on their faces. One woman inched past with her left hand on the steering wheel and her right on the chest of her son, who looked to be about four and rode in the passenger seat beside her. Garish restaurants and small shopping centers crept by on both sides. Warner asked the driver to turn on the radio.

The slow traffic jacked up the fare considerably, but he barely noticed. He paid off the driver and waved away the skycaps, picking up all his luggage according to the one workable system he had devised, the two largest bags in his hands and the two smallest under his arms. The doors parted for him, and he shuffled, grunting, toward the ticket counter. The terminal was like a huge gymnasium, high-ceilinged and climate-controlled. Everything echoed softly and was hard to understand. The sun shone weakly through the tall windows and the haze.

When he checked in he dropped all his luggage save for one bag through the gap in the ticket counter. He saw the bags being tossed on the conveyor belt and moving quickly out of his sight. When he walked away with only the bookbag over one shoulder he felt as light as if he were walking on the moon. On the video display mounted on the wall, he found the gate number for his flight to London.

You could be blindfolded and dropped at a train station just about anywhere in the world, and when they let you look around you could get a fair idea of what city you were in. But an airport was an airport the world over, at least on the inside. It was meant to be soothing, perhaps, but for Warner it was dislocating. Maybe this was as it should be. Airplane travel was in most ways the very opposite of travel. There were no sights to see, no people to meet along the way, no chance events. When you got on the plane you were in one place, and when you got off you were in another. As a rule, you weren't even permitted to touch the ground between the plane and the faceless airport. If you didn't wear a watch you might have only your own body —a headache or nausea or the sweat and fatigue of having slept in your clothes—to let you know that anything had happened to you at all. Warner listened to the music and watched the blue carpet stretch before him as he searched for his gate. The ubiquitous advertisements, set into the white walls, stayed stubbornly at the corners of his vision. Even the people who swept past him seemed less distinctive to him than they might have in another environment; the setting reduced them all to a common denominator.

There was a surprising crowd of people seated in the molded plastic chairs by his gate; he looked at the temporary sign over the small counter and saw that he was so early that a flight from Madrid due to arrive at the same gate had not yet come in. He found an empty seat. Across from him was a row of chairs with tiny coin-operated television sets attached to the armrests, twenty-five cents for twenty-five minutes. Those chairs were filled, mostly by children. There was almost no conversation. The gentle, universal voice of the public addresss system was just loud enough to be heard. Beyond the ranks of chairs, people continued to hurry by in both directions. Warner still had The American Earthquake in his bookbag. He took it out but could get through only one short essay before distraction got the best of him. He kept looking up at all the people going by. He read the first paragraph of the next essay four times before giving up and putting the book away. He was very nervous now. This didn't seem like a good place to be. The child sitting to his right was staring at him, and he realized his leg was bouncing rapidly. He forced it to stop, and when it did, it came to him suddenly that what was making him nervous was a kind of subconscious fear that someone was going to come looking for him here. It was absurd. He stood up with his canvas bag and went searching for the bar.

Airports themselves were depressing places, but airport bars were so depressing, Warner thought, especially when you were by yourself, that it became funny, a commonplace; it lightened the heart. He found the nearest one and ordered a scotch and water, which he took to a threadbare banquette. The darkness was nearly complete. The only light seemed to come from the television; the bartender was watching the news with the sound turned off. The lead story concerned the one billion dollars the Congress had just apportioned to Colozan — now that the fighting was virtually over and a new government installed — to raise again all that the U.S. armed forces had leveled. The screen flashed an image of what Warner, like most people, now easily recognized as the Colozan City airport. It looked like any other airport—much like, aside from the palm trees, a smaller version of the airport he was in now. He smiled wearily and looked away. Beyond the bar's large windows, which were tinted, the human traffic moved according to its own laws, in bright silence. It was like a trip to the aquarium. The scotch was too expensive and tasted of smoke. But once Warner felt himself hidden from things, he began to relax.

He hadn't told anyone that he had no real plans to return from London. He had kept it to himself mostly because he was worried he would let himself be talked out of it. Everyone— Kendall, Lewis, his family—expected him back in New York in four or five weeks. His parents, in fact, had mentioned more than once that they expected he might want to return home for a while, since he had not lined up an apartment for himself. What little furniture he owned he had asked Kendall to keep while he was away; she was happy to have it, at least until she could replace it. He was most worried about leaving his family behind, but he knew that this was not a genuine hardship; he did not see them that often, and though they were all on good terms, none of them could be said to need him, any more than he truly needed them. They saw each other once a year or so. They kept in touch mostly by telephone; calls from London or from New York, so far as he could see, were little different. The same could be said of airplane flights, in case he had to come home for some emergency; from one city or from another, it didn't matter. Even as he sat in the bar, he tried to come up with some compelling reason for returning to New York in one month, or six. It would not change his plans; still, if he could tell himself that he was sacrificing something, leaving something behind, he could perhaps convince himself that what he was doing was brave or daring. Other people, he knew, would probably see it that way. But all he could summon now when he thought about his flight were feelings of failure and loss.

As his eyes became accustomed to the dark, he noticed a woman sitting alone on the other side of the bar. She, too, was watching the television screen. She had a strong, boyish face. Her long hair disappeared from his view behind the bar. She seemed quite tall, though perhaps it was just an effect of the barstool. Men often bought women drinks in such situations, he knew it to be true; it wasn't just the stuff of films. It happened in a certain kind of real life. He stood up and brought his empty glass to the bar. The bartender lifted his chin by way of a question. Scotch and water, Warner reminded him in a soft voice. The woman did not take her eyes off the screen. She was drinking wine. Then the scotch was in front of him; he paid for it and returned to his banquette. Anyone looked good in this light, he decided; he probably didn't look too bad himself. He smiled, toasted himself, and looked out the window.

By the time he returned to his gate, every sensation was a pleasant one. When he moved his head it took his eyes an instant to catch up. All the signs at the gate had been changed for his flight. A small crowd was forming. He overheard an attendant telling one family that they wouldn't be able to board for another half hour. There was no question of reading. He thought maybe he could handle a magazine but didn't want to wander off looking for one. Instead he took a seat by the window facing the tarmac and watched the planes. Inside, their high roar was barely audible. None of them moved, though odd, parasitic jeeps and carts dodged in and out of their paths, carrying fuel or baggage or nothing at all. He saw that his own plane was already pulled up alongside the gate. It was growing darker. The seats filled up around him. Not exactly drunk, he was in a kind of alcoholic limbo; he had a small headache and felt as though he needed a shower. Either he would have to continue drinking on the plane, or stop completely and ride out this feeling until he was sober again. He decided against alcohol; I need to think, he said to himself, then mouthed those words silently as he looked out at his plane.

As soon as they saw the attendant lift up the public address microphone, overanxious passengers began lining up at the entrance ramp. Warner knew he had some time before his seat number would be called. He found a water fountain and drank as much as he could stand, and then splashed some water on his face. When he straightened he felt dizzy for a moment, but once that had passed he felt better than he had expected. A few drops of water rolled from his chin. He heard his number called as he headed back to the gate. He had been using his boarding pass as a bookmark; once on the slow-moving line, he opened his bag and got it out. Suddenly, he saw in line, about ten people ahead of him, the woman with the long hair from the bar. He felt a familiar rush of pleasure and fear; but as soon as it came it was gone again, and he found himself regretting that she was there. He showed his boarding pass to the stewardess. He took each movement very seriously now.

In his seat by the window he put his bookbag where he could feel it with his feet and buckled his seat belt. He looked quickly at the contents of the in-flight magazine and replaced it in the elasticized net on the seat in front of him. The roomy plane seemed full of activity. He slid up the plastic window shade. It was nighttime now. He could see the highway, the countless sweeping lights. In the darkness, only the lights in the landscape gave off color; the cars, the grass, the silver dividers, the deep green road signs, all were shades of gray now. In the distance, an elevated sign outside a large turnpike restaurant burned powerfully. Blinking lights moved in a circle around the restaurant's name. Other, more distant signs were harder to distinguish. The landing lights of another airplane flashed in the sky above the cars. The window framed a populous square of American country, filled to capacity at any given moment with people who had not been there a moment before. No one, Warner thought with satisfaction, knows what is in my mind right now.

He sat through the various disaster briefings acted out by the stewardesses with gestures and expressions that seemed to have been borrowed from synchronized swimming. The plane taxied to its place on the runway. He thought of London. He had not been there in years and so tried not to put too much trust in his memories; still, as he recalled, it was civil or loud, sociable or private, according to one's whim. It seemed possible to live there. It redeemed the very notion of a city. He did not feel that he was going to a foreign place. This had something to do with language, he realized, but not that much. He felt as foreign in his native place as he expected he could feel anywhere new.

The captain announced that they were next in line for takeoff. A stewardess, coming by to check that every seat belt was fastened, looked into Warner's lap, smiling, and moved on.

What is it, he thought, that binds a man to his country? What were these ties that he did not feel? He would wake up tomorrow in a different nation. Would he ever feel some loyalty to it? It wasn't a matter of simple political opposition but something deeper and more confounding. He was forced to abandon the idea of his own opposition because that opposition, even in his daily life, was useless and unrecognized. Nothing he did, on any level, had an effect; none of it would last. He felt himself outside of the history of his own time. His country was a monument to a brand of injustice, to the tyranny of power and beauty in all their forms; he had always sided with the victims, but the more he felt himself to be one of them, the less attractive or honorable or romantic they became. In distant countries, bloody victories were claimed in his name, on behalf of principles twisted into the most grotesque postures. He did not even know what a proper response to this might be. Those who let him down did not care that they were acting on his behalf. There was nothing for him here.

The stewardess knocked on the bathroom door a few rows in front of him; the woman from the bar emerged, smiling apologetically as the stewardess rather sternly pointed her back to her seat. She was just two rows ahead of him, in the center of the plane. As she walked back, she caught his stare, and this time she smiled at him. She was as beautiful in fact as she had looked to him in the darkness of the bar. Her hair fell all the way down her back; he saw that when she sat down she had to brush it over one shoulder. It hung like a private curtain from her face all the way to the armrest. He cursed himself. He had to get his thoughts in order.

And then the volume of the engines' sustained music increased, the cabin began to rattle, and they sped down the runway. The takeoff took Warner by surprise. He had been on planes before, of course, though not recently; but he did not remember this special, threatening sensation of speed. There would be no such sensation, naturally, once they were in the air. But now he held his breath. He looked out the window and saw the wing shaking. Then the rattling was silenced and they were off the ground. They banked quite sharply into the black sky. Warner's fingers were white on the armrests, but he felt no fear. His thoughts began to disentangle; in the air all the confusion and the doubt and the regret gradually drained away, and his mind was clear, except for the one remaining, irreducible, surprising thought—the prideful, secret essence of belief in his own superiority, and in the romantic and memorable quality of his own exile—crossing slowly, stealthily within his mind, like an airplane in a clear night sky.

I am going to a new country, he thought. I am starting again. If my country's history troubles me, then there is still a political recourse left to me and that is to renounce that history, to make it not mine. And that is what I am doing. I am removing myself from the course of events, and I can reintroduce myself when and where I choose. I have a new past to learn, because I will arrive without one. This is what it means to be empowered. I can recreate myself; who can do more? No one knows me. I have no advantage or disadvantage. I'm taking with me only the things that I believe in, the things that I know to be just or unjust. Everything proceeds from that, from me. The world takes shape around me. I can not change.

Holly called Julian and asked him out to dinner. They hadn't seen each other in a while. On the phone, he seemed quiet and unemotional; she was concerned, though she didn't say anything, and offered to pick him up at his apartment. He agreed. They went to an old German restaurant in the Yorkville section, an inexpensive, dispirited little place; an electric train, stalled on its tracks, sat in the window.

Before any small talk, she knew there were two things she had to ask him. He had been out of the city for the past few days. His mother, just two weeks earlier, had suffered a relatively minor stroke. She was a vigorous woman, and to say that it was unexpected, Julian said, didn't begin to capture it. It happened in her sleep—she might not have been aware of what was happening, though she would never remember those minutes now—and had traumatized Julian's father to a degree he could only guess at. The ambulance crew that his father had summoned that morning had had to let themselves into the house; they found him lying silently on his back, staring at the ceiling, in the bed beside his unconscious wife. She was going to be all right, or so Julian had been told; there would be some paralysis, but the doctors, who praised her strength, expected a good recovery. He wasn't sure he could say the same for his father, who seemed much older suddenly, and depressed to the point of self-indulgence. The doctors would begin to give him instructions on how to help his wife through her rehabilitation, how to ease her life in these new circumstances, and he would simply stop listening, close down, like a child. Julian thought it was possible that he would have to return home himself for a while until both his parents found a way to take care of each other again; he hoped he could avoid it, though, as he found himself, like his father, a little afraid to return to a home that had changed so.

Then Holly asked him how he was taking the breakup with Kendall, if they had been in touch. He didn't want to talk about that, he said; but he asked it so gently that Holly, disarmed, had no choice but to honor it. They ate the rest of their dinner in near silence. The waiter, an unhappy-looking man in an immaculate white shirt, glumly took their plates away.

Julian looked down at the check, then up into Holly's face

for a long moment. I'm sorry, he said. I don't know why I'm being so boring. It's good to see you. I haven't even asked about you at all.

She smiled. It's all right, sweetheart, she said. You can talk to me or not talk to me. I'll still love you. If you're just not in the mood, I understand. Let's just pay up and I'll drop you home.

He shook his head. No, he said. Let's go out.

He wanted to change first, so she waited in his living room, examining everything on the walls and shelves uninhibitedly, as if she were in a museum. She recommended a club down in the meat-packing district. Sounds like heaven, Julian said.

When they got there, the doorman saw Holly and nodded, unclipping the velvet rope. She touched his cheek as they passed. His expression, that of a professional executioner, did not change. Inside, Julian felt mercifully bombarded by noise and light. It was impossible to think. He saw one or two people he knew and met a dozen friends of Holly's. A group of them were admitted to a small private room. He was asked to dance once or twice and declined; but other than that, he took part in the life completely. He had four or five drinks, and there were drugs. He felt connected now. He asked someone to tell him what time it was and she refused.

Nothing was said when Julian and Holly left the club and stepped up to the line of cabs which formed there in the morning hours. A ragged-looking man ran over to hold the cab door for them and asked for money in return. Julian gave him a dollar. Holly leaned forward and pronounced her address. The door closed. The cab pulled out of line and started off.

In silence, Julian paid the driver. Holly did not look back as he followed her through the front door and into the elevator. He felt his heart pounding from the cocaine. It had been a while for him. Inside, he went to the bathroom and when he came out she had made them each a drink. They sat apart from each other and looked out her windows. The vodka helped to cut his feeling of edginess, to soften his nerves. They talked a little about the night, and the people they had seen.

Holly watched the empty river. I'm not very good at this, she said. If you want to stay with me tonight, you can.

They were too far apart to touch. A minute passed. Julian nodded, and though she was not looking at him, she saw. In another minute or two he had finished his drink. He stood up. She turned out the light; they walked into the bedroom like two members of a jury.

Nothing was said. They undressed in the dark, she with her back to him. Their first surprising touch under the sheets was like the sudden drop of an elevator. There you are, she said. They kept their faces close together, and their eyes gradually closed. It was awkward and surprisingly tender. Afterward, she traced his back with her fingertips; he settled his face against her neck and listened to her breathing as it slowed. He thought how quiet it was here, how dark. Her hands stopped moving. After a while, they gently pushed apart.

Near dawn, she was awakened by the sound of mock gunfire in the street, and she thought she heard him crying. She raised herself on one elbow and rubbed at her eyes.

What, she said.

His back was to her, and he faced the wall; his knees were drawn up near his chest. His eyes were open. I'm so happy, he said. I've wanted you for so long.